MY FIRST, MY LAST

A FRIENDS-TO-LOVERS NOVEL

BROOKELYN MOSLEY

85 MEDIA LLC

OTHER WORKS BY BROOKELYN MOSLEY

Novellas/Series

No Fraternizing, Pt. 1
No Fraternizing, Pt 2
No Fraternizing, Pt. 3
First Came Love: The Love, Hate & Revenge Prequel
Love, Hate & Revenge, Pt. 1
Love, Hate & Revenge, Pt. 2
Love, Hate, & Revenge, Pt. 3
Girl Code
Mr. & Mrs. Jones
Forbidden: An Anthology
They Call Me Mello
A Love Deferred
Indecent Arrangement
Last Comes Love
Ebb & Flow
PRIDE
Meant To Be
LUST

Loveless
GREED

Short Stories

Just Friends
Chateau Luxure
Lena's Ex-File
Dream Boss
Unsilent Knight
Twice In Love
Home For Christmas
Rekindled

PREFACE

My First, My Last is officially my fourth published friends-to-lovers story. When I set out on this journey to becoming a self-published author, never did I imagine that friends-to-lovers would be *my* thing. But it is and what I've created here in this story solidifies my love of this trope. Ayla and Hassani challenged me to my core. I honestly can't believe I fell in love with a pair of characters who frustrated me so much. These two put me through it, so trust me when I say it surprised me when I missed them and wanted more of them after typing "the end." This story is a love story but touches on the tragic events that occurred on September 11th, 2001. As a born, raised, and still lives in New York, New Yorker, recalling this day well enough to capture important elements for this story was tough but healing too. If you were deeply affected by the events on this day, my heart goes out to you. Also, please keep this in mind before you read. The premise for their story came to me in a dream and this is what I created from it. Enjoy.

To the lovers who were friends first.

INTRODUCTION - THE STARTER BLOCKS (2013 - PRESENT DAY)

Ayla

Falling in love is a lot like running a race. Before you get started, you're confident and uncertain about the outcome, but you're determined to give it your all. Some of us are sprinters, we fall in and out of love fast. For others, hurdles are put in our paths and need to be jumped to cross the finish line. Many of us go the long distance, committed to winning a love that lasts a lifetime. The rest of us are in the romantic relationships where we're running out of it, passing the baton so we can catch our breaths and take a break to prepare for the next lap around love.

When you compete, regardless of how sure you are, nervous energy courses through you. Your palms sweat, your pulse races, and your heart pounds at a rate that mimics a drum... a lot like what happens when you find love.

A race is also a series of choices. And just like falling in love, those choices must be made in hope and not in fear.

I never realized how much fear influenced my decisions.

It's not like I experienced any of my fears in real time, anyway.

I witnessed the people around me take risks and live life with brave hearts. They often returned with an anthology of stories to tell, too. Meanwhile, I watched at the sidelines protecting mine as if getting my heart broken would cause my demise.

One of my biggest fears in life was regret. I wanted every decision to be made with the right heart and sane mind because I didn't want to regret or even think about what would happen if I chose differently. So, I prepared for the bad by expecting the worse, thinking I was protecting my heart, but I was robbing myself of love instead. Looking back on things, I could have used that energy to create a good outcome in my head instead of creating a bad one. Because whatever energy I chose to align with, I was creating either way. Everything would become clear years later, though. Twelve years to be exact. And the stopwatch started in 2001... when I met a boy named Hassani.

PART I
ON YOUR MARKS

CHAPTER 1

AUGUST 2001 - LONG ISLAND, NEW YORK

$\mathcal{A}$yla

"WHY ARE WE INVITING THEM OVER FOR DINNER?"

Seated on a cushion in the corner kitchen nook, I switched between snapping photos of my mother and sipping on a glass of lemon iced tea through a plastic bendy straw. I calibrated the lens on my camera and zoomed in on her dainty hands as she chopped the last of the tomatoes. She planned to add the diced tomatoes to the garden salad she prepared for dinner.

"Because your father wants to make a lasting first impression on his new boss. That's why," my mother, Sonia, replied. Her eyes were trained down on the wooden butcher's block when she added, "I would think you'd be enthusiastic to meet someone your age being the new kid in Long Island and all."

I placed the camera down and blew air through my lips, rolling my eyes and leaning forward to help myself to another sip of my drink. I knew better than to roll my eyes while she faced me. My mother was the sweetest person you'd ever meet, but she wasn't that sweet where she wouldn't check me for being rude.

I liked saying things every now and again to mess with her though. Case in point…

"Am I meeting this new kid in Long Island so he can be my boyfriend? Or…"

She glanced at me over her shoulder. "Say what?!"

"Boys are for dating, not for being friends, remember? Didn't you tell Aunt Laurie that just the other day?"

"Your hardheaded aunt was lying to herself about a man she —*oops!*" My mother slapped her hand to her mouth. "I did it again" She slapped the counter's surface next and mumbled, "I swear… the way you speak to me, Ayla, sometimes I forget you're only a child."

I couldn't hold back my giggle. Just the mention of my aunt's name made me peek down at the shiny gold charm bracelet she flew back here with from her trip to Paris three weeks prior. I toyed with the dangling Eiffel tower and beret charms, momentarily dreaming about being just like her when I grew up.

My mother cleared her throat and resumed dicing the final ingredient for her salad. "First, let's get something straight - I told your aunt what I told her for a specific reason that is a little too grown for your ears to hear. Men can be friends… just not *with* her. And I think it's also worth noting I said *men* and not *boys*, so there."

I snickered.

"Second, what did I tell you about eavesdropping in on my conversations with your aunt, nosey? Because I know for a fact you weren't present when I said that to her"

"But you said it, right?" I arched a brow. "And correct me if I'm wrong but don't boys become men?"

"I am not answering that, little miss *nosey*." My mother laughed to herself as she leaned to her left to peek out of the kitchen. "Gosh, and while we are on the subject," she whispered this time while scooping up a handful of chopped tomatoes, "you better not let your father hear you say a thing about boyfriend anything, because he will not find it as funny as I did."

I bit back my laugh.

"For Ayla Samuels, according to him at least, all boys are to be *only* friends to you and that's it. Okay?"

"Okay, but mama, what am I going to talk about with this boy? My gut tells me nothing because we are clearly from two different worlds."

My mother rinsed her hands under the running water in the sink. "And how do you know that?"

"Because half the boys I've seen out here so far might as well be nerds."

"Well, beloved." My mother glanced at me over her shoulder once again, this time sporting a knowing grin. "Nerd or not, we can't change him into anything he isn't in time for dinner, so you're just going to have to find some way to find *something* in common with him... and in the friendliest and most cordial way possible. If for anything else, do this for your dad. What do I always tell you?"

"Not everything is about me."

"Not everything is about *you*." She held one finger up for emphasis. "Precisely."

I conceded with a sigh and a nod.

It was the last Saturday in August and the last week of my summer vacation. I'd turned 14-years-old that March and was spending the last few days of warm weather on the very quiet, quaint, and quintessentially boring Long Island. Thanks to my father's new job in the city, Aden Samuels thought it was the best time to move his tiny family out of Brooklyn and into Long Island. He'd been eying the two-story property in Nassau County for well over a year. Had a cork-board in the home office that wore the clipped and pinned picture of his dream house. He called the cork-board his vision board. He would stare at the thing for hours on end. I thought he was crazy until we drove out here for the open house, and I realized it was the same house in one of those magazine clippings he kept pinned to the board. My father spent several sleepless nights brainstorming ways to increase his income to afford the house he wanted his daughter to start her high school academic career living.

The house was okay, I guess, if you were into that long-block-of-huge-houses-in-the-middle-of-nowhere vibe. Compared to our three-bedroom two-family rowboat house on Flatbush Avenue in Brooklyn, our new home in Long Island was definitely more spacious and quieter. Did I mention how quiet it was? So quiet, if you listened well enough, you could hear other people's thoughts while out and about. An exaggeration, yes, but it was that quiet to me. And for a Brooklyn girl, silence bored me.

"Everything all set in here?" my dad asked as he stepped into the kitchen. Like my mother, my father dressed himself up like he had somewhere important to go. I lifted my camera to make my dad my subject this time. He struck a pose immediately, like he always did whenever I held my lens within view.

I laughed. "Just act natural, dad."

"Not when I look *this* good." He placed a hand on his chin. "Make sure you capture me at the perfect angle."

"Oh, always," I confirmed, playing along.

He sported a short-sleeved navy-blue button-down shirt with dark slacks and shiny cognac colored oxfords while my mother wore the prettiest floral chiffon dress with a hem that moved with the breeze blowing through our opened backyard door. I couldn't understand why this dinner was such a huge deal. So much so, my father had to beg me to replace my denim shorts and Converses with a yellow and gold summer dress, and the matching slingback thong sandals. I wore the same getup down to the shoes at the last Easter Sunday service we attended at our church in Brooklyn.

"Yes, everything is just about ready," my mother answered, glancing his direction while smiling at him. "Just adding the finishing touches to the salad now."

I watched as my father moseyed up behind my mother and wrapped his long arms around her slim waist, hunching his tall frame forward to plant a kiss on her neck. I snapped a photo, and then another, before placing the camera down on the table below me so I could finish off my iced tea.

She giggled like a schoolgirl, like he was kissing her for the very first time. She always did that when my father laid his lips anywhere on her.

I made kissing noises behind them, so they'd hear me and stop. They were never shy about showing affection in front of me. Sometimes it was sweet, other times annoying.

The two of them laughed to themselves before my father turned to approach me.

"And how about you?" he asked, sliding into the nook across from me. "Ready to make your dad look good for his boss the way you make me look good in those pictures you're always taking?"

"Now you know you don't need me to help you do any of those things, dad. You're a natural."

He smiled that smile that made it seem like everything was right with the world. My father, Aden Samuels, was one of my favorite people on the planet, next to my mom and my Aunt Laurie. He was funny, smart, charismatic, and understanding. Not to mention extremely affectionate with the woman who stole his heart their sophomore years in college.

"Yeah, but with my baby love." He reached over to pinch my cheek, "I'm sure I'll shine even more."

I blushed. "Dad, if your boss can't like you for you, then I know the problem ain't with you."

He pointed while nodding. "Ayla, when you're right, baby, you're right. But listen..."

I cocked my head to the right.

"I want you to be hospitable to their son when he gets here, all right?"

I had to keep my eyes from rolling again.

"He's your age, and the two of you will attend the same school next month. It'll be great if you two hit it off. You can have at least one person you know at a new school. I think it will make for an easier transition."

"What's wrong with him?" I crossed my legs beneath the table and leaned in. "He's a geek, huh? Uppity? An Oreo?"

My father sputtered a laugh. "A what?"

"Well, mama told me you told her your boss's son grew up here in Long Island and so far, the black boys I've seen here, which are very few by the way, are Carlton Banks-like."

He furrowed his brows. "Carlton Banks-like?"

"You know, ultra preppy and stuffy. Probably buttons his perfectly pressed white shirts all the way up to his collar and wears his sweater's sleeves around his neck."

"My daughter." He scoffed a laugh while shaking his head. "Hassani is an athlete. From what his father has shared with me over lunch, Hassani is a track runner. Has won a few medals and trophies for his junior high school. That's the reason he's attending Garvey. The coach for Garvey's track team sat with Hassani's parents and asked that Hassani attend Garvey High School and run for the school starting at the varsity level. That's rare. And from what his father tells me, he's pretty good, too."

I bit at my bottom lip. "Interesting."

Ding-Dong.

All our eyes moved toward our front door without us uttering a word.

My dad peeked down at his silver wristwatch while my mother undid the knot on her apron in record speed.

"Seems like they're on time." My father glanced my way. He was up and out of his seat, running his hands down his shirt, then over his head nervously.

"Dad, you look fine," I assured.

He smiled at me before inhaling a deep breath. He brushed his hand down the top of his head a second time.

I'd never seen him so nervous until that day.

My father's new job was a big deal. He'd secured a position at an investment firm in Manhattan. A firm with an office in One World Trade Center, to be exact. A huge upgrade from the tiny office suite he slaved at in Jamaica, Queens. That place was literally a hole in the wall spot that sat beneath the underpass of the Long Island railroad. How ironic, right? The trains he worked beneath would travel the route that would one day bring him to his dream home.

He didn't have to go there anymore though. The sky was the limit that year. My dad worked close to the clouds on the 95th floor in the North Tower of one of the most iconic buildings in the world with a firm that, according to my mother, was as famous as the building itself. At my age, none of that mattered at the time though. It all sounded great in theory, but I didn't really know how major it was. I would be lying if I said I didn't know enough to be at least proud, though.

"How do I look?" my mother asked my father as she tossed her apron on the bronze hook by our kitchen's entrance.

"Like a woman I can't wait to turn in with later tonight," my father replied, wrapping an arm around her waist to draw her close to him.

The two of them were a vision of perfection, to be honest. I used to tease them a lot, but I loved their love and how willing they were to show affection in front of me. Even back then, I wished that when I grew up, I would find the perfect somebody and nurture a beautiful relationship with my other half. I also hoped I could have the freedom I often saw missing in romantic relationships. The freedom to do as I pleased and see the world without restriction, just like my Aunt Laurie.

I released a loud and exaggerated sigh. "Don't we have guests to let in?"

My father snickered as he made his way around my mother to approach the front door.

She turned to me and pointed. "Be nice, be kind, and treat Hassani the same way you would like to be treated by him, understood?"

He's a Carlton Banks.

"Of course, mama," I assured.

There were voices before faces became visible.

"Wow, he's taller than me," I heard my father say from the front of the house.

"*Hmmm*," I hummed. "A tall geek."

"Stop that," my mother whispered.

"Oh shoot!" I heard a woman with a slight accent exclaim from a distance. "I forgot the rum cake in the car. Hassani, run out and get it for us please."

There were a few more unintelligible words exchanged between the men. Deep voices didn't penetrate the air like higher pitched ones, so I couldn't make out what they said. A bass-filled laugh followed before my father informed, "Everyone is in the kitchen, please follow me."

The chorus of footsteps started toward my mother and I and my curiosity had me leaning in my seat to see around the corner wall to get a glimpse of the people we had to impress for the next few hours.

First, my eyes landed on an older gentleman with a salt and pepper beard who appeared to be a year or two older than my father. My view then landed on a woman who was considerably shorter than the man. She had the prettiest and most sincere hazel-green eyes I'd ever seen on a person. I liked her instantly.

"Percy, Joslyn, this is my wife, Sonia," my father introduced, and the gentleman greeted my mother with a soft handshake. "And this is our daughter, Ayla."

I stood from my seat, something I knew my parents wanted me to do without being told.

"It's a pleasure to meet you, Ayla," the gentleman greeted first. "Your father speaks of you often."

His voice had an authentic Caribbean twang, and I immediately traced its origin to Jamaica. I would know. Back in the city, most if not all our neighbors were originally from the islands, often Jamaica. The rhythmic tenor of his accent in his bass-filled speaking voice reminded me of where I considered home to be, Brooklyn. And just off that, I liked him as much as I did Mrs. Franklin.

When he extended his hand, I accepted.

"Ayla, this is my boss, Percy Franklin."

"Nice to meet you, Mr. Franklin," I greeted with a smile.

"And his wife, Mrs. Joslyn Franklin," my father added.

"Ayla," Mrs. Franklin spoke after leaving my mother's side. She too had a Jamaican accent. A porcelain doll face and a bright smile rounded out my first glance of her.

Mrs. Franklin took my hand and held it in a gentle grip. "It's lovely to meet you, my dear." She glanced at my father then turned my mother's way. "She's gorgeous."

My smile transformed into a toothy grin.

"She's aight," I heard near the kitchen's entrance. "I guess."

I switched my eyes in that direction and jerked my head back at the boy standing at the entryway.

He was... wow. So *not* a geek.

"Ayla, don't mind this one," Mr. Franklin explained, stepping toward the tall teenager sporting the sly grin feet away. Mr. Franklin took a Tupperware bowl out of the boy's hand and handed it to my father. "Hassani enjoys saying things to get a rise out of people."

"Oh, well, Ayla likes to do the same," my mother spoke next, then winked at me. "So, I know she and Hassani will get along just fine."

Mrs. Franklin giggled. "Hassani, this is Ayla. Ayla, this is our knucklehead of a son Hassani."

Our eyes met for only a moment. That's because I shifted mine away from his analytical stare. His eyes glowed like gold-green marbles; fancy marbles collectors would obsess over. Instantly, I realized Hassani inherited his mixed eye color from his mother. But while her eyes were sweet to gaze at, on Hassani they were intense on impact, shaded by naturally heavy lids and black feathery lashes. His skin mirrored the mellow reddish-brown that colored the mornings during a sunrise.

Hassani was... wow.

If only he was less wow and more like what I expected.

After my mother introduced herself to Hassani and all formalities were out of the way with everyone, I noticed the tenseness in my father's shoulders calm some.

"Percy, Joslyn, please let us show you around," my mother insisted. "We haven't had family out here yet. My sister is in town and is visiting tomorrow night, but I am dying to give someone a tour of this place right now."

Mrs. Franklin smiled with all her teeth. "I would love that! We live a few blocks north of here and every time we pass this property, driving Hassani to school, I'd always gawk at its beauty from the outside. So, I would love to see what you've done with the place."

As they all filed out of the kitchen, my father was the last to leave. He peeked at me over his shoulder before turning the corner to enter our living room.

"Please be nice," he mouthed, moving out of sight.

I turned my head to face Hassani, who stood with his back against our counter.

I looked him up and down, taking in his white tee, blue jeans, and crisp black and red Jordan sneakers.

Why did I have to dress up and he didn't?

I folded my arms and asked, "What kind of name is Hassani, anyway?"

He snorted a laugh.

I honestly didn't know what else to say. I wasn't expecting him to be... *him*. My thing back then was to never show cute boys the attention they were so used to receiving for doing nothing besides entering a room. Childish, fine, but gawking or fawning? Ayla Samuels was way too cool for that.

"What kind of name is Ayla? And how do you spell it, anyway? E-Y-E-L-A?"

His voice was deep for a fourteen-year-old, and he was really tall too. Far from lanky. At his young age, he had broad shoulders and rolling hills for arms. Hassani looked for sure like he spent his time playing a sport. He had the most unwavering eyes too, but they weren't intrusive, nor did I find it rude of him to stare. Oddly enough, he didn't make me feel uncomfortable, which was a feeling I experienced in the company of boys like him back in Brooklyn. To say Hassani was cute would be lazy because he had certainly outgrown that years ago.

"It's spelled A-Y-L-A, and it's Arabic," I answered, lifting my chin with pride. "It means moonlight. My aunt named me. She went to Arabia, heard the name and loved it so much she begged my mom to name me Ayla."

He shrugged a shoulder. "Cool."

I leaned back in my seat. "And Hassani means...?"

"Handsome." He smiled wide, revealing two rows of white teeth including peeks at his back molars. His teeth were perfect, annoyingly perfect. I'd just had my braces removed a few months earlier after getting them installed at 11. I doubt he'd ever worn two tracks of metal in his life, and it was clear he wouldn't have to.

"Couldn't you tell?" he added, rather arrogantly.

I rolled my eyes at his cockiness and he snickered, while pushing himself off the counter.

"What y'all got in here to snack on before dinner, anyway?" he asked, approaching the fridge and pulling the door open.

I sat there in complete shock, watching him survey the shelves inside our fridge before deciding on a can of cheese.

"Um, what are you doing?" I asked, jumping to my feet. "Is that what you Long Island boys do? Go to strangers' homes and go through their fridge without permission?"

"You're not a stranger though," he retorted, shaking the aerosol can of cheese and popping off the top with his thumb. "You're a girl name Ayla who's name means moonlight. Your Aunty named you, after her trip to Arabia." He winked then leaned his head back, dropped opened his mouth and squeezed cheese onto his tongue.

"Oh my God, ew," I groaned.

He leveled his head to focus on me, his cheeks puffed out and full of the liquid cheese. I gagged, not at how he looked because I was sure there wasn't anything he could do that would make him look bad. I gagged at the thought of his mouth being filled with liquid artificial cheese. My father used to love that stuff on crackers. I hated it. Just the sound of it oozing out the can turned my stomach.

"Yo, A, you know who you resemble?" Hassani asked once his mouth was empty.

I shifted my eyes to his and arched a brow at his comfort in calling me by only a letter after meeting me minutes ago.

"Lauryn Hill." He slid into the nook opposite me, sitting the can of cheese down on the table in front of him. "You got the same eyes and face shape as her. You're lighter than she is, but you look just like her. The only thing missing is locs."

Hassani wasn't the first to say that. Ever since Lauryn Hill made her debut with the 90's hip-hop group, The Fugees, years prior, people had been comparing my young almond eyes and heart-shaped lips to hers. They did it so often, I dressed myself in a similar red hat, red jacket, and baggy blue jeans - like the getup she wore in the "Fu-Gee-La" video - for Halloween my last year of middle school. My friends went wild over that.

I smiled at the memory.

With some hesitation, I took my seat again, this time across from him. "That's what people tell me."

He was quiet for a moment before he told me, "I'm gonna call you A. Boogie."

I couldn't help the laugh that fell from my lips. "A. Boogie?"

"Yeah, get it?" he asked. "Lauryn goes by L. Boogie, so you A. Boogie?"

I giggled and nodded. "I get it, Hassani."

He sat there for a couple of breaths, staring at me as my smile settled on my lips. Those eyes of his were so analytical, observant, bold, and beautiful. He stared, but again, not rudely. More so as if he were trying to record something to memory. It was charming and an aspect about him that would be my favorite for years to come.

His eyes fell on the camera. "Yours?"

"Yeah."

"You're into photography?"

I toyed with the mode dial on the camera. "It's just a hobby."

"Cool. I think they have a photography club at Garvey High. My dad said you'll be going there too next month."

I nodded. "My dad explained the same."

"Starting in the same grade and everything."

"Yup."

"When is your birthday?"

"March 3rd." I crossed my legs and leaned in his direction. "You?"

"April 30th."

I sat up in my seat. "I'm older than you!"

"By a month."

I shrugged. "Older is older."

"Yeah, whatever," he said through his laugh. "So since we're going to the same school, starting the same grade and all, I think we'll be hanging out a lot."

I fought to keep my smile from showing again and instead wrinkled my brows. "Just because we'll be going to the same high school doesn't mean we'll be seeing a lot of each other."

"Why not A. Boogie?" He grinned. "You're cool, I'm cool. You got all the cool snacks in your fridge, and I like to eat. This seems like a friendship I can get with."

"A friendship?" I questioned.

"Yeah," he said with a smile, one that did not reach his eyes. His eyes questioned my question. I didn't have the balls to point that out though not even when he asked, "You cool with that?"

Back then, I thought Hassani was way out of my league. He was a student athlete; I wasn't. He had charm, which I thought I lacked. I was far from having low self-esteem, but I also never considered myself to be the "it" girl, nor did I strive to be her or anything close to a black Barbie to match his black Ken energy. But even back then, I knew there could have been more to us. Just the idea of having a simple connection with someone as dope as him was enough for me, though.

So... I settled.

"Yeah." I conceded with a smile. "I'm cool with that."

"Aunt Laurie!" I shouted, running down the case of stairs, two steps at a time.

She dropped her luggage to the floor and splayed her arms out wide to receive me. "Ayla!"

The moment I made impact with her slim frame, I hugged her tight, feeling her hug me just as tightly back.

"You two are too much." My mother shook her head. "Y'all act like y'all didn't just see each other right before we moved out here."

"Aunty, this place is *so* dull. No character."

"Ayla!" my mother shouted

"What, mama? It is."

Aunt Laurie cackled. "Favorite girl, I know exactly what you mean."

As a child, my aunt was everything I wanted to be. She was a free spirit, an avid traveler, with a love for all things new. Aunt Laurie lived the life I thought I wanted.

"Come here and let me look at you." She grabbed me by the hand and spun me around. "Fucking gorgeous... like me."

"Oh, please." My mother scoffed, placing a hand at her waist. "And language, Laurie."

Aunt Laurie tossed her head back and laughed. "Oh! Where's my big brother? You know I have to watch my words whenever he's around too. House just full of cuss police."

My mother pointed at my aunt. "Don't do that."

My aunt shrugged while holding back her laugh.

"Aden went to hang with some friends. He'll be back later tonight."

Aunt Laurie clapped once. "Perfect, Ayla..." She turned toward one of her luggages to push her hand inside the side pocket closest to her. "Look what I got for you from Milan."

I gasped at the wrapped present. "What is it?!"

"Go upstairs and open it to find out." She beamed, moving her eyes from me to my mother. "You'll be able to see it better when you put it on in front of your mirror."

She didn't have to tell me twice.

I peeled off for the stairs.

"Aht, Ayla?" my mother scolded behind me.

I stopped in my tracks, knowing exactly what that voice meant. I turned briefly and focused on my aunt. "Thank you, Aunt Laurie."

"Aw, favorite girl, you know you don't have to have any manners with me."

My mother shoved my aunt. "Laurie!"

Aunt Laurie laughed. "Go 'head upstairs. I'll be up there in a moment to see how good it looks on you."

I ran up to my room and straight to my empty work desk, pulling apart the shimmering gift wrapping paper without taking a seat. The second I lifted the lid on the long slim box, I gasped again.

In gold was my name written in script on a heart pendent that hung from the matching thin chain.

I held the necklace around my neck and smiled from ear to ear before clasping it in place.

"She always gives me the best gifts," I whispered to myself.

I knew she told me she'd be up to see me, but I also knew that was her excuse to get some alone time with my mother so they could have a little girl talk.

See, my mother was right. Back then, I used to eavesdrop all the time. I wish I had a sister of my own to girl chat with. My parents never had time to make that happen for me, though.

I tiptoed out of my room and stepped down three stairs, taking a seat on one step and leaning in to the conversation they had on the living room's couch.

"You are so hardheaded, I swear," my mother chastised. "Laurie, when are you going to settle down?"

She giggled. "Girl, please."

"I'm serious," my mother continued. "Don't you get tired of flying from city to city?"

"I'm a buyer," Aunt Laurie reminded. "For one of the top luxury brands in the world, I might add. The only way I can know about all the latest fashion is to be where the latest fashion is."

"Yeah, but you can be a *buyer* in one city."

"Oh, here we go with this conversation again." She sighed heavily with exaggeration. "I'm not trying to have the life you have, Sonia, you know that."

My mother pursed her lips while shaking her head.

"I don't need a man."

"Shit, neither do I," my mother insisted. "But they are nice to have around."

"Yup, true. On-call sex is definitely a plus."

My mother gasped, leaning forward in her seat to no doubt check if I was listening. I lifted my legs quick, so they were out of sight.

"You are too much," mom accused. "You know that, right?"

"Big sis, what I'm saying is I can't do the husband and the child thing. I am so in love with my freedom. I treasure it. I can get up and go wherever I want to whenever I please without having to check in with or answer to anyone. I'm not about to give any of my good years to a man. They're always looking to tame you for their own egos. And you know what happens after they do that, right?"

"What happens?"

"They go looking for the person you used to be."

I twisted my lips to one side and moved in even closer to the conversation.

"Laurie—"

"Uh-uh, nope, no thanks! The life I'm living, this is the life I love living, and that's a fact."

"But do you at least date Laurie? It must get a little lonely being out and away all alone."

"I date all the time, in fact." Aunt Laurie scooted closer to my mother. "I'm taking a trip to Turks & Caicos next week and I'll have some company. This business guy I met on my trip to Venezuela."

"A business guy, huh? What kind of business he into?"

"Girl, I don't know. Something that's paying, I'll tell you that much. But what I do know, though?" Aunt Laurie whistled while fanning herself. "That man is all man."

"Oh yeah?"

"Oh. Yeah." She bit her bottom lip before shivering in her seat.

"Uh, nasty!"

Aunt Laurie giggled. "But we're just having fun."

"But you like him?"

"Am I eight or something? Do I like him?!"

My mother released a loud laugh before slapping her hand to her mouth. "You know what I mean."

"He's nice," Aunt Laurie sang. "And big. He's nice and *big*."

My mother shoved my aunt and the two of them fell back in their seats laughing.

"Let me go run upstairs to see how cute my niece looks in her new chain."

"I hope you didn't spend too much on it, Laurie."

I had already left my spot on the stairs and was back in my room, so I didn't hear her response. After sliding into the seat at my work desk, I turned to face it as if I'd been sitting there the whole time.

"So?" she asked, poking her head in my door.

I turned in my seat at my desk to face her as she stood at the threshold. "I love it!"

I was out of my seat and in her arms again, wrapping my arms around her.

She gave me a big hug as always, then held me back at a distance. "Let me see it on you."

I stood with my neck straight and a smile on my lips.

"Gorgeous!" she squealed. "As always."

Hearing that from my aunt always made me smile until my cheeks hurt. She was the gorgeous one, with a pageant grin like Whitney Houston's, eyes like Angela Bassett's, and a laugh more infectious than Jackeé Harry's. She stopped the world whenever she spoke, at least through my eyes.

For the next half an hour we talked about any and everything *I* wanted to talk about. My aunt was my everything, I wanted to be more like her than my own mother.

"Ready for school in the next few weeks?"

I nodded. "I am."

"Those boys won't know what to do with themselves when you grace those halls with your presence, girl. You know that, right?" She gave me a high five. "I promise you they won't."

I cheesed until my cheeks hurt again. She mentioned boys, but only one boy crossed my mind. And as much as I wanted to stop thinking about him, I couldn't. After just one meeting, Hassani had worked his way into my thoughts and was living rent free.

CHAPTER 2

$\mathscr{H}$assani

"HASSANI!" I HEARD OVER MY SHOULDER.

I stood in front of my locker, pulling out the brand-new spiraled notebook I'd need for AP math. It was my first day of high school. I'd watched enough television shows to know what to expect, or so I thought.

Students flooded the halls, some new like me, others looked a few years older than I did and were probably the upperclassman. You could tell the new ones. Most of them stood alone in front of their lockers, their eyes shifting from left to right, absorbing their new environments. Me? I was a freshman, true, but half of my junior high 8th grade graduating class had enrolled at Garvey High School. I was in good company. And even if they weren't there, I'd still find my way at Garvey just fine.

"Hey Marcus," I said, closing my locker door. I extended my hand in his direction for a pound. He accepted, then stuffed the last of a cinnamon bun into his mouth and crumpled the cellophane paper into a ball, pushing it into his pocket.

My mother made sure I had a balanced breakfast before I left the house. Yams, boiled green bananas, a dumpling and all of that topped with salt fish and ackee. This was the standard in the house for first days of school and other special occasions. She swore eating all that now and then made me run fast on the track. My parents seemed more excited about my first day than I did. Honestly, I could understand why too. The track and field coach for Garvey sought me out to attend this high school, specifically to run track wearing the school's uniform. The coach, of the track team, Coach Briggs, visited my home to petition to recruit me, which was a little uncommon for incoming high school freshman. Usually that kind of interest took root for high school seniors, especially in this school. Apparently, it was the main hub for college coaches to snatch up players straight off the field in anticipation for the following college year. But as my father always told me, I was the exception in everything.

Marcus pressed his back to the locker door beside mine, lifting his Timberland-clad foot and pressing it flat against the metal behind him. "Man, have you seen these girls?"

I peeked over at him and chuckled to myself.

"I can tell already I'm going to love high school. The summer done changed half of them. You saw Tonya Palmer yet?"

I shook my head. "Nah, why?"

"She's gotten..." Marcus held his hands in front of his chest, splayed his fingers apart and grouped them in the shape of a dome to imitate breasts. "She got... prettier."

The laugh that bellowed out my mouth echoed down the nearest hall. He laughed in response.

"I'm serious," he continued. "And she's not the only one. Keisha Morgan, Vanessa Brown. Even Zora Levy grew a pair and you know when we graduated a few months ago, we could iron our track uniforms on her chest."

I shook my head and moved my eyes off him. He continued listing the girls we graduated middle school with and how the summer had been good to them.

I'd known Marcus my entire time in junior high school. We'd clicked in our sixth-grade homeroom class on the first day and had been inseparable ever since. Marcus and I spent our summer apart, but it was refreshing to see nothing had changed with him.

He tapped my arm with the back of his hand. "Now, *she* is someone I haven't seen." He blew air through his pursed lips. "Who is *that?*"

It wasn't what he said that drew me out of my thoughts. It was how he said it. His words came out slow like blackstrap molasses, and the energy behind them were fully charged.

"Who?" I asked, my eyes searching the halls for who had his attention.

He tapped my arm again and pointed a few feet ahead of us. "Her."

I followed the direction he gestured with my eyes. My view collided with a cloud of coils and curls that framed a familiar heart-shaped face. She dressed herself in all denim. Her jeans were high-rise and cinched at her tiny waist by a thick leather belt with the letter A as the buckle. A dark t-shirt peeked below the cropped denim jacket she wore, failing to hide her young curves I could still make out from a distance.

My brows piqued when she turned toward Marcus and I and recognition relaxed the lines on her forehead.

She shifted the two spiraled notebooks she held in her hands onto her arms to lift the opposite hand to wave at me.

I waved back, then gestured with the same hand for her to approach.

"Wait," Marcus whispered. "Did she just wave at you? Why is she waving at you? She knows you?"

"Yeah."

"From where?!" Marcus's voice went up an octave. "Did she go to Carver? There's no way she went to our junior high. I would have noticed her before you, for sure."

All I did was chuckle. She was within a foot of us before I could even think to answer any of his questions.

"A. Boogie," I said to her. She rewarded me with a smile.

Ayla was exceptionally pretty. Besides the fact that she resembled one of my biggest crushes in my teenage youth, there was a unique twist to her beauty that I hadn't seen in girls my age. She had a city girl and a shy disposition, which was ironic to me. I always considered city girls livelier. She was lax but bold in presence. Ayla stood out in a crowd with little effort on her part. I liked that a lot about her.

"I see the nickname still stands," she replied. Her eyes briefly wandered over to Marcus before returning to mine.

"Hi," Marcus greeted, stepping forward. He pressed his hand to his chest and added, "I'm Marcus."

"I'm Ayla," she replied.

"Ayla," he repeated, like he was repeating the name of a menu item.

My eyes moved between the two of them when silence settled over our little huddle. I cleared my throat and her attention returned to me.

She parted her lips to say something but stopped when Marcus questioned, "So... how do you know Hassani and not me?"

I shut my eyes tightly. I hated when he did that.

"Our parents," she clarified. "Hassani's dad is my dad's boss."

Marcus formed an O with his lips.

"We just met a week—"

"Where's your first class?" I interjected. Truthfully, Marcus didn't need to know anything other than what he'd already been told.

She pushed her hand into her jeans' back pocket and pulled out a piece of paper with handwriting on it. Ayla peered down at it, then looked up at me, turning the paper to face me.

"Across campus," she answered. "AP math."

I couldn't stop the smile from pulling at my lips. "Me too. We can walk together."

Marcus exhaled audibly beside me in response.

She balanced her weight on one hip. "*You* have AP math?!"

I tilted my head to one side. "Yes, *I* have AP math."

"Hmph."

"Hmph, what?"

She shrugged her shoulders. "Nothing, I guess. I just figured you were an athlete and—"

"And athletes can't take AP math?"

We stared at each other for a moment, her fighting back her smile and me trying my hardest not to give in to mine.

"What other classes do you have?" Marcus spoke again, moving in closer to her. "Maybe we have a class or two together too."

I scratched the back of my head, silently saying a prayer that they didn't.

"I'm enrolled in only advanced classes." She smiled politely. "Are you taking any advance classes this year?"

Marcus twisted his lips to one side.

"Marcus is the athlete you think I am and has regular classes." I turned to face him. "Right, Marc?"

His jaw protruded a bit. Probably because he clenched his jaw in response to what I said. I chuckled at the sight.

"Well, maybe next year then." Ayla turned to me. "You ready?"

I held out my hand to Marcus, and he accepted, gripping my hand tighter than normal. I didn't care. I hadn't known Ayla for that long, but I knew her long enough to know I didn't want her getting too close to Marcus.

Ayla and I stepped out the doors of the main building, the sun greeting us when we walked out. Garvey High School was one of the largest high school campuses in Long Island. The largest in New York State, actually. Five buildings made up the school, and they all orbited the massive center lawn. Garvey High was a sought after high school campus. It had everything from a large football field with an equally larger track that outlined the field's grass. An indoor recreational pool and outdoor tennis court were the other highlights of Garvey High School.

"Marcus is nice," Ayla opined to my right as we made our way across campus.

I peeked over at her to find her looking right at me. "He's cool."

"*Hey Hassani.*" When I turned to my left, I found a group of girls waving my way. I recognized them from my junior high school.

I chucked my chin their way. "What's up?"

"How long have you two known each other, anyway?" Ayla asked, forcing my focus back on her.

"Who?"

"Marcus, duh!"

I knew who she was talking about, but I wanted to play dumb. I didn't like that she was asking about him.

"Oh." I scratched the back of my head. "Since junior high."

"Hmph." She nodded. "Cool."

I dipped my hand into my pocket in search of the school's map. There were two identical buildings near where we needed to be, so I wanted to be sure we entered the correct one. My father had given me the map of the school's grounds the week prior to my first day so I'd know how to get around campus confidently.

I pulled the map out of my pocket and unfolded it, immediately locating the building Ayla and I needed. I'd placed a red dot, using a red pen, on its location from the night before.

"You dropped something."Ayla stopped walking to bend down to pick something up off the floor.

I turned to see the white paper with blue lines in her hand.

"Oh, that fell out of my pocket. It was in there with the school's map."

She stared down at the white paper she picked up, saying nothing.

"I brought it to show it to my art teacher during 7th period. I heard he used to be an architect."

Before I could think to reach for the paper in her hand, she unfolded it completely. She peeked up at me before refocusing on the paper. "What's this?"

I shoved a hand in my pocket. "Oh, it's nothing. Just a little design."

"Of?"

"A house."

She looked up at me.

"I made it at architecture camp."

"Architecture camp?" she questioned. "I didn't know that was a thing."

"Neither did I until my dad signed me up." I reached for the paper and she pulled it out of my reach to continue her observation.

"And this is what you did there? Draw blue lines on white paper? They look like just lines."

"The design of the house is on the other side. What you're looking at is the floor plan. But yeah, at camp, I drew pictures along with other designing stuff." I reached for the paper again and she pulled it back once more. "But this is mad geeky—"

"I like geeky."

We held our stares for a moment.

"I like this." Her attention returned on the paper. "Who is the house for?"

"My teacher in the program gave us an assignment to design two houses for the people in our lives but the houses had to be for the future. The design had to be futuristic. Since my mother and father would live in just one, I designed a house for them."

"This one?"

"Nah, another one."

"Then who is *this* house for?"

"You're nosey, huh?"

She shrugged. "A little."

I looked around us. "We're going to be late to class."

"We can go after you tell me."

I scratched at my head again and mumbled, "The other house is for my wife."

"You're what?"

I sighed, a little frustrated I had to repeat myself. "My wife."

Her brows shot up.

"I told you it was geeky. The assignment was to focus on the future." I laughed nervously. "You got me sharing too much info."

"*Hi Hassani,*" another girl passing Ayla and I in the opposite direction called a few feet away. "I didn't know you were going here."

"Now you do." I replied with a grin, honestly grateful for the distraction.

"Cool," she said, returning a smile. "Now I'm glad I decided to go here, too."

I nodded my head, watching as she walked away, switching her hips.

Marcus wasn't lying. The summer had been great to a lot of the girls we knew.

"Mister popular," Ayla remarked, drawing my attention back to her.

I glanced Ayla's way again and chuckled. "Not really."

"*Hey Hassani*," Ayla mocked in the same airy voice the other girls said my name in. "*Hi Hassani*. Whew! Those girls are in la la love with *Hassani*. You can practically see the hearts in their eyes when they look at you."

I laughed out loud.

"The good news is that you won't be short of options for wives around here."

"*Whoa*, I did *not* say I was looking for all that." I held my hands up in defense. "I just told you what the assignment was about. It was for the future. I had to pick someone from the future. That's it."

She giggled, glancing down at the drawing again.

"Well, I don't know how to read this but..." She turned the paper over to look at the design of the house. "If this is for your wife, and you're designing it, there should be a bunch of skylights and in every room so she can gaze up at the stars at night. Girls like that kind of stuff. I know I do." She handed me my design and walked off.

"Hmph," I huffed, folding the paper design and placing it back in my pocket.

A few steps later, we approached the building's entrance, and I pulled the wooden door open by the handle for her to enter.

"For what it's worth," she said as she stepped past me. "I kind of get the hype."

"What hype?"

"All the *Hassani* love." She rolled her eyes playfully. "I get it."

My cheeks warmed from blushing.

"But don't let that get to your head."

Too late.

～

"PASS ME THE RATCHET, PLEASE, SON," MY FATHER INSTRUCTED FROM beneath his truck's hood.

Under the setting sun the evening after my first day as a high school freshman, my father and I were outside in our driveway working on his truck.

My father drove a Range Rover back then, still does to this day.

"I like the way these things drive on the road," he'd always say whenever it was time to upgrade the vehicle.

"Flash the light a little more this way, Hassani," he directed, his head still buried under the hood.

My dad didn't believe in spending money on things he could take care of himself. If he didn't know how to do something, he'd spend the time and effort learning how to do it before paying someone. The way he saw things was, if he knew how to complete the work, whenever he outsourced, he would know if the person completed the job well.

"Hey dad," I said beside him. I held the flashlight at an angle that gave him an excellent view of the truck's spark plug. "Can I ask you something?"

"Can you ask me something," he repeated then huffed. "With you, Hassani, it's never just one question you got, boy."

I chuckled beside him.

"What's on your mind?"

"More like *who* - Ayla."

I had been thinking about her since we left her house two weeks prior, and seeing her in school earlier that day made my stomach do things that were new to me. Things I kind of liked.

"What about Ayla?"

"What do you think about her?"

My father peeked up at me, keeping his hands busy beneath the hood. "What do I *think* about her?"

"Yeah."

He stared at me for a moment before returning his focus to the truck, laughing while shaking his head. "Why don't you just come right on out with what you really want to know, Hassani?"

"Okay." I squared my shoulders and took a deep breath of confidence. "I think I like her and I want to know what you think about me asking her out."

That got his full attention.

He stepped back from the truck and placed the ratchet down on the edge of the Range to stand up straight in front of me. "Is that right?"

"Yeah," I answered with a nod.

The neighborhood was quiet, it was always quiet. We lived in the deep part of Long Island that was less than an hour away from Manhattan. Not much happened out here, so meeting a girl like Ayla who was born and raised in the city was one of the most interesting things to happen to me.

"Hassani, you like a lot of girls."

"That's not true."

He removed his work gloves and placed them down on the truck too. Running his hands down his black t-shirt he asked, "And what about Sabrina?"

I scratched the back of my head. "She and I are cool."

"And Natalie?"

"Uh—"

"What about that other little girl you invited to your birthday party at the bowling alley a few months ago? The one who was pitching a fit every time she saw you talking to all the other girls at your event? Now that one was something else." He cackled, and I shook my head while biting back my smile. "What is her name again?" He snapped his fingers as if that would help him remember. "Her name is at the tip of my tongue too, you know."

I dropped my head back between my shoulders. "Vanessa, dad."

"Vanessa!" He shouted a laugh. "Ha! That one wanted to beat all them little girls up over you. Your mother and I laughed about it all night."

I sighed with forced annoyance. "Come on, dad!"

My reaction only made him laugh harder.

"Dad, what is your point?"

He held a hand up, signaling for me to give him a moment so he could get the last of his laugh out.

I folded my arms.

"My point is *this*, son," he clarified with one final chuckle. "You've never had a friend of the opposite sex before, and platonic friendships with girls are necessary, especially when you get older. Now Ayla is a great person to have as a friend. She's smart, very mature for her age, which makes her an excellent influence on you—"

"Dad—"

"Your friendship with Ayla is a friendship that can last a lifetime. I see how you are with girls you like." He said "like," with finger quotes. "Your interest in them never lasts more than a couple of weeks."

"Dad, I—"

"And that's not a bad thing," he interjected once again. "I tell you that all the time. You should date, have fun, not get serious with anyone. Not right now. Not at this age."

"Ayla's different, though."

I don't know why I admitted that out loud. Why it was even a thought, but it was. She *was* different. I knew that the second I stepped into her parents' kitchen and locked eyes with her. It wasn't only because she was beautiful, because she was very much that, but it was more than that. I just couldn't explain what it was, and definitely not at that age.

"They're always *different* to you until they aren't."

I sighed while sagging my shoulders.

"Trust me, Hassani, you'll want to keep things as friendly as possible with Ayla. Your track record of getting bored with these girls concerns me. But it's fine because like I always say, these are the years to do what you're doing... just not with Ayla."

"But, Dad—"

He pressed both hands on each of my shoulders to stop me from speaking. "Son, I work with her father. Things not working out between you and Ayla could make things awkward at the office. Mr. Samuels and I are still getting to know each other." My father patted me on the shoulders. "Don't mess things up because you think she's *different*. She's a good girl—"

"And I'm a good guy," I insisted. "No?"

"You are. So, remain that way." He returned to his position underneath the hood when he added with finality, "Anyone but her. Ayla is just a girl you know. Trust me on this. Am I ever wrong?"

"Never," I mumbled.

I ran my tongue over my gums, knowing better than to push the issue. My father was a man of few words and when he gave his opinion on something, I seldomly went against it. Looking back at things, that was probably the one time my father was wrong.

CHAPTER 3

yla

"My God, he is so fine."

I turned my head slowly to glance at Tiara.

"Just look at him. Ugh!" she exclaimed as she continued to gawk from a distance.

We sat outside in the stands with a view of the football field and track.

Tiara and I met on our first day at Garvey in the same spot on the bleachers. Well, we'd been seeing a lot of each other in school, being that we had the same classes. Us talking and becoming friends happened in time.

"And he's only the homie to you, right?" She asked, glancing my way. "I don't want to step on any toes."

I stuffed the last of my turkey sandwich into my mouth and forced my head to nod up, then down. "Yeah, only friends. You're good."

I dusted my hands of breadcrumbs and peered toward the field, deciding to lift my camera out of my backpack. I pointed the lens in the direction she gawked.

The *"He"* who was the topic of my and Tiara's discussion was Hassani. Most of my discussions in the first few days of school with my new girlfriends revolved around Hassani. It was like the only reason they spoke to me was to get close to Hassani.

I rolled my eyes at the thought as I snapped one last photo, then returned my camera to my backpack.

He and his teammates were in the middle of track and field practice. Though school had only started three days ago, their coach was very serious about getting them in tip-top shape for their first race against a rival school. Their coach had them running several laps around the track, stopping only to complete drills midway around the field. And this was just in the mornings before school. The afternoons, like that afternoon, Tiara and I sat outside watching, their practice was unforgiving. The coach's demands that day were far more demanding than the first two days of school.

"His arms are so cut up," she gushed beside me. "And his smile, *ahh!* I want to faint every time he smiles. He doesn't have a girlfriend, right? *Please* tell me he doesn't have a girlfriend."

I shrugged a shoulder. "Not that I know of."

Tiara released a sigh of relief. "Good. I mean... it wouldn't have mattered if he did, anyway, to be honest."

I leaned away from her to get a better look at her before I scoffed a laugh.

Exactly why he's just my friend.

Hassani was my focus again. I watched as he laid his tall frame out on the football field's grass to stretch his long legs.

Although we were in the earlier part of September, the weather still offered that summer heat. And that heat created a sheen of sweat, glossing his arms and legs.

"Do you know if he has a type?" Tiara probed. "Short, tall? Like, what's his preference?"

I inhaled and exhaled the air, slowly growing irritated. It seemed all she cared to talk about with me was Hassani. And honestly, who could really blame her.

"To keep it real with you, Tiara," I started, "I don't know all that much about Hassani. We literally met last month."

"I know, but," she whined. "Do you think *I* might be his type?"

I pointed at Hassani, who I noticed had abandoned his teammates and his exercising to approach Tiara and I. "You can ask him yourself. He's headed this way right now."

"Oh my God." She perked up in her seat and ran her hand down her long black curly hair. Tiara turned her body to face me. "How do I look? Do I have anything in my teeth?" She blew air into her hand and cringed. "I knew I shouldn't have packed tuna. My breath reeks of fish."

As she continued to fire off questions and self-criticisms in a panic while ironing her already perfectly coifed hair down with her hands again, I made eye contact with Hassani who flashed a smile the moment he saw me looking.

"I see you haven't passed out yet from running and completing drills," I teased. "Good for you."

"Oh, that?" He pointed briefly behind himself. My eyes did a slow crawl down at his exposed stomach when he lifted his track shirt to clean the sweat off his face. "That's nothing. This feels like a warmup, to be honest with you. I was hoping coach would've started the day with a real challenge."

"Hmph," I huffed.

"But school just started, so I guess he's taking it easy on us."

Tiara scooted closer to me and nudged me against my rib using her elbow. If by any chance that didn't get my attention, she cleared her throat for emphasis.

Taking the hint, I asked, "Hassani, have you met Tiara?"

His hazel-green eyes roamed over to an eager Tiara before he rewarded her anxiousness with a smile. The girl practically melted against the metal beneath her.

"Hey Tiara," he greeted.

"Hi, hey, hi, Hassani," she said in one long stream of breath, bending a lock of her curly hair behind her ear. "You look great out there."

"Thank you." He smiled while folding his bottom lip into his mouth and running his teeth over the fullest part.

Tiara sighed beside me, and I had to bite my tongue to keep from laughing.

"So, Hassani," I started. "Tiara wanted to know if—"

Tiara elbowed me a second time against my rib, this time harder than the first nudge.

"*Ow!*" I howled, twisting my head in her direction. "What the *hell* was that for?!"

Tiara smiled at me nervously before looking Hassani's way again.

Hassani lifted a foot and placed it against the metal railing that divided Tiara and I from him. He leaned in.

"If, *what*?" he quizzed.

"If," she spoke in haste, her fair skin becoming red right before my eyes. "If you think we'll beat Lincoln High in our first game?"

His brows furrowed before he checked over his shoulder. I stared at Tiara from the corner of my eye.

"Uh, yeah, I think so." Hassani lifted his shirt once more while he took steps backwards to return to the track.

"Practice is about to start again so I'll check you later Ayla," he said, turning to jog off.

"Later," I said as he turned to leave.

"It was great meeting you," Tiara hollered.

Hassani turned to face us, now jogging backwards. "Nice meeting you too, uh..."

"Tiara," she reminded. "It's Tiara. T-i-a-r-a. Tiara."

His eyes switched to me, and I tucked my lips in my mouth to keep from laughing. Hassani fought back a laugh but still managed a wave and a nod before pivoting on his feet to run toward the track, leaving Tiara and I alone again.

I twisted in my seat to face her. "No, you did not just spell your name out for him."

She slapped her forehead with her palm.

"What was that?"

"I wasn't ready!"

"Tiara." I squinted an eye. All the rambling about him you were doing earlier. How weren't you ready?!"

She shrugged a shoulder. "He makes me so nervous. I didn't think he'd make me *so* nervous!"

"Alright, check it, we haven't known each other for long, fine," I stated as I gathered my things, "but you cannot be elbowing me like that and still be able to breathe this air out here. I have had to handle my friends back in Brooklyn for doing less, so *please* understand how lucky you are."

She giggled. "I'm sorry girl, but I wasn't really expecting you to put me on blast like that."

"Well, how else was I supposed to answer any of the questions you asked me?" I grabbed the Tupperware my mother packed my sandwich in earlier that day, stuffing the plastic container into my backpack.

"Well, not like *that* and definitely not right now." She crinkled the empty bag of potato chips she'd been eating from, turning it into a foil ball. "Ask him when it's only you two and *then* tell me in homeroom tomorrow."

I chuckled while shaking my head.

For the rest of our lunch period, Tiara and I remained on the bleachers, watching Hassani and his teammates complete drills before running their allotted laps around the field.

His calf muscles became the center of my attention. How they flexed when he picked up speed on the track. Hassani cut through the air like a bullet, his arms steady with the wind he created from his quick pace.

His long legs aided in him taking up space on the track. Hassani breezed past his teammates, completing his laps around the field just as the coach requested, and in record speed like it was nothing. While the other guys, including Marcus, showed their exhaustion all in their faces, Hassani appeared relaxed and focused, as if he were just going for a casual stroll around the track.

"Are you sure I'm not getting in your way with Hassani?"

I whipped my head so fast in Tiara's direction. For a moment, I'd forgotten she was even there.

She sat with her arms folded in that instance as she stared at me with wrinkled brows.

I fanned my hand in the air. "Didn't I tell you you're good?"

"I mean, yeah, you did." She paid another glance his way before returning her view to me. "But the way I just saw you looking at him..."

"We should go." I shot up from my seat. "You know Ms. Ramirez warned us on the first day she will lock the door to English if we ever arrived late and we only have five minutes to get to class."

Tiara jumped to her feet too. "Oh, true, true! Let's go."

As Tiara gathered the rest of her stuff, I treated myself to one last view of Hassani.

LATER THAT EVENING, I STARED DOWN AT MY HISTORY TEXTBOOK, trying my hardest to record the passage I read to memory. I felt myself nodding off as the text floated right before my eyes. Out of all the subjects in school, U.S. History was my least favorite because of all the reading about things I considered boring to read.

I was two seconds away from nodding off again when the phone I kept on my desk – a phone I begged my parents to allow me to have in my room the first day we moved in - rang with a call.

The cries of seagulls the moment I answered the phone brought a smile immediately to my face.

"Hey Aunt Laurie," I sang before she even spoke a word.

She laughed. "Now, how did you know it was me calling?"

"The only person I know who is anywhere besides here in boring Long Island is you."

She laughed again, sighing once she got the last of her amusement out. "How's my favorite girl doing?"

I dog-eared the page in my history textbook. "Hanging in there. Studying."

"Good girl." In the distance, I heard music playing. "Study so you can get all you want out of life once you get to my age."

"Are you still in Turks and Caicos?"

"I am."

I smiled. "Will you bring me back something pretty?"

"You know I always do."

My mother used to describe my aunt, her baby sister, as miss wild and free. Aunt Laurie had a travel bag permanently strapped to her shoulder, it always seemed, and a travel bug she couldn't quite shake when I was younger. My aunt got her passport stamped so often, it was always exciting viewing the latest one. And there was always one that was new to view.

We spoke a lot on the phone. I could count on my fingers the amount of times she actually stayed still long enough in a home of her own where we could visit her and not her always stopping by our house whenever she was in town.

"Laurie, you ready?" the bass-filled voice permeated the phone line. My brows went up instantly.

"Okay, my favorite girl," she told me, "I have to go."

That made my brows arch even higher. "Running when a man calls, huh?"

"Ha!" She shouted a laugh that made me giggle. "You better not let your mother hear you talk like that. She'll blame me for it, like always."

I smiled big.

"But between you and me, *that man* that's got me running when he calls? Might be your new uncle."

Light taps on my opened bedroom door broke my focus and made me twist in my seat at my work-desk. It was my father.

"Aunty, I'll talk to you later. Dad just arrived."

"Give him and your mama my love." She blew a kiss through the phone.

I blew one back. "Love you, bye."

"Love you more. Bye-bye."

When I turned to face my dad completely, I noticed the two white saucers he held in each hand. On each plate laid a slice of strawberry shortcake. My eyes widened at the sight.

"Your Aunt Laurie?" he asked at my door's threshold.

"You know it! She told me to give you and mom her love."

"Hopping from plane to plane again, I assume." He shook his head with a smile on his lips. He held up the two plates of cake.

I wagged my finger. "Now, dad, you know mama does not like—"

"*Shh,*" he shushed. My father checked over both shoulders and I giggled. "Sometimes having dessert first is a good thing. I doubt it'll spoil our appetites before dinner, anyway."

I cocked a brow, knowing he was full of it.

"And besides." He winked. "These are tiny pieces of cake. I was mindful while slicing them, see?" He held the plate out in front of himself and closer to me for me to examine, and I tucked my lips in my mouth to keep from laughing. "So technically they don't really count. Now, eat this with me or I'll have no problem eating them both and you know it."

I needed no more convincing.

I quickly closed my textbook and waved him into my room. He chuckled, leaning forward to plant a kiss on my forehead when he was close before placing one plate down in front of me on my desk. He then took a seat at the foot of my bed, opposite me.

I'd spotted the orange and white Juniors bag in his grip the second he stepped out of the car in the driveway earlier. My new bedroom window faced the side of the house with the perfect view of the driveway. Ever since we moved to Long Island, my bedroom's walls would light up whenever he returned home. That's because his car's headlights cast a glow through my window curtains at the same time every weeknight when he returned from work in Lower Manhattan.

"So." He forked a piece of the sweet cake into his mouth. "It's been three days at Garvey High. What's the verdict?"

I shrugged. "It's cool I guess." I took a bite out of the sweetness and smiled at the familiarity and memories the sponge cake, whipped cream, and fresh strawberries elicited. I missed Brooklyn so much.

"The teachers are cool at Garvey; the campus is huge, as you already know."

"*Mm-hmm.*"

"I like it."

"And Long Island?"

"Well, now Long Island..."

He scooted forward in his seat, curious. "Yes...?"

"It's quiet, dad. Too quiet." I scraped my fork against the plate to get some of the whipped cream off the prongs. "Perfect-horror-film-backdrop quiet."

He laughed.

"Practically nothing happens here, dad. But I guess that's what makes it peaceful to you, huh?"

"Yup. Exactly how I like it."

I rolled my eyes playfully and dropped my attention down on my cake.

"And... how about Hassani?"

I lifted my eyes out of my plate. "What about Hassani?"

"Has he made your transition from Brooklyn to Long Island better?"

I shrugged a shoulder, hoping my non-verbal response appeared as nonchalant as I was forcing it to look. "I guess."

He smiled to himself while focusing down on his plate again.

I closed my eyes briefly, already annoyed with myself for asking, "What dad?"

He fought back his smile. "Nothing."

I waited, knowing there was more. There was always more.

"I thought I noticed something there between you two the day he and his parents came for dinner."

I cutout a big slice of the cake with the side of my fork and shoved the piece of cake into my mouth. I figured, if my mouth was full, I wouldn't have to answer.

"You know your mother and I were friends in college."

My eyes moved in his direction quick.

"You were? I mumbled.

"*Mm-Hmm.*" He grinned to himself before taking another piece of cake onto his fork to shovel into his mouth. "*Good* friends, too... until we became more."

"Well." I shifted in my seat uncomfortably. "Hassani and I are *only* friends."

"Hmph."

"And even if we weren't," I said, keeping my eyes glued on my plate. "I doubt he'd ever notice me with all the girls who are constantly in his face, doing everything to get his attention."

"If he's as smart as I know him to be, I'm sure he's realized by now none of them compares to you."

I pursed my lips together to keep from giving into the smile, trying to pull them up. "You *have* to say that."

He wrinkled his brows. "And why is that?"

"Because you're my dad, dad."

He shooed my comment away with the wave of his hand.

"Besides, weren't you the same one who clarified me dating was a no-no?"

"Things are changing," he acknowledged with a smile. "*You're* changing. Getting older. You're a high school student now." He sighed. "I suppose I'm coming to terms with the fact you're no longer my little baby, Ayla. You'll always be *my* baby, but you're not *a* baby. Dating, I must understand, is a part of your teenage life. Marriage, inevitable—"

"Whoa." I held a hand up. "Marriage talk now?"

"Yes." He chuckled. "And while we're on the subject, make sure you do me one favor - marry rich, okay?

"Dad, rich?"

"Yes." He confirmed. "Marry someone rich with integrity, honor, respect, and devotion..."

I dropped my head back between my shoulders. "Dad—"

"All right, all right." He conceded. "I guess it *is* a little too soon for all that, I get it. But look, all I'm saying is I will not stifle your growth because I want to be unrealistic. I can't keep you in a bubble. There isn't one large enough for you in actual life. I checked. Twice."

I laughed.

My father back then wasn't strict, but he'd always clarified having a boyfriend was not even a thought I should consider. School was a priority, my extra-curricular activities a close second. To hear him bring up dating was like hearing him speak to me in a foreign dialect.

"I like Hassani," he continued. "He's a good kid."

"Where is this coming from, dad?"

He shrugged a shoulder. "I just wanted to let you know that if you *were* interested in him..."

"I'm not."

That was a lie.

"We're *just* friends."

And there's no way I'm willing to compete, or worse, fight with those girls at school for his attention.

My father stared at me for a moment before shrugging a shoulder and simply saying, "Okay."

I nodded to myself, relieved he didn't push the issue.

"It may not be clear to you now, Ayla," he stated. "But when you get to my age, you'll see why being friends with the person you love is an excellent foundation for a lasting and healthy relationship."

I nodded, even though at the time his words didn't really resonate with me. Eventually they would though, many years later. My dad had a way with living in the future. How we ended up in our house was the biggest proof of that.

"Now finish your cake baby love before your mother finds us in here ruining our appetites."

I gasped. "But you said—"

"Less talking Ayla." He told me with a full mouth. "And more eating. I think I hear her heading this way."

My mother clearing her throat behind us made my dad turn quick.

"Oh, *she's* already here." my mother said, tossing the dishrag she carried over her shoulder. "And what are you two doing?"

I stuffed the rest of the cake in my mouth, trying my hardest not to spit it out while laughing.

"Nothing," my father mumbled through a full mouth, his cheeks bulging with the cake.

My mother scoffed while shaking her head. "Aden."

"What?" He approached her, pulling her into a hug.

She played along trying to free herself from his hold, but I knew my mother well enough to know she wouldn't have wanted to be anywhere other than in my father's arms.

"I saved the best piece for you," he informed, leaning in to peck her on the lips.

"Oh yeah?" She grinned, coiling her arms around the back of his neck one at a time. "And where is it, handsome?"

He pecked her again, and I cringed at the thought of them moving their kiss into one with tongue. They've done so too many times to count in front of me.

"Seriously, guys?" I stood from my seat and took steps out of my room. "You two should do that in *your* room." I took my father's plate, stacked it on top of mine. They snickered behind me while I made my way toward the stairs to head down to the kitchen.

"One day you'll be in love too, Ayla," my mother promised. "And you won't want to show love in only one room."

CHAPTER 4

$\mathcal{A}$yla

"SO, WHAT YOU'RE SAYING IS, I CAN BORROW YOUR NOTES, RIGHT?"

Hassani and I were making our ways to third period math like we'd been doing since the first day of school. We'd only started school a week ago, but already we'd fallen into a routine.

"Hassani, school started seven days ago and you're slipping already?"

He adjusted the strap of his backpack over his shoulder. "Not slipping, just dotting my i's and crossing my t's like my mother always tells me to do."

I pursed my lips together.

"Mr. Raymond is all about these formulas, man, I don't get it." He shook his head. The sound of our sneakers pattered against the pavement as we shortened the distance between ourselves and our class. "I can solve the equations fine in my head using my own way but he's always like, *you have to follow the formula Hassani*," Hassani mocked. "Personally, I think he's ego trippin' but whatever. You're a good note taker." He bumped his shoulder with mine. "And you use those index cards and everything. Mad organized with it."

"You mean index cards you can get from the stationary store like I did?"

"Come on, Ayla."

I paused in my step to turn and face him.

Hassani stuck out his bottom lip in an exaggerated pout and I sighed.

"Do me this one thing, please."

I gave him a blank stare.

"I thought we were friends."

Right. *Friends.*

When he'd originally suggested that very thing in my kitchen the month earlier, I thought it was... interesting. The idea of being friends with a boy like Hassani was both intriguing and frustrating to me. He wasn't the type of guy a girl could be friends with. He was the type of guy a girl would crush on. But I'd willingly friend zoned myself because teenaged Ayla believed being his friend was safer and more achievable than being anything more. After the conversation my dad and I had several nights before, though, I was second guessing my decision.

If only I were brave enough to admit that, even if it was only to myself.

I stared up at Hassani, then broke eye contact when he flashed his signature boyish smile.

That smile had the girls at Garvey High awestruck, even the girls in higher grades than Hassani and I.

They were so interesting to watch. Planting themselves on the bleachers to watch him practice. Going out of their way to stand behind him in the lunch line or to pass by his locker while he was getting his books so they'd have an opportunity to exchange words with him. The girls in our school would stoop so low as to befriend me, or at least know me on a first name basis, with the primary goal of getting close to him. It was offensive they thought I didn't realize what they were doing. And we were only in the second week of school. It was too much, and it was for that very reason I knew better than to even think about wanting more with him. I did not need the stress, certainly not at fourteen. Besides, Hassani showed no signs he was checking for me in the least.

Because of that, I'd done well with not staring at him for too long whenever we were alone, although he was well worth the attention. He made my stomach muscles flutter and my heart do weird things I couldn't quite recognize at fourteen.

And it wasn't only his looks that did those things to me. It was *him*, in his entirety. His energy, I guess? His looks were for sure hard to ignore. Not to mention, his piercing hazel eyes that had specs of green. The green was more pronounced when he wore any variation of the color, I learned in the short time we knew each other.

I teased him the first day of school when the girls flocked to him like lint to his track and field uniform but, honestly? The fanfare made sense. I over-stood and inner-stood the fanfare, actually. As a teenager, Hassani was truly a sight to behold, and he was well aware of that fact. Which was why I refused to tell him how captivating he was or even worst show him.

"We *are* friends," I answered, punctuating my words with a gentle punch to his arm.

His bicep was hard, solid. I hated myself for noticing.

"I'll give you the notes when we get to class," I conceded. "Promise."

A shriek a few feet away from us made Hassani and my shoulders jump before we turned toward the loud cry. A girl went running past us next with tears in her eyes and her hand covering her mouth.

Everything moved fast after, but way too slow at the same time. Voices fluttered around us. A bunch of students took large steps or ran quickly to enter the surrounding buildings. Panic swelled like a wave in seconds.

"What the hell is going on?" I asked lowly, to more so myself.

"I don't know. Aye, excuse me." Hassani reached out to stop another girl who tried to breeze past us in the opposite direction. She wore the same panicked yet puzzled look on her face as the others around Hassani and I. "What's everyone's problem?"

She inhaled a stuttered breath, raising a shaky hand to her forehead. "A plane hit one of the twin towers in Manhattan."

I felt the blood drain from my face instantly.

"Wait, what?" Hassani questioned beside me. I guess what she revealed sounded so unreal to him, he thought he misheard her.

Instead of responding, she burst into tears.

I looked up at him. "Did she just say—" I couldn't complete my question. My mouth had suddenly become dry. I held my hands up in front of me and tried my hardest to breathe in enough air to remain on my feet. There was no way she'd said what I thought she'd said.

"The twin towers?" Hassani asked. "As in the World Trade Center, twin towers?"

"Yeah," she said through her cries while backing away from us. "I have to go. I have to call my father. He works in that area."

My dad.

"How's AP math going," my dad asked me earlier that morning. The day had started as it did every other day. Shards of sunlight fought for entrance through our kitchen window blinds, tattooing the walls with sun lines. It was only he and I in our kitchen. My mother was up in her room busying herself in the mirror, applying her makeup like she always did while my father and I ate cereal seated in the kitchen's corner nook.

I swear she wore makeup for my dad more than for herself. A lot of the girly things my mother did back then was more for my father than for herself.

"I do it to make him happy because he makes me happy," is what she always told me whenever she did something she was only doing because he liked it.

"It's going," I answered my dad.

"I hear you and Hassani are in the same math class." My father spooned Honey O's into his mouth and grinned.

I rolled my eyes. "Dad, please don't start with this again."

"What did I say?" He shrugged innocently. "All I did was ask about math."

"No, you asked about Hassani, indirectly." I folded my arms.

"Ayla, I tell you all the time you're too smart and too sharp for me"

"Well..."

He chuckled "Who's the adult here again?"

I balled my lips to keep from laughing. "I already told you Hassani and I are only friends."

"And how is that going?"

I tried to hold back my smile, but it was getting increasingly hard to do that with my father wiggling his eyebrows at me from across the table.

He laughed. "Is it a crime I like someone for you? Especially when I know their parents and like them too?"

"Most girls my age would say it is."

"Well, baby love, you're not like most girls."

"And these days you've changed so much you're obviously no longer like most dads."

He bowed in his seat. "Why, thank you."

I snickered. "Most girls would also think it's a bad sign when their father likes a boy."

He tilted his head. "Oh yeah? Why's that?"

"Dads don't do that, dad. You should know that. And when they do like a boy for their daughter, the boy is always a dweeb."

My father leaned in. "Is Hassani a dweeb?"

"Far from it.

"So..." He tapped his chin. "When do I get the ticker tape parade? Why aren't I being celebrated right now?"

"Because you're being weird. Wanting me to like a boy? That's very un-dad like."

He threw his hands up. "Oh, I'm sorry. I've never been a dad before to a girl your age. It's all so new to me, so please forgive me."

I giggled.

"It's not like there's a manual on this or anything."

"Hilarious." I got up to place my empty cereal bowl into the sink.

"You ever seen your face whenever you talk about him?"

I turned to face him.

"Obviously you haven't since it's impossible to without a mirror."

He had my attention.

"It lights up." He smiled. "Like how my face lights up whenever I talk about your mother."

"Dad." I feigned annoyance. "Please stop."

"You should ask him out."

I pointed. "Look, if you want to do things dads don't do, you can go for it. As for me, I will not do what girls don't do."

"Your mother asked me out," he revealed.

I jerked my head back. "She did?"

"She sure did." He smiled big. "She got tired of waiting for me to do it, so she asked me out and her doing so impressed me. I fell even more in love with her because of it."

My brows rose with surprise. "Wow. I would have never guessed that."

"Ask him out," he challenged. "Then later tonight you can tell me all about it. I'll get Juniors."

Hassani and I stared at each other for a beat, both of our chests rising and falling in sync.

I parted my lips and said, "I have to call my—"

"Yeah." He grabbed my hand and pulled me in the opposite direction of the building that housed our AP math class. "Come on. I have to call my dad too. We can use the phone in the main office."

~

HASSANI

OUTSIDE HER HOUSE HAD AN ENERGY I IMMEDIATELY SENSED WHEN I stepped out of my father's truck. Night had set when my parents and I arrived at Ayla's home. Earlier that day, when I called the bakery from the school's main office phone, my father answered and told me to escort Ayla home.

"Dad, is everything okay?" I asked, peeking at her over my shoulder as she kept the phone to her ear with one hand and the other on her forehead. In the short time I watched her, I observed how she placed the phone down on the dock and lifted it again, pecking at the numbers on the dock and then placing the phone back to her ear.

"Just make sure she gets home as soon as possible," my father stated.

When she and I received the news, my mind went straight to my dad. He and my mother usually drove me to school in the mornings before they went to work. They'd done this together from the time I started kindergarten. My father would drop me off first, then he'd drive my mother to our family bakery in Long Island City, which was on the western tip of Queens, before hopping on the FDR Drive and taking it to Manhattan for work. Turns out, he did things differently the morning of September 11th because he never made it into his office in the city.

When my parents arrived at the bakery, my father noticed a leak in the cellar. A pipe had burst and flooded the basement with at least a foot of water. So, he stayed at the bakery with my mother until the plumber arrived to repair the pipe, then my father drove back home to work from our home office since he feared traffic would be too heavy at the late morning hour. When I called my mother at the shop, because I couldn't get my father on his line at his office, I released the longest sigh in my life when he was the one who answered the shop's phone.

I thank God to this day for the shop's busted pipe.

Later that night, my mind raced with a thousand thoughts as my parents and I made our ways up the paved path leading to the Samuels' front door. My mother rushed up ahead of us. She'd grabbed one of the ready-made carrot cakes from a stand at the bakery to bring to their house.

"Dad," I said in a tone above a whisper.

He looked at me with solemn eyes. "Yes, son?"

I'd never seen him so sad before that day. He was also quieter than usual. It was weird, but I understood enough not to question it.

"Wh-what do I say to Ayla?"

My father sighed and wrapped his arm around my shoulder. In that moment, I was so grateful to feel his embrace. Something I would have wiggled myself out of before that day, I was so relieved to feel in that instance. Things could have gone a completely different way if he'd actually made it into work.

"I wish I could tell you," he answered. "Just say whatever comes naturally to your heart."

Up ahead, the house's door had opened and Mrs. Samuels stood at the threshold with sagging shoulders. Her eyes were red rimmed and her hand clutched the door's knob like it was the only thing keeping her on her feet.

When my mother was close, Mrs. Samuels fell into my mother's arms sobbing so loud, her voice pierced through the night... and my heart.

"I am so sorry, Sonia." My mother tried to console Mrs. Samuels in her tight embrace. She handed off the cake to my father, who'd power-walked up the paved walkway to meet them at the door.

I pushed my hands into my pockets as my mother escorted Mrs. Samuels back into the house. Mrs. Samuels clung to my mother in a way I will never forget. She looked like she relied on my mother for something no one else could give that night.

"Son?" my father called when we'd arrived inside of the house. "Place this on their kitchen counter, please."

I nodded and did as I was told.

"This is a nightmare," Mrs. Samuels cried. "A complete nightmare. I can't believe this is happening. He was *just* here this morning."

My mother rubbed her back as Mrs. Samuels rocked from side to side.

"I don't know what to do. It's nothing but rubble over there." Her eyes went wild. "Will I get his remains? Will they even find Aden under all of the—" She stopped to take a breath. "I don't know where to start with this."

"Don't think about that right now," my father insisted.

"My sister won't be here until the morning..." Mrs. Samuels stared out into the distance. "Probably not *even* the morning because they've canceled all flights in and out of New York. She's stuck in another country, and she's a complete wreck over this. I don't know what to do—"

"I will stay with you for as long as you need me to, Sonia," my mother insisted, pulling Mrs. Samuels in with another tight embrace. Instead of it providing comfort, it seemed to make Mrs. Samuels cry even more.

My father cleared his throat and asked, "Where is Ayla?"

At the mention of her name, I stood with my shoulders tense.

Earlier that day, after I hung up with my dad, I tried to walk Ayla home like he asked, but she refused for me to follow her. She ran out of the school's office in a panic, and I let her. I hated myself for letting her do that.

Mrs. Samuels exhaled a sigh that said it all.

"Ayla's in her room," she answered. "She's been there since she returned from school." Mrs. Samuels brushed her hand through her pressed hair and choked back a cry. "I'd been trying to calm myself down in time for her return. I didn't want to tell her anything until I knew something but..." She shut her eyes tight. "Ayla figured it out the moment she saw my face."

I still hoped Mr. Samuels was okay. Deep down, I hoped he too didn't make it into work and was without communication to let Ayla and Mrs. Samuels know.

"If I hadn't spoken to him while he was at the office a half an hour before..." She swallowed hard. "Before it happened, I could confidently tell her everything would be okay. But I can't lie to her. She'd see right through it." Mrs. Samuels held a trembling finger beneath her nose, trying to fight back her cry. "She's been in her room all day. Hasn't spoken a word, shed a single tear. She's been sitting in front of her window, waiting... for hours."

"Waiting?" My father questioned.

Mrs. Samuels nodded. "Yeah, waiting for her father to back into the driveway like he does every evening."

"Oh God," my mother whispered, before swiping away a tear from her eye.

My father peered over at me and I read his expression immediately.

"Son?" he asked with arched brows.

"Aight," I answered, knowing exactly what he wanted me to do.

My feet felt like they weighed a ton beneath me. Each step was harder to take as I made my way up the stairs. The house was quiet, all of Long Island was quiet the night of September 11th. So many of the students at our high school had at least one parent who worked in the city. You could slice through the worry in the air with a machete, that's how thick it was in Long Island. Living in Long Island was safer than living in the city, according to my father. So many people moved to the island for that reason. Believing it was dangerous to work in Manhattan would have been crazy until that day. I knew then, even at fourteen, things would never be the same.

In front of Ayla's room, I peeked in through the crack of the door to see her doing exactly what her mother said she'd been doing all day - sitting at the edge of her bed in front of her window, waiting. I'd never been in the position to console someone before. Death was a mystery until the day of the attacks.

I swallowed what little confidence I had in the moment and pushed the door gently. It creaked opened, and Ayla gasped softly while turning quick in her seat on the bed to glance my way.

"Dad?!" she shrieked, stopping herself when she noticed it was me. Her brows relaxed, and she closed her eyes for a moment before opening them again. She stared at me for a beat, her shoulders sagging in defeat before she turned to face the window again. I took careful steps into the room, taking in the posters of R&B artists taped to her purple-painted walls. She sat at the side of her bed, wearing the same jeans and TLC t-shirt she'd worn earlier that day. Ayla had drawn her curtains wide open, her eyes were as wide as she fixed her pupils straight ahead.

I stopped beside her and kept my eyes on her as I took a seat next to her. She never broke focus from the window. Didn't say a word even after I sat mere inches away from her. Her inhales were stuttered, and her bottom lip trembled like she was holding back those tears her mother said she had yet to shed.

So, I sat there with her for a few minutes, as quiet as she was. I honestly didn't know what to say and feared saying the wrong thing. I feared the same thing she feared when we heard the news together hours earlier, and if she was anything like me, nothing anyone would say would be enough to soothe the pain of losing my dad.

I scooted forward in my seat, leaning toward the window. Exhaled against the glass, fogging the surface with my breath. Over the condensation I wrote "I'm sorry" with my finger and sat back.

The moment she read my message on the window, her inhales became audible, and I watched her body vibrate as she fought her damndest to keep it all in.

I wrapped my arm around her and pulled her close to me, and that's when she let it all out. The tears, her cries.

Ayla fisted my shirt in her hand and clung to me the way Mrs. Samuels did to my mother and I held her.

"He has to be okay," she cried against me. "He has to be okay."

I held her tighter against me, hoping the closer I pulled her to me, the more her pain would be easier to bear, but it didn't. She just cried harder, so I held her tighter.

I let Ayla cry against me for what felt like hours until she fell asleep from exhaustion in my arms.

CHAPTER 5

yla

THE BIRDS COMPETED WITH THE SUN FOR MY ATTENTION. THEY WERE loud. Their chirps intruded on my sound space, distracting me from what I was doing. It sounded like there were hundreds outside, but I'm sure only two, maybe three, sat perched on a tree branch close to our house. I wondered, had they always been loud? Was it possible I'd never noticed? I probably never realized the volume because usually when I sat in the kitchen nook, mine and my father's voice and laughs would be the ones bouncing off the kitchen's walls. Not the birds.

A week had passed since we buried him, two weeks since he perished. My dad's remains were one of the first few found during search and recovery. My mother told me we were one of the *lucky ones* because we could bury his body while others were filling the caskets of their relatives with rocks. I didn't feel lucky. At least if they did not find him, I'd still have hope he was alive somewhere out there.

The scene at the cemetery would remain burned in my memory

forever. My mother bawling her eyes out, being held back from approaching my father's casket as the mahogany wood descended lower and lower into the deep plot. She'd been sleeping a lot. Unable to muster up the strength to see me off to school on my first day back.

"You can take another day off," she rasped as I got ready in the bathroom earlier that morning. "Your principle is aware of our situation. He said you can take as much time off as you need Ayla."

"I'm fine, mama."

I wasn't.

I was far from that.

But if I spent another hour in the house, listening to my mother trying to stifle her tears in her bedroom while the absence of my father's voice haunted me, I'd lose what left of my mind I had.

The morning I returned to school, I moved around the house carrying out my usual routine, hoping I'd feel like my old self once I concluded them. Toilet, sink, tub, then down to the kitchen for a bowl of cereal. I'd pulled out the cereal, the bowl, and the milk, sat everything on the nook's table, and slid in across from them all. Then the birds started.

"I can take you to school."

The rasp in her voice was hint she'd just finished crying yet again. She stood at the kitchen's entrance still wrapped in her robe, her silk headscarf tied securely to her head. Knowing her, her shoulder length hair laid wrapped and pinned in place from three nights ago. She hadn't done her hair in days. My mother was dressed for rest.

"I'm going to walk," I told her.

Her eyes moved to my breakfast setup. "Your bowl is still clean. Did you eat?"

"No." I shrugged. "I guess I'm not hungry."

She sighed. "Let me get changed—"

"Mama, it's fine." I stood from my seat and lifted my backpack off the floor. "I prefer to walk this morning."

Closing the space between us, I approached her once each strap of my backpack clutched the tops of my shoulder blades. The whites of her eyes bore red lines, and the bags forming beneath them had taken on a puffy appearance. My mother, Mrs. Sonia Samuels, strongest woman I knew, looked so defeated.

I inhaled a stuttered breath.

I hope I never love someone as hard as she loved my dad, I thought to myself.

"I promise I'm fine walking." I leaned closer and pressed my lips to her cheek, leaving a kiss there.

When I pulled back, my mother took my chin in her hand. She said, "It hurts to not see you smile."

I stared back at her.

"I know it'll be a while, but I just..." She took a breath and sighed. "I wish there was something I could do, something anyone could do to make you smile at least once today."

"I'm fine, mama," I repeated yet again, but this time I spoke the words more so to myself. I wanted to believe I was okay so bad. "I'll see you later, okay?"

Inhaling the outside air the moment I stepped out of the house didn't give me the same satisfaction it gave my dad. Every morning before school, we'd exit the house together in route to the car and the second his foot touched the welcome mat below our front door, he would smile this genuine smile that shined brighter than the sun.

I stepped down the stairs and down the paved walkway, heading toward school. It was only my fifth week at Garvey High, and I wondered how things would be after everything. The news stations wouldn't stop talking about what they called "terrorist attacks" and every time they mentioned "9/11" I was mentally transported back to the horrifying day, wishing the moment in time was only a nightmare I'd eventually wake up from. Since they wouldn't stop talking about it, I stopped watching TV altogether.

If it wasn't the news anchors force-feeding reminders about the day, it was the neighbors or my family members constantly asking me if I was okay every time they saw me. Death had a way of keeping people around when I wanted to be left alone. Uncles and cousins asked me repeatedly if I needed anything. I couldn't so much as swallow in the days following my father's death - especially after his funeral - without someone asking me if I was okay or if I needed something.

Of course I wasn't okay and of course I needed something - *someone* - my dad.

My dad had died, but I sure didn't want everyone to coddle me because of it. It's not like doing so made anything better. The only thing capable of doing that was bringing my father back. And since bringing him back wasn't possible, I wanted to be treated like they treated me before he died or simply left in my grief.

"Ayla!" I heard shouted behind me.

I twisted my head in the voice's direction to find Hassani rolling up on a red seven-speed bike.

I hadn't seen him since the funeral. We spoke little that day because family surrounded my mother and I keeping us busy. Truthfully, I didn't feel I knew Hassani well enough to talk to him about anything besides school. The one thing about him I knew was I liked him but kept trying to convince myself I didn't.

"Hey," I mumbled, turning again to continue pacing toward school.

Hassani pulled up as close as he could before hopping off the bike and holding onto both handles, walking the bike beside me.

"I hope you didn't bring any books with you," he said, accompanied by his usual smile. "We haven't been doing much in school."

"All of my books are still in my locker." I adjusted the strap of the bag on my shoulders. "All I have in here are pencils and my notebook."

"Cool."

We continued to walk silently. Only the sound of a lone car driving by and the clicking and clacking of his bike's chain filled the silence.

"Let me give you a ride to school. I can't do all this walking."

"I'm fine walking, Hassani," I retorted.

"You're not." Hassani pushed the front wheel of the bike in front of me, blocking my path and forcing me to stop walking. "We don't have to talk about anything you don't want to talk about, Ayla. I promise."

I stared at him for a moment.

"Especially if what we talk about isn't Mr. Raymond's math quiz because I failed that thing with flying colors."

I snorted in response. It was the closest thing to a laugh in two weeks.

He gestured with his head toward the back of his bike. "Stand on the stunt pegs so we can go."

I waited for him to return to his seat on the bike, and I stepped onto the stunt pegs as instructed. One hand at a time, I placed my palms on each of Hassani's broad shoulders, tightening my grip. A second later, he began peddling, and we took off.

I closed my eyes as the breeze caused by Hassani's speed combed through my thick coils and curls.

"You ever had fried ice cream?"

I furrowed my brows before opening my eyes again. "Fried what?"

"Ice cream."

"No." I stared at the back of his head for a moment, fighting my smile, relief setting over me at the prospect of talking about anything other than my grief. "How is that even possible?"

"How is what possible?"

"Ice cream to be fried. Wouldn't the ice cream melt under heat?"

"You would think so, right? But nah." He shook his head. "It's a scoop of real ice cream rolled in crushed cereal, frozen together, and fried. Mrs. Louis, you know, the nosey old lady who lives in the big brick house across the street from me? She claimed fried ice cream ain't nothing but the devil's work, and I kind of believe her. Because how that thing tastes got to be a sin for real."

This time I didn't snort. I laughed a good hearty laugh, unintentionally releasing some of the weight off my heart.

He laughed too. "It's really good, though. You have to try some." Hassani glanced at me briefly over his shoulder. "I had some at this new Japanese place that just opened a few miles from us. I'm gonna get you some. I think you'll like it."

I smiled.

I smiled all the way to school that day.

Hassani made it possible for my mom to get her wish.

*H*assani

SHE WASN'T IN CLASS.

"Everyone take out your books," our math teacher, Mr. Raymond, instructed from the front of the classroom. His back faced us as his hand and arm moved in record speed, adding equations to the blackboard at eye level. The long white chalk in his grip tapped and scraped along the surface. "We'll keep things light to work us all back into routine."

I sat in the back of the room. I always sat in the back. Sitting at a distance was easier to go unnoticed in class. But Ayla, she'd been sitting up front from the very first day of school. Which was why I noticed her absence. She was in school. We entered through the school's doors together.

But where was she right now?

I twisted my head toward where Ayla usually sat and did one last scan of the room to see if she was there. Maybe she sat in another seat today. She wasn't herself when I saw her earlier. We'd only known each other for a little over a month but she was different that day, understandably.

"So." Mr. Raymond turned to face the class. "Who wants to try their hands at this equation?"

Ayla's hand would've been the first to go up if she were here.

We rode to school on my bike that morning. I found her walking to school from a few feet away and peddled my way faster to her. My parents told me how important it was for me to do my best to be there for her in whatever way I could. I didn't know what they meant or how I would be there for her if I didn't even know *how* to be there for her.

My hand shot up.

Mr. Raymond's salt and pepper brows went up as fast, and a smile spread across his thin lips even quicker. "Mr. Franklin," he said, impressed. "What a delight to see your hand up! What say you?"

"Uh," I pointed at the classroom door. "Can I go to the bathroom?"

His smile slid off his face faster than it appeared. Instead of responding with words, he shook his head and gave his approval by fanning his hand in the air. "Anyone else?"

I stood to my feet and swaggered to the door, pulling the door opened and stepping out into the empty hall.

School had yet to return to the way things were the first week. It was my first year at Garvey High, but compared to the first day, everything was somber. The halls were strangely empty. Fewer students were in attendance since a lot of their parents worked out of one of the twin towers or in the surrounding area. For the first few days of school before 9/11, I would always find at least two people in the halls, either students by their lockers or a teacher posting some kind of bulletin to the pebbling school walls. These days the halls were empty and grief still lingered in the air like a smell that took too long to go away.

I had no intentions of going to the bathroom. Well, maybe part of me did, looking to get away from boring third period math, but I also went looking for Ayla.

The moment I turned the corner, I found her. She was in front of her locker, rummaging through the metal compartment. The sounds of her moving around papers, books, and pencils echoed down the hallway.

She tossed printed handouts over her shoulder like they were nothing. I was only feet away, but from where I stood, I could tell she was searching for something in a panic.

"Where is it?!" she spat, her voice echoing around us.

"Ayla," I shouted as I made my way to her. "What are you doing out here?"

She didn't answer, just kept searching.

"What are you looking for, anyway?"

That question went unanswered too.

The closer I approached her, the more I heard her mumbling to herself.

"Ayla," I called again when I was close.

"I'm looking for my pen," she pointed out, eyes still in her locker, her hands moving around the contents inside.

"Your pen?" I questioned. I moved behind her to get a better view of her locker. The container was clean, orderly. Of course her locker was clean. Besides the fact we'd just started school five weeks ago, Ayla herself was someone who prioritized order, something I noticed almost immediately about her.

With that knowledge about her, it was hard to comprehend how she misplaced something.

"Class started five minutes ago," I informed. "I'm surprised Mr. Raymond didn't lock the door yet, but you know how he gets down."

She kept moving around the things in her locker.

"Look." I pointed from behind her when I spotted a blue BIC pen. "There goes a pen right there. Take that and let's—"

"I don't want to use *this* one," she shot back.

"Well, I'll give you a pen," I insisted, grabbing for her arm before she jerked her forearm free.

"NO!" She screamed, and the shriek in her voice made me jump back. Ayla turned to face me for only a moment to say, "I *need* the pen I'm looking for."

Her chest heaved as her nose flared. Her beautiful brown eyes were red and watery, like she'd been crying.

"Ayla," I whispered.

"My dad gave me that pen, Hassani. I *have* to find it." Ayla's voice trembled. She turned to face her locker again and instead of continuing her search, all she did was stand in front of it with her back to me.

Just the mention of her dad made my heart sink and I knew her saying that out loud did worse for her.

Her shoulders shrugged uncontrollably and her sniffing back her tears got louder.

I turned to look down both sides of the hall, hoping someone would appear so they could help. Specifically, help *me*. Because in that instance, I really did not know what to say to get her to stop crying.

Her loud sniffles transitioned into a soundless cry. So, I did the first thing that came to mind, the first thing that seemed right.

I turned her by the shoulders and wrapped my arms around her, and she leaned in without missing a beat. Like the night me and my parents visited her home, Ayla pressed her face into my chest and muffled her cries against me. I felt the warmth of her tears as they seeped into the fibers of my blue tee. Something in me told me to hold her tighter, and I did, and her crying became even quieter.

"I want my dad," she whispered against me.

"I know you do," I said back.

I'm not sure how long we stood out there for, but Ayla never made it to class. In fact, she left school and didn't return until the following month. That day though, I spent the rest of third period with Ayla's head against my chest and my arms wrapped tight around her shoulders, understanding our bond was something more than superficial and Ayla, despite what my father told me, could never be just another girl I knew anymore.

PART II
SET

3 YEARS LATER...

CHAPTER 7

MAY 2004 - LONG ISLAND, NEW YORK

$\mathcal{A}$yla

"I THINK I'M GOING TO DO IT," MY FRIEND CHLOE SAID INTO THE PHONE.

I moved my eyes off the page in my book and focused on my ceiling.

"I really love him, Ayla, and he's been patient."

I rolled my eyes. "So... to you that means you should have sex with him?"

"I mean..."

I snorted to myself while refocusing on my novel. What was happening between the pages was far easier to escape to than into the arms of a boyfriend, like Chloe was proposing.

A TLC track played low from the boombox I kept on my dresser. Each time the bass dropped; the radio vibrated against the mahogany wood. On that wood sat a line of picture frames, each one holding a picture I took of my father. It was my favorite spot in the house to stare at. Each photo reminded me of what he said before I clicked the shutter release button.

"So, you think it's a bad idea?" She asked, pulling me back into the now. I imagined lines forming on Chloe's forehead, the way they always did when she became concerned.

I nodded my head in time with the beat and hummed the lyrics while turning the page of the novel I read.

I paused humming long enough to tell her, "I think it's a very serious decision that you should really take your time considering."

It was just me in the house, filling up my time until my mother returned home.

Mom was spending a little extra time at her shop working on a wedding dress for one of her clients. It was the spring, which meant it was officially wedding season, the busiest time of the year for her.

My father passing three years prior strengthened my relationship with my mother. Back then, all we had was each other, and, that made our bond stronger. We'd both coped with the untimely death of my father in our own way. I drowned myself in music, phone calls, and novels, and she spent more time at her bridal shop designing and sewing wedding gowns long after the wedding season was over.

When I wasn't reading or listening to music, I'd taken up a babysitting business, babysitting my neighbors' children after school, during school breaks, and during the summer months. Their parents believed I was a godsend, but honestly, they were godsends to me. I loved being around children. They helped with distracting me from the pain I still felt from my dad's absence.

The line beeped with another call. I moved the phone off my ear to peek at the caller ID. My mother insisted on getting me call waiting and upgrading my phone to a phone with caller ID when I kept missing her calls because I was on the phone all day.

The moment I saw Percy Franklin in my caller ID window, I smiled.

"Chloe, let me call you back."

"I'm meeting up with Kevin tonight," she informed. "I'll tell you what happened tomorrow."

I sighed, "Ok, fine."

After switching over to the other line, I answered with, "Hey, Mr. Franklin."

"Ayla," Mr. Franklin said on the other end the moment I answered. "How are you?"

"Good," I replied, sitting up in bed.

"And school?"

"Great," I answered.

"Your mother told me you're on track for being Valedictorian of the graduating class."

I grinned.

"So, asking about your grades and what they are like would be silly, huh?"

"All A's of course."

"Of course." He chuckled. "That's fantastic."

Receiving phone calls from Mr. Franklin wasn't out of the norm. He'd call every so often to check on me, to see if I needed anything. The bond my mom and I formed with the Franklins over the years was one I didn't even realize I needed until I did. If it weren't for them, I'm not sure my mother and I would have known how to get through life out there in Long Island, far away from family and practically in the middle of nowhere.

"So..." I moved my phone to the other ear. "Is everything okay?"

"Everything is fine," he answered. "I'm calling because I need a small favor if you may."

I smiled in response to his Jamaican accent that, to me, exalted his words. I'd spent enough time with the Franklins to understand they had a knack for turning their accents up a notch or lowering it just enough when they needed to code switch. But on any day, their accents, especially Mr. Franklin's couldn't go unnoticed even though Mr. and Mrs. Franklin had been in the states for well over two decades.

"Sure. What's the favor?"

"As you know," he started, "Hassani will retake the regents in a few weeks..."

"Mm-hmm." I reached for my bookmark and wedged it between the pages of my book.

The regents were a series of tests given to New York State high school students in the subjects of Math, English, and Science. The Board of Education administered the first tests at the start of the year. Students who failed it the first time retook the test twice more, once in June and then again in August. For graduating seniors like Hassani and I, it was our last chance to pass so we could march in graduation and not have to return for summer school. I'd passed the first series of tests. Hassani failed Math but passed the English and Science exams with flying colors.

"After the talk I had with his math teacher—"

"Oh, you mean, Hassani's favorite teacher in the whole wide world?"

"Yeah, right," Mr. Franklin confirmed, laughing at my sarcasm. "After the talk I had with him, I'm not confident Hassani will pass the regents with even a passing grade to graduate next month without a little help."

"Okay..."

"And since you're a math wiz, and not to mention a soon to be Valedictorian, I was thinking you could tutor—"

"Mr. Franklin?"

"Yes, Ayla?"

I tucked my lips in my mouth for a beat. "Is Hassani aware you're asking me for this favor?"

"Not exactly." He chuckled. "Hassani knows the work, this is true, but he's having trouble with memorizing the formulas to show his work and he'll need to do this to pass the test."

"I know." I twisted my lips to one-side.

"And you also know, Hassani doesn't like to ask for help with anything, especially from you."

That was true. Hassani had an ego back then that didn't allow for him to ask for help because to him asking for help - from me, especially - was like making an admission that I was better than him at something... which I was.

"Yes, I know that too." I sat up and nodded. "Okay, fine, I'll tutor him."

"Perfect."

"But..."

"Oh boy."

"It has to be during the weekends and in the morning. Saturdays and Sundays before noon."

Mr. Franklin sighed. "You know as well as I do Hassani is not an early bird."

"I can only tutor him in the mornings, Mr. Franklin." I reiterated. "After school, I babysit and during the weekends I babysit at night. Most of my neighbors with babies go out to dinner in the evening and nighttime, which means big business for me."

"Look at you, sounding like a real business woman on the other end of my phone." He laughed. "Balancing work and school flawlessly is a trait that will take you very far in life. Ayla, I am so proud of you and I know your father would be too."

My heart ached at just the mention of my father. I took a sharp inhale of the surrounding air. "Thank you, Mr. Franklin. I appreciate you saying that."

"Of course, and anytime."

The Franklins had become a staple in my life. Besides me being friends with Hassani, my mother and I visited their home, and they visited ours at least once a month for dinner. And even though I was grateful for their presence, knowing they didn't have to do any of that, nothing could make up for my dad being gone. My father only worked with Mr. Franklin for all of a few weeks, but they formed a friendship in that short time. I loved the Franklins, but it's like I said, nothing could fill the void my father's passing created. There wasn't a day that went past that I didn't wish I could hear my father's voice again. What I wouldn't do to listen to him say Mr. Franklin's words.

"Perfect, then. The weekends before noon," he repeated. "I'll let Hassani know."

"So." I bit back my smile. "Would it be unreasonable to make him admit that I'm better than him at Math before he arrives here for tutoring?"

"Ayla, please."

I giggled. "I'm only kidding."

"I'll let him know he will spend his next few weekends with you."

I nodded. "Sounds good."

~

"OH, RICARDO," AUNT LAURIE SHOUTED IN LAUGHTER. "YOU ARE TOO funny, baby, stop it!"

My mother and I exchanged a look while we sat amid probably one of the most awkward dinners ever.

It was eight that evening and my favorite and only aunt, Aunt Laurie, was in town for one night only, like always, except for this visit, she invited company.

She and her "friend" Ricardo were stopping in New York while Ricardo, whom she affectionately called Ricky, handled business. Aunt Laurie would purr his name when she said it. And I wanted to vomit every time.

"Isn't he funny, y'all?" She asked, searching my mother and my face for an amused reaction.

We gave it to her. I did it because I honestly didn't want to be rude. I'm sure my mother felt the same way but was too sweet to say otherwise. Plus, she was probably just happy Aunt Laurie brought a man home because to my mother, this meant my aunt was ready to stop jet setting around the world and now had a reason to settle down.

From the time they arrived at the house, I got a bad vibe from Ricardo.

"You can call me Uncle Ricky if you like," is what he told me, which almost made me gag.

As if...

"Mr. Ricardo is what I'm comfortable calling you, but thanks," I politely told him before gladly leaving the room to help my mother set the table.

He was handsome with slick back silky hair. His sandy brown skin and sharp eyes made him look like he was mixed or something. My aunt insisted Ricardo had Native American blood pulsing through his veins. Mentioned it as if it were some type of badge of honor.

"Have you two been to Mumbai?" Ricardo asked between bites of his vegetable pilaf. I did not know what a pilaf was, nor did I like the soft taste of it in my mouth. I'm sure my mother wasn't a pilaf person either, but she wanted to impress Aunt Laurie's "friend." I thought it was so odd when my aunt introduced him to us as her friend. I would later ask her why and she would tell me, "Because these days I am too grown to have a boyfriend. He's my friend until he marries me."

Marries her?

When did that become an expectation? Something to look forward to? Who was this woman?!

Hearing her use the word married almost made me fall out of my chair. Out of all the people who I knew would never wear a ring on their left ring finger, it was Aunt Laurie. All my life, I'd never seen her with a man. Heard her discuss them with my mother in private when they thought I wasn't listening, but I never actually *met* those men... until that night.

What was so special about this one?!

"Mumbai?" My mother questioned. "No, we haven't. Where is that again?"

He grabbed the white napkin with the clip of his middle and index fingers, bringing the cloth to his mouth to clean. "It's a large city in India. The people are adoring and the food is divine. Your pilaf kind of reminds me of there."

My mother blushed. "Oh, does it? I hope that's a good thing."

"It's a great thing." Ricardo peeked down at his plate, then looked over at my aunt.

As if they'd communicated to each other in some unspoken language, my Aunt Laurie sat up immediately in her chair and leaned over in her seat and in his direction. Turned his plate like a turntable so that the steak my mother broiled faced my aunt. What my aunt did next made me lean forward in my seat with a brow piqued.

Aunt Laurie lifted the silver fork and knife out of her plate, then started cutting up Ricardo's meat.

My eyes moved to my mother's, and she wore the same shocked expression on her face. Unlike me though, she could recover before being noticed.

Aunt Laurie and my eyes met, and she gave me a closed-mouth smile. "Ricky likes his meat to be a certain size."

"So why doesn't he cut it up himself? His hands seem to work fine," is what I wanted to ask. But all I did was smile politely. I smiled politely for most of dinner.

She was different that evening. Usually the life of the party, my bubbly Aunt Laurie that night was strangely more reserved. Every time she was about to say something that was so Aunt Laurie or whenever she was about to make one of her usual jokes, she would stop herself. She'd dimmed her light. And for the first time in my life, I didn't like her very much. In fact, that night, without saying it to myself, I resolved to being no one other than myself to have a "friend."

assani

I CLIMBED TWO STAIRS AT A TIME. THE SOLES OF MY JORDAN SNEAKERS thudded against the concrete steps as I headed toward the big brown wooden door. Once in front of the door, I knocked twice.

"Hassani, how long you plan to be here for?" Raphael asked behind me.

"Word," Marcus echoed, draping one arm over the iron banister. "We only have fifteen minutes to get to practice and we're walking so you know it'll take forever to get there."

I waved their comments off behind me. "Not long. Just chill." My attention returned to the door in front of me. I rapped on the surface again and rang the bell this time. "Why is she taking so long to answer?"

Sunday's sun beamed down over Ayla's house as I waited for her to greet me at the door. Summer had arrived early in Long Island. The high was 75, but it felt more like 89 degrees with all the walking my teammates and I had to do. We'd have to get used to the heat, at least according to our coach. As team captain, for weeks, I stopped at all my teammates' homes to pick them up in route to school so we could arrive to practice together. Since most of them didn't live within walking distance of our high school, it was my responsibility to assign them to partners who lived near the school so we could meet up at the same time. I'd gotten the meetup place down to one house that day - mine. Our coach swore this would encourage team camaraderie in time for our last meet in four weeks. If we arrived as one, we'd run more unified, according to him. This was the last competition in my high school as a student and a part of me was nervous, but I wouldn't show it. Being appointed team captain my last year at Garvey High was major for me. My new position on the team made my father proud and made me feel like I accomplished something. Me running all those years earned me a scholarship to study architecture at Langston University later that year.

I huffed out a stream of air, dropping my head back.

"Is she even home?" Raphael asked.

"Of course she's home. Where would she be?" I turned to face the door again and knocked harder. "All she does is study." I mumbled that last part to myself.

I didn't even plan to stop by Ayla's that afternoon, but my father insisted I speak with her when I kept complaining to him about having to be tutored by her early in the morning. Tutoring didn't start until the next weekend, but I wanted to get ahead of everything. I'd known Ayla for all of three years at that point and knew she wouldn't budge. That didn't stop me from trying, though.

I balled my fist to tap the door again when she pulled it open. She stood there, balancing a chubby toddler on her right hip.

"Where's the fire?" she asked, rocking the boy in her arms. Her eyes moved off mine when she realized I wasn't alone.

"Right here in the flesh," I started, holding my arms up at my side.

"Aht, aht," she teased. "Watch your tone when addressing your elders."

"Ayla please. You're older than me by *one month*. Stop this."

"Older is older."

"Man, whatever. I ain't even here to go back and forth with you about this for the trillionth time."

She rolled her eyes. "So then… what's up, Hassani?"

"*What's up* is this tutoring hour you chose for next weekend? It's *way* up as in too early." I grunted. "Why are you doing me like that?"

Her eyes focused over my shoulder. "Why did you bring the entire track team to my porch? To jump me?"

Laughs echoed behind me.

"Coach said we have to go to practice together," Raphael answered.

"On foot," Mason, another one of my teammates added.

"Damn," she drug out, lifting the toddler higher on her hip. "And he expects y'all to run when y'all arrive?"

"Yup," Raphael confirmed with a nod.

It was just the four of us on her porch while the rest of the guys stood on the other side of her gate. I turned briefly to check on them to find them raising their hands impatiently, signaling me to join them to leave.

Ayla sighed as I turned to face her again. "I have to babysit in the afternoons and the evenings. Like I'm doing right now. Mornings were all I had available to tutor your stubborn ass. If you would have been studying like I always tell you to do—"

"I really feel you picked mornings to get under my skin."

"And *why* would I do that?"

"Because you're Ayla," I retorted.

"And?" she challenged.

"That's it," I answered. "Because you're you and a lot of times, there's no reason you do the things you do with me."

She bit back her smile and her doing that made me do the same. There was this new tension between us that had formed in the three years we'd been friends. When she returned to school the second time, after her father passed, she was different, understandably. More sarcastic, slightly argumentative, still one of the prettiest girls at

Garvey even though she bragged more about her brains and never her looks. But she was the homie, something I had to remind myself of constantly. And if I forgot, my dad was always around to remind me too.

She and I never discussed her breakdown in front of her locker freshman year, and that was cool with me. We were friends, so not much needed to be said about it. Under all that, though, there was something special about our friendship, something that meant everything to me. Something that had no name, but that I knew she felt the same way about. My girlfriends in the past claimed the tension between she and I was actually flirtation, but I promised that wasn't my intention. At least I thought it wasn't.

"Hey Ayla," Marcus greeted over my shoulder.

Her eyes moved off mine and switched in his direction. I didn't like that.

"Hey Marcus."

"What's good?" he replied in a soft voice. I hated when he dropped his voice to a Keith Sweat octave. He did that all the time whenever speaking with girls. It annoyed me to no end.

Honestly, I wasn't sure if it was really his voice or the fact he was addressing her that bothered me. When I look back at it now, it was probably the latter.

I snapped my fingers in her face, so she'd refocus on me.

Ayla rolled her eyes my way. "The time stands, Hassani."

"Aight, well you know I'm gonna be late, right?"

"What?" she whined.

"Don't worry about it, Ayla," Marcus said to my right. I turned my head to look his way, and he kept his eyes on her and a slick smile on his lips. "I'll make sure he gets to you on time."

"Thank you." She shifted her eyes off Marcus and onto me. "You know, Hassani, you sure are lucky to have such a responsible friend."

"*You sure are lucky to have a responsible friend,*" I mocked in her voice. "Please spare me."

She giggled.

I shook my head and turned on my soles. "Y'all come on before we're late."

"Bye guys," she sang behind me. "Have a good practice."

"Thanks, Ayla," Marcus said, stepping down the stairs behind me.

I grunted to myself and kept walking.

Raphael, Marcus, Mason, and I led the way once we started toward school again. Our teammates followed close behind.

"Aye," Marcus said beside me. "You know if Ayla got a date to prom yet?"

Prom was only one month away and was the only thing anyone could talk about. Not me. I was more concerned about our last meet. The meet would earn the school another trophy and offer me an opportunity to set a new record for Garvey as the fastest time completed in a sprint at an at-home meet. If we won.

I honestly couldn't care less about prom. If I could miss the event, I would. But I knew back then that would have crushed my mother, and I wouldn't dare do some stupid shit like that.

"I don't know if Ayla has a date. Why do you ask?"

"'Cause," Marcus started. "I'm thinking about asking her to go with me."

"Well..." I peeked inside of my gym bag to make sure I had my running sneakers packed. "*Stop* thinking about it."

The words slid from my mouth with ease before I could even think to stop them.

Marcus jerked his neck back. "What you mean stop thinking about it?"

I shrugged. "I'm not trying to have my two friends getting together. What happens when you two fall out?"

"It's *just* prom, man." He bumped me with his shoulder. "I ain't asking shorty to marry me."

The humor that crinkled the corners of his eyes made me clench my jaw.

"Aye." I stopped and turned to my other teammates behind me. "Y'all can go 'head. We'll catch up."

When our teammates were far enough ahead of us, I asked, "Can you just not?"

Marcus just stared at me.

"You're my homeboy and she's the homie. I'd like to keep it that way. You're always falling out with these girls you get involved with and Ayla ain't like none of them."

"Exactly," Marcus replied. "She's better. I'm supposed to upgrade, do better. Plus, I see her eyeing the kid."

It was my turn to jerk my head back. "Man, Ayla is not looking your way."

"I couldn't tell." Marcus crossed his arms over his chest. "You got feelings for her or something?"

I glanced up ahead of us, watching as our teammates created more distance between us.

"Y'all been friends for mad long, but I haven't seen you make a move." He threw his hands up. "So, what's the problem?"

"Look, it's like I said, Ayla is the homie and so are you." I tapped his chest with the back of my hand. "But if you hurt her, which you know you will, it'll put me in a position I don't want to be in."

"Hmph," he huffed, staring at me through squinted eyes. "Aight then, fine."

I nodded, walking off. "Cool—"

"I'll race you for her."

I turned to face him quick. "What?"

"I'll race you for her," he repeated. Marcus pointed up ahead of us. "The first one to get to the school's track wins. If I win, I'm asking Ayla to prom. If you win..." He shrugged. "... then I won't."

I rolled my eyes up toward the sky, considering the challenge. I was going to race Marcus anyway because back then, and really still now, I liked a challenge and he loved to challenge and compete with me."

"Bet." I crossed the strap of my gym bag over my chest to secure the bag in place then lifted one leg at a time to stretch my hamstrings. "You ready?"

"Born ready," Marcus replied.

"Aight, then." I rolled my head around my shoulders once. "On your mark, set—"

Before I could finish, Marcus took off in front of me.

"Cheater!" I shouted as I took off too, feeling the muscles in my calves activated and flexed as I did my best to close the distance between us. I pumped my arms and pounded my feet against the pavement. Inhaled and exhaled at a patient rate as not to tire myself out too soon. It only took a few seconds for me to gain enough momentum and speed to blow past Marcus and to hear him grunt in response.

Our teammates cheered us on as they took off running behind us. I heard my name and Marcus's chanted until the only name I could hear was mine.

I felt energized and charged, and picked up even more speed. The ache in my ankle went ignored because losing wasn't an option. I peeked behind me when I saw our school's building come into view. Everyone was far behind, Marcus a few feet ahead of them but still where he belonged - behind me. My lungs were burning, thighs begging for relief. I hadn't properly stretched or warmed up, but I didn't care. I wouldn't stop. Marcus challenged me, and that was enough motivation to keep going.

I'd finally reduced speed and came to a gradual stop when we arrived in front of the gates to our school's field. Our track outlined the bright green grass that stretched over the football field where our school's football team trained and played.

I hunched forward and pressed my hands to my knees. My head was between my shoulders as I tried to steady my breathing. As my teammates entered the field, I felt their pats on my back or heard their compliments on how fast I ran. Marcus was the only one who stopped beside me before heading through the gate.

"Damn," he exclaimed before continuing onto the field. "Was that competitive Hassani or the Hassani who just didn't want me to ask Ayla out?"

"Competitive Hassani, of course. You already know what happens when you challenge the God," I boasted through breaths.

"Yeah, okay," Marcus shouted from his distance in front of me.

I knew then like I knew now that it was the latter. Keeping Ayla away from Marcus was my motivation. The reason I claimed I was doing it for was the lie.

~

"GOAL!" MY FATHER SHOUTED BESIDE ME AS HE SHOT UP FROM HIS SEAT. "*Bredrin*, what did I say? Didn't I say these boys got suited up to play?"

The thundering claps from his two friends who sat on chairs around the room filled the space.

We all lounged in the basement, a spot my father had renovated at least three times in the previous year alone. He kept having the room redone until it resembled a man cave unique to him, one he loved escaping to.

A billiard table sat in the middle of the space with a man-made bar only feet away. We all sat near the center of the room with our eyes focused on the entertainment center that housed my father's beloved flatscreen television.

"I should've placed my bet on Mexico," his friend Fitz mumbled.

My father kissed his teeth while lowering the spout of his beer bottle from his lips. "Shoulda, coulda, woulda. Make sure you leave *mi paypa* on the bar before you even think 'bout stepping one foot out of here."

Everyone laughed, including me.

On a Saturday evening, I basked in the company of my father and his friends Lloyd and Winston, who we all called Win. My dad had known these guys since he was a kid climbing mango trees in Montego Bay, Jamaica.

We'd all just finished eating the dinner my mother prepared and were allowing our food to digest in front of a soccer game my father recorded a month earlier. The game was really for them, not me. I couldn't care less who played and often had trouble following the game, anyway. Soccer, to my father's horror, wasn't my favorite thing to enjoy.

"Aye, Hassani," Win called from his seat. "You ready for your race in June?"

I shrugged. "As ready as I will be, I guess."

My father placed a hand on my head and moved my head around playfully. "What is this *I guess* you telling the man?"

I chuckled.

"Hassani's bringing another trophy to place on the mantle in the living room," he asserted.

I shook my head while fighting back my smile. "Dad..."

"Dad, nothing." He balled his hand into a fist and tapped me on my bicep. "What I always tell you? See it here..." He tapped his temple. "...before you can get it here," he reminded, holding out his hand. "You understand?"

"I understand."

He nodded with pride. "When am I ever wrong?"

"Never," I answered with confidence, like always.

"I bet he's not as modest with thcm *lickkle gyals* he got blowing up your phone line, eh Percy?" Lloyd quizzed.

"Ha!" My father shouted before laughing. "Runnin' the phone bill up for the phone in his room like he got money to put down on it when time comes to pay it."

They all laughed in unison.

"But you know what?" My father peeked over at me before directing his attention to his friends. " I'm not mad at him 'bout it. That's what he's supposed to do."

"Yes, big man," Lloyd concurred.

"This the time to line 'em up," Win added. "Have a different girl every day of the week."

"You understand," my father confirmed. He pointed at me with his thumb. "I tell the boy all the time that before his mother, I couldn't sit still with just one girl."

"Truth," Lloyd confirmed.

"Your teenage years are not for settling down," my father contin-ued. "This is the time to date them all, commit to none. Finish school, start your career, then concern yourself with that other stuff. For now, explore your options."

He took a swig of beer. "You hear these kids talking about they in love and that so and so is their man or their woman. See the world and achieve some goals with no distractions before you come talk to me about love."

"That's the truth right there," Win shouted, clapping his hands twice for emphasis.

My father's words were nothing new. He'd always say the same thing, and so often that I never expected him to say otherwise.

"I love your mother," my father admitted, eyes trained on the screen. "But I would have never known she was good for me if I didn't know what bad was."

"But what if..." I scooted to the edge of my seat. "What if you met mom young... like at my age?" My eyes were on him while he kept his eyes glued to the screen. "Would you have passed her up back then based on your views now?"

Lloyd chuckled to himself.

"Yes," my father asserted, refusing to take a moment to mull my question over. My father turned his attention to me. "Because I wouldn't have known what to do with a woman like your mother. A woman like your mother takes time to create. Life and life's experiences does that. Equally, it takes time for a man to mature enough to recognize and honor the thing that makes her so incredible and not abuse or misuse it. Takes him another set of years to realize he can't use her for her greatness and not pour greatness back into her too."

I folded my lips in my mouth as I considered his words.

"A man has to decide what he's willing to sacrifice to have a woman like your mother. And a boy who thinks and acts like a boy can't do all that at your age, son." He scooted to the edge of his seat when the team he rooted for gained control of the ball. "Woi!"

Lloyd and Win stood from their seats in awe as the player kicked the ball with no obstruction into the opposing team's net, winning the game.

My father clapped. "Mi picked the winning team nuh?"

As he and his friends applauded the player's moves, I sat there processing my father's words.

It's like I mentioned, this wasn't the first time we discussed finding love young and his strong views regarding the subject. He's always been against falling in love young and showed how much he was against it leading up to when I started school at Garvey High. But even at my young age, although I respected my father immensely, I wondered if his rule had an exception.

yla

"How could I be so stupid, y'all?" my friend Chloe mumbled beside me. "How?"

I sat at the foot of her bed with my legs folded below me. Another friend of ours, Raina, sat with her legs extended. Chloe laid with her head on Raina's knees as Raina stroked Chloe's hair softly.

Chloe swiped a finger across her wet lids. "You know what? Just never fall in love."

I exhaled a deep sigh and slowly let the air escape from my nose.

"I just thought..." Chloe sniffled. "I thought we were ready. He claimed he loved me."

Raina scoffed while shaking her head, never losing pace of brushing her palm over Chloe's hair.

"I can't believe I fell for that shit."

Chloe's room was the scene of sadness. She was someone governed by her feelings back then. When Chloe was happy, everything around her reflected that. And when she was sad, her surroundings mirrored that too.

Crumpled tissues littered her carpet below her bed, Mary J. Blige played low in the background. Old photos of her and her now ex, Kevin, were reduced to strips of glossy paper after she took a scissor to them.

"That's exactly why I lost my virginity to a random over the summer," Raina admitted. "Some kid from Midwood Prep who was friends with my cousin."

I moved my eyes off the crumpled tissues to focus on Raina. The day she did what she confirmed she did, Chloe and I were the first to know about it. We were all tight in high school. My relationship with Hassani was more solid, but in terms of girlfriends, they were them.

"There was no way I was going to start college still a virgin." Raina shook her head, continuing to stroke Chloe's hair. "And there was no way I would lose my virginity to one of these liars at school."

Chloe sat up from her recline against Raina's leg. "Well, I can't take it back now."

"What is Kevin saying?" I asked.

"I wouldn't know." She scoffed. "He won't answer my phone calls. Every day this week he told me he had to get to football practice so he couldn't talk to me or see me. Before we had sex, he made time though, so I know the reasons he says he can't see me aren't true."

I shook my head.

"Conveniently, he's become so busy since we had sex and that shit isn't lost on me one bit," Chloe dragged her hand down her face to clean her tears. "I hate him."

Chloe and Kevin started dating at the start of the school year. He was the new kid in school from New Jersey who gained popularity by his second week at Garvey after helping the school win a game against one of our rivals. He and Hassani became fast friends, even though they played different sports. The two bonded over athleticism and a love of girls, I guess. Chloe took notice of Kevin immediately and did everything for him to notice her. He eventually did, and they became inseparable. Before having sex with him, Chloe prophesied he would be her first. I thought she was insane but cute too because they really were couple goals. Popular cheerleader and football star together was such a cliché. But it worked for them… until it didn't.

"Ayla, Who'd you lose your virginity to, again?" Raina asked, pulling me out of my thoughts.

"No one," was what I wanted to answer with. I wasn't "saving it" as my friends would say back then. Nor was I in a rush to give it away either. I'd already avoided relationships for most of high school. I'd gone to the movies and the local diner with a boy. Shared a kiss with a few, many of which were student athletes at other schools, but that was the farthest I'd ever gone with them. Honestly, sex hadn't become a topic amongst me and my circle of friends until we started our senior years. At that point, being a virgin was vintage.

Peer pressure was such a bitch.

"Uh..." I shifted in my seat. "I don't really remember his name."

There was no way I would tell them otherwise. Especially with Raina being so *Raina* that night. She was always so cavalier about sex, even before losing her virginity for reasons I could never understand.

A huge approving smile sprawled across Raina's face as she pointed at me while turning to face Chloe. "See? That's how you're supposed to do it. This whole pedestal people put virginity on only gets us in shit we can't get out of, like this funk you're in Chloe."

Chloe's face balled up first before the tears stained her cheeks again.

"Ayla, if you hadn't lost it," Raina said, looking my way once more. "I would've suggested you do so with Hassani. A friend is way better than a boyfriend, I would imagine."

I twisted my lips to one side, my eyes moving in the other direction.

"Look." I cast Raina's words out my mind, at least for the time being. I reached for Chloe's hand to console her. "It's okay. It happened, you did what you thought was right, and it didn't work out. Never regret doing anything you did with your heart."

Raina shook her head in my peripheral.

"It's Kevin's lost. There's only six weeks left in school. Soon he'll be a distant memory. You'll find someone much better; I promise."

"Oh, girl," Raina whispered, extending her hands to check her cuticles. "*Never* make promises that break themselves because these losers are a dime a dozen. They're like candies in a Pez dispenser. Remove one and another one pops right up to take the other ones place." She cringed, then shook her head. "Don't keep hope alive on them. They will disappoint you every time. I'm telling you. I learned that fact the hard way."

I waved Raina's comment off with my hand. "You're going to be fine, Chloe, all right?"

A ghost of a smile pulled at the corners of her lips that she refused to give in to. That was enough for me to know that she would really be fine.

And although I viewed Raina's approach as jaded and cavalier, she'd made a point that I'd decided was worth exploring.

I'D BEEN HEARING CRYING ALL DAY, SO WHEN I HEARD IT AGAIN DURING the early morning hours, I didn't hesitate to sit up in bed.

The hour was minutes after 2 a.m. I know that because the alarm clock on the night table beside my bed displayed the time in bright red. I'd fallen asleep a few hours earlier, but I must have not been that deep into my sleep to hear my mother crying.

I stepped off my bed, one foot at a time, and made my way to my bedroom door while doing my best to rub sleep from my eyes.

My mother wasn't an early riser, but a night owl she wasn't either. Knowing she was up definitely set off a few red flags in my head.

The second I opened my bedroom door, I heard laughter and voices belonging to a room full of people. Their voices sounded a little distorted, so I knew immediately no one was actually in the living room with her.

"I'd like to propose a toast to my beautiful wife."

My father's voice stopped me cold in my steps. Goosebumps

pimpled my skin next. I pressed my hand to my chest as if I could feel for my heart to stop it from beating so hard.

"How good it feels to say that."

The volume was courteously low. Knowing my mother, she did so to keep from disturbing me. The living room from my view only a few feet away was dark with only the glow from the television set providing all the light the room would need.

"Isn't she beautiful today?" The crowd wherever my father made his speech applauded his words. "You look so beautiful, Sonia."

When I got closer, I peeked around the corner to find my mother seated on our couch with her legs folded beneath her. She stared at the TV screen, her hand holding a ball of tissue as she sniffed back her tears with every breath. The light from the screen in front of her highlighted her wet cheeks.

I switched my eyes to the screen to see my father. He stood over an elaborately decorated table with my mother seated below him. To her left was my aunt and a few of my mother's friends. My mother's friends wore light pink dresses, my aunt a deeper hue of pink, and my mother donned a pure white dress. She looked beautiful. Her hair swept up in an intricate top bun. Freshwater pearls adorned her earlobes and decorated her neck.

My father wore a black tux that laid against his frame like how tailored garments laid pinned to mannequins. His hair was short in its usual Caesar haircut. The only thing different about him in the wedding video was that his face was smooth and hairless.

"Thank you all for joining us tonight," my father spoke into the microphone he held in his hand. "This is one of the most magical night's I've ever experienced in my life and I am blessed to be sharing it with you all."

I turned quick to press my back to the wall. Slapped my hand to my mouth and held my palm tight over my lips to keep my cry from being audible. The more I heard his voice, the more my heart ached. To the point I felt myself getting weak.

I pushed myself off the wall and took quick steps toward my bedroom, closing the bedroom door slowly once I was inside.

Hearing my father's voice for the first time in three years made me feel all the emotions, all the feelings I experienced the day I realized I would never see him again. Emergency responders recovered his remains, identifying him using his dental records, but a part of me still wanted to believe he was still out there, somewhere, really far away but still there.

I climbed into bed and reached for my bedroom phone before my head could touch the pillow. Lifted the phone off the receiver and started dialing the number by heart.

"Hello," he answered on the second ring. Sleep was heavy in Hassani's voice, making it raspier than usual.

I said nothing in response. Couldn't think of the words to say in that moment. Instead, I sniffed back the new tears that formed and threatened to fall from my eyes.

"Ayla, it's okay," Hassani whispered. "You're okay."

I ran a hand down my face to dry it of my tears.

"You wanna tell me what's on your mind?" he asked. He traded the sleep in his voice for concern. There was rustling on his side of the phone as I'm sure he waited for me to say something, anything.

Hassani just like me had caller ID on his phone, so there was no doubt he glanced at it before answering. That late-night phone call did not differ from the more than dozens before it. If I had a dream about my father, I would call Hassani. If I found something that belonged to my father that went missing once upon a time and then suddenly found, I would call Hassani. He became very much my support during that time. And although I would do things, little things, to get under his skin, Hassani meant more to me than I would ever admit out loud.

"Aight," he said in response to my silence. "Then let's talk about how horrible of a tutor you are."

I gasped. "I resent that."

He barked a laugh on the other end of my phone and his humor at my response made me laugh too.

"Well, we're going to see how good it is with this math test Mr. Torez has coming up this week."

"You'll pass it," I mumbled. "I'll see to it."

"Yo, did you hear what happened at lunch on Friday?"

I smiled, feeling my spirits lift by the late-night distraction that was my friend Hassani.

"No," I lied. Of course, I'd heard about it. Everyone did. A mini-food fight had broken out during our lunch period that had led to a few expulsions only a month before graduation. I was in a yearbook meeting and missed everything but heard all about it. I played dumb when Hassani asked though because any reason to hear Hassani speak in that moment was worth playing dumb. "Tell me what happened."

For the rest of the call, Hassani did well with taking my mind off my father. We spoke on the phone until the sky broke enough to let the sunshine in.

CHAPTER 10

assani

THE RUBBER BOTTOMS OF SNEAKERS SQUEAKED AGAINST THE HARDWOOD floors. Basketballs, too many to count, bouncing out of sync, echoed around the gym while the impact of the balls against the hardwood made the surface below my soles vibrate.

I was in the expansive basketball gym at Swoops Center, a few miles from my home. It was the largest sports and events complex in Long Island and my heaven on earth as a teenager.

"I'm open," I shouted, extending my arms high above my head, signaling Marcus to pass me the ball.

Of course, he didn't listen.

We were playing some random kids, same age as us. They had four players and so did we, so in the spirit of competing just because we agreed to a game.

Marcus faked left, the guy guarding him immediately recognized Marcus's pattern. He'd been playing the same predictable way since we walked on the court that day. Marcus leaped as high as he could,

93

angling the ball toward the basket only to have the guy guarding him knock the basketball clear out of his hand.

Marcus grunted while going after the ball. The ball had bounced too far away from him though.

I sucked my teeth as I ran for the ball. The moment I got it in my grip, I swiveled on my right foot, gained my balance as quick as I could. I jumped a few inches behind the three-point line, aimed for the net, flicked my wrist and propelled the ball toward the hoop.

By the time I landed back on my feet, I heard the sweet swishing sound of the ball going through the net.

"Game!" Kevin shouted while clapping his hands.

Kevin and another one of my friends Jason ran up to me to bump fists in celebration of our win.

"We should've placed a bet before playing," Jason admitted, giving me another pound.

Marcus was slow to approach, bumping fists with me when he finally came around, never congratulating me, though.

I balled my fist and playfully punched him on the arm. "Let's get you some water," I told Marcus while smiling big, draping my arm around the back of his neck. "You seem a little salty."

"Man, whatever," Marcus replied while pushing me off him. "That guy was all up in my face. I couldn't see the basket."

"Yeah, okay," I replied.

"I would have made that shot, no problem, and you know it."

Kevin and Jason both had their fists at their mouths, laughing into their hands while shaking their heads.

It's a wonder any of us had any energy after playing three rounds of laser tag less than an hour prior.

Trips to the sports complex was our version of going to the movies or for girls, going to the mall to shop. The center was a place we'd go during the weekends or after school on a Friday... if our parents gave us the okay like on that day. I only got permission to go if my grades were good that week. Truth be told, going to the center was my primary motivation for putting in most of my effort at school.

I loved Swoops Center because of the range of sports I could do there. Mountain climbing, ice hockey, ninja parkour - I loved doing it all. Competing was what thrilled me the most, though. Me and my little crew liked to go head-to-head against each other over everything from who could score the higher points in Mortal Kombat in the center's arcade to who could tie their shoe laces the fastest. Especially me and my boy Marcus.

"Y'all want to grab something to eat at the food court?" Jason pointed to the food stands.

We all nodded and made our ways there.

Four orders later and after we found a spot at a table to accommodate all four of us, we were all stuffing our faces with our selected meals.

"Guess who finally let me hit yesterday?" Kevin asked while taking a huge bite out of his hot dog.

All of our heads popped up from our individual food containers.

Kevin was the player of the group. Every other week he had another girl hanging off his arm. He swore I was his inspiration and I let him believe that but, honestly? We were nothing alike. Some would say we were similar since I fit the bill for changing out girls faster than he did, but to keep it real, looks in this case could be extremely deceiving.

"Shamaya Lawson?" Marcus asked. "You had sex with her already?!"

"Already." Kevin smiled with all his teeth, his cheeks bulging with food. "She was aight. Talked a lot of shit about how she knew what to do to make me fall in love with her, but she couldn't stay on top long enough for me to get into it."

"Damn." Marcus threw his napkin to the table while smiling from ear to ear. "Y'all *just* started talking this week."

Kevin nodded with pride.

"Man," Marcus added. "Please, teach me. Show me the way. 'Cause..."

They all laughed while I scoffed, then chuckled.

"Didn't you just break up with that chick, Chloe?" Jason asked next.

Kevin shrugged his left shoulder. "She gave me no choice. Shorty was getting all clingy. Following me everywhere while at school.

Calling me every day after we hooked up." He cringed. "I needed my space. She was doing way too much."

I stayed quiet, keeping myself preoccupied with the cheeseburger I held in one hand.

"She was a virgin anyway," Kevin continued. He pushed his hand into his food container and moved around the fries a bit before picking one up and placing the fry in his mouth. "I rarely mess with virgins because they get mad attached after. Wanting you to damn near marry their ass. Wanna talk about love and shit." He shook his head. "I tell them what they wanna hear, but I don't mean that shit."

Jason and Marcus chuckled.

"I know Hassani knows what's up." Kevin chucked his chin my way. "Right, man?"

I scoffed another laugh and shook my head, focusing my attention down on my container.

"See, Hassani is the real player," Kevin added. "You remind me of a lot of the dudes from my block in Newark. Real quiet with your moves, but I see what's up. I can't keep up with all the girls you run through."

"Man." I shook my head. "It ain't even like that."

"Ha!" He laughed. "I bet. I'm doing my best not to mess with the same girls you mess with, but it's hard, you know?"

"For real," Jason chimed in through his laugh. "Hassani done practically gone through the whole graduating class of girls."

It was no secret, I liked to date. Back then, I loved the company of girls. Loved how they smelled, how they felt against me when we hugged. I appreciated the sound of the soft moans that escaped their lips whenever we kissed. They had the softest hands and the sweetest smelling hair. But all I did was date. I never got physical with any of them... a fact I would never admit out loud to those guys.

"Not the whole graduating class. That cutie Ayla is the only one left." Kevin smirked. "She's next on my list."

My head popped up fast again.

He pointed my way. "Now I know for a fact you ain't never got with her."

I grabbed the square white napkin at the middle of the table to clean my mouth.

"Hook me up," Kevin insisted.

"If Hassani's going to hook *anyone* up with Ayla," Marcus jumped in while patting his chest. "It's most definitely going to be me. I've had my eye on her since freshman year."

"That's true," Jason confirmed.

"Well, you snooze, you lose." Kevin took another bite out of his hot dog. "What are you waiting on to make your move, anyway, Marcus?"

"For Hassani to quit playing and come through." Marcus pointed his eyes at me. "Hassani's been cockblocking since forever with Ayla. Like a damn gatekeeper. Dude raced me the other day just to keep me from asking her to prom."

"Whatever," I insisted.

"If you ask me," Jason spoke next. "I think he's keeping Ayla for himself."

"She's my friend," I explained, making eye contact with each of them. "So I would never hook her up with neither one of you fools."

They all grumbled their responses while flipping me the bird.

"And how would that even look, Kev?" I asked Kevin. "You trying to get with Ayla when you just broke up with her friend Chloe? You know they're super close, right?"

"Don't worry about that," Kevin insisted. "Hook me up and I'll take it from there."

"Nah." I shook my head while taking a bite out of my fry. "Not gonna happen."

"See? See?!" Marcus shouted from his seat across from me while bringing his fist to his mouth to laugh into. "Cockblocker."

They all laughed at my expense and I let them.

I'd let them say whatever they wanted to say about me because Ayla, to them and everyone else I knew, was off limits and would continue to be off limits as long as I could control it.

Beyond her being a friend to me, she was special. How special would become clear to me sooner than I expected.

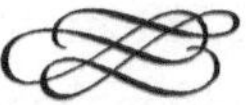

yla

"Well, I'll be damned." The thud of me slamming the book closed echoed around us. "I think the kid has finally got it..."

Hassani grinned widely beside me, popping the collar of his white tee for emphasis.

"... after three thousand years of tutoring."

His grin turned down into a frown.

I giggled in response. "I'm only kidding."

I'd been tutoring him in math for the past three weekends and fourteen weekday evenings, and the grueling favor was finally paying off.

Originally, I'd only agreed to weekends, but after he asked me to tutor him during the evenings after school, I caved.

"It don't even matter," he insisted. "I solved that last equation faster than you could've."

I scoffed. "Yeah, you wish."

He chuckled.

"You've got it, but you ain't got *it* like that, homie." I climbed off my bed to drop the textbook on my work desk.

I'd been giving Hassani mock equations since he arrived at my bedroom door, and until that very moment when I closed the textbook. My mother let him in on her way out. She had plans to spend the weekend in Silver Spring with my Aunt Laurie. Aunt Laurie had shocked us all by getting engaged a month prior. By shocking us all, I meant mainly me. My mother was beyond thrilled, which is why she jumped all over helping Aunt Laurie plan the wedding along with sewing my aunt's wedding dress. My aunt was in no mood to wait, she wanted to get married as soon as humanly possible. So, the wedding date was quickly approaching with a date for late August of that year. With that in mind, my mother drove to Silver Spring for another wedding dress fitting. My aunt's dress was gorgeous - an off the shoulder masterpiece that hugged my aunt in every place she thought was right to be hugged. It was perfect for her.

"*I don't want to look like a princess on my wedding day like you did Sonia,*" I remember Aunt Laurie telling my mother on the phone. "*I want to look sexy!*"

Aunt Laurie skipped the typical white puffy dress and requested my mother sew her a sleek blush one instead. So that is what my mother drove out to Silver Spring to do, fit my aunt to the dress, along with other things.

"You stay trying to play me." Hassani chuckled as he leaned back in my bed, resting his head against my headboard. He crossed his socked ankles, threaded his fingers together and wedged his hands between his head and the headboard. "I'm a math wiz now. Don't hate."

With his elbows at the sides of his head, the hem of his shirt rose to a level that offered a peek at his abs.

I tilted my head to one side, my eyes gradually working their way off his stomach. Our eyes connected and I noticed the sly grin on his lips.

"I'm not hating."

I turned quick to face my desk, pulling open my desk's drawer to retrieve a menu for the local pizzeria a few miles from my house.

It was a Saturday around 6 pm. Like I said, my mother had gone out-of-town leaving me home alone, which I preferred.

I didn't have any parties planned, nor did I consider meeting up with friends at any point in the night. Teenage Ayla was very low key, and she played it really safe. I never snuck out the house or skipped curfew. I figured my mother had enough shit on her heart, so it made little sense to stress her in any of the ways my friends stressed their parents.

"Let's get pizza," I suggested, my eyes scanning the menu below me.

"Moms left you money for that?"

"*Moms,*" I mocked in his voice, "left enough money to buy pizza for the entire block."

"Cool," he replied, hopping off my bed. "Order it then. You know what I like. I'mma run to the bathroom."

"Extra cheese and extra pepperoni," I said, reaching for my bedroom's landline.

"That's right," he confirmed on his way out my bedroom door. "Because I'm a growing man."

I mouthed that last part, knowing he'd say it. He always said that. We'd hung out enough times for me to know Hassani was that predictable.

As promised, I placed the order for two large pizzas - one with extra cheese and pepperoni and the other with ham and pineapples. Less than an hour later, the pies arrived and Hassani and I pigged out on our individual orders.

"Pineapples are so nasty on pizza," he said before leaning his head back to angle the point of the pizza over his mouth. "I don't know why you always get it."

"Because it's the bomb, duh." I picked a pineapple chunk off the pie and held it in front of his face. "You know you want it."

He pushed my hand away. "I *want* to throw it in the trash where it belongs."

I pressed my lips together to keep from laughing.

"Yo, I *hate* pineapples."

"Weirdo," I teased. "What kind of person doesn't like pineapples?"

"The kind with good taste, obviously."

I shrugged, continuing to eat my pizza. I aimed my slice at the center of my mouth when I peeked over at Hassani and asked, "You know what I hate?"

His cheeks bulged with food, but he still reached in front of him for another slice. "What?"

Before taking a bite, I answered, "A guy who takes advantage of a girl and makes her fall in love with him only to break her heart."

Hassani sighed beside me, shaking his head, and avoiding eye contact. "Ayla, please don't start with this."

"A guy who lies just to get in a girl's pants."

"Don't get involved, I'm telling you."

I grunted and dropped the rest of my slice in the pizza box in front of me. "Has Kevin mentioned anything to you about Chloe?"

"Ayla—"

"She's heartbroken because of him."

Hassani shook his head again and focused ahead of himself. "I don't know too much about the situation because I mind my business."

"So, he's said nothing with his low-down dirty ass, huh?"

"Look." He turned to face me. "Graduation is only five weeks away. Before she knows it, Chloe will be away at college not even thinking about Kev."

"I don't know about that, Hassani." I closed the lid of my pizza box and moved the box to my side table. "Them breaking up really broke her. I honestly can't believe she's so hurt over his sorry ass. Crying and questioning her decision to get with him. Especially when he's been slithering around here with Shamaya Lawson on his arm like the creep he is."

Hassani used his tongue to clear food from his gums. "She'll be aight, man. I really don't want to get involved or even talk about this stuff right now. Can we talk about something else?"

"Okay, sure. When did *you* lose your virginity?"

The question sent Hassani into a coughing fit. His light eyes reddened right before he shut them tight, heaving in air, doing his best to catch his breath.

I patted his back. "Are you okay?"

"Are *you*?" He got one last cough out, then cleared his throat.

"I'm fine," I answered. "Just curious."

His head was still turned toward me. He tucked his lips in his mouth, then released them slowly. "Yo, you girls have been wild lately. For real."

"And yet, the question is still unanswered."

"Why are you asking me that?"

I'd thought about asking that question the moment I returned home from Chloe's. It's crazy how it wasn't clear to me when it happened, but my friend Raina had planted a bug in my ear I couldn't get out.

"I'm just asking."

"*That* though?!"

Hassani jumped off the bed, dusting his black joggers of the pizza crust crumbs.

My eyes rolled down from his chest to the bulge in his pants. I twisted my lips to one side, eyeing and trying to measure the size of him through the fabric. When I'd given up and finally finished gawking, I lifted my gaze to find him staring right at me.

He quirked a brow and scoffed a laugh.

I pinned my bottom lip between the bite of my top and bottom teeth, swung my legs beneath me, and balanced the weight of myself on my knees. I moved so fast, Hassani had little time to question me further as I positioned myself in front of him and leaned in.

"Whoa." He stepped back while holding his hands out in front of him, creating some space between us. "What are you doing?"

I tucked my lips into my mouth, maintaining my stare with him.

He slammed his eyes closed. "Oh, hell no."

"Okay, hear me out."

"Ayla?" Hassani placed a hand on each of my shoulders and lowered his face so it was in line with mine. "*What* are you doing?"

"Do I have to say it?"

"Were you..." He tilted his head to one side. "Were you trying to kiss me just now?"

I bit inside my cheek.

"Because that's what it looked like."

I exhaled through my mouth.

"Ayla?"

"Yes, I was."

"What? *Why?*"

"Because I need you to do me a favor... a kinda *huge* favor. Colossal."

He motioned with his hands for me to continue.

"I need you to..." I inhaled the surrounding air and held my breath for a moment. "I need *us* to..."

"Spit it out."

"Do it."

"Do, *what?*"

"*It.*"

He wrinkled his brows, still confused.

"Have sex, Hassani."

All he did was blink. He blinked a lot, in fact. I remember standing there, doing my best to read his thoughts. I was both amused and offended he took so long to respond.

And when he finally did respond, I wasn't expecting him to say, "No."

He said it so assertively, I wasn't sure I'd heard him correctly.

"What?"

"I told you, *no.* Hell no, actually."

"What?" I questioned again. "Why not?"

"Ayla." Hassani took me by the hand and escorted me back to my bed, sitting me down and then crouching down in front of me. "Wouldn't you want to do that with someone special?"

I shook my head quickly. "That's the last thing I want to do."

He leaned back and into a seat on my carpet.

"I would hate to love someone as much as my mother did my

father and end up losing them or worse, think I love someone so much only to learn they don't feel the same way about me."

"Is this about Chloe?"

"It's about everything Hassani." I sighed. "Why are you being so weird about this? Any other guy would do flips right now."

He lowered his head to pinch the bridge of his nose.

"I want to give you my virginity. Why are you trippin'?"

His hand found a home at the top of his head, before he ran his palm down and over his face. Hassani's fingers smoothed down the waves of his hair as if he were passing his digits over silk. I watched as he turned his head away from me, shaking it from side to side swiftly. "Nah, I can't. *We* can't."

I jerked my head back. The wrinkles in my forehead relaxed the moment something occurred to me... *he didn't like me like that.*

Of course, he didn't like me like that. For all the years we'd known each other, he had never crossed the line, *ever.* Never allowed himself to even come close to that line.

"I'm not your type." I said to more so myself. I looked his way and asked, "That's what it is, right? I'm not your type?"

He shook his head.

"Listen, I'm not asking you to love me, Hassani. I just need this one thing. And I get it. I'm not model tall like your ex Cynthia or have wavy hair down my back like your other ex Stephanie, but I'm kind of cute. I mean, not today." I glanced down at myself. "Today I look like a troll. I thought about wearing something else and getting my hair done but I didn't want you to get all weird or anything because I knew I wanted to ask you—"

"Ayla." He placed a hand over my mouth, stopping me from continuing. "Can you just... be quiet for a second? You talk so much." He exhaled a long stream of air before removing his hand. "It's not any of what you said, okay?"

"Then... what is it?"

He exhaled audibly again.

"Oh!" I lifted my hand to my mouth and blew into my palm. "It's my breath. It still smells like pineapples and you hate pineapples."

He snorted a laugh, which made me laugh too. I was grateful in that moment things hadn't completely changed between us.

"What if we do that..." He attempted but failed to hold back his smile. "What if we do that and things change?"

"Nothing will change, I swear it. I won't make things weird or awkward. I won't even expect anything from you after. I just need to do this."

"Why?"

"I can't go to college in the fall with this thing."

"*With this thing?!*" he asked. "Your virginity?"

"Yes."

"It's never been a problem for you before."

"Well." I shrugged. "It is now."

He scratched at the goatee sprouting from his chin, shaking his head for what felt like the millionth time. He had been consciously growing his mini-beard all senior year in time for prom. Next to his eyes, it was the second-best thing about his face senior year.

Before he could tell me no again, I revealed, "My dad liked you."

Hassani's eyes shot over to me.

I needed him to know that. Honestly, if I didn't *need* him to know that, I wouldn't have told him. Just the mention of my father made me almost skip a breath, but it was something, probably the only thing I knew that held enough weight to make Hassani change his mind.

"He liked you... for *me*."

Hassani parted his lips to speak, but I held a hand up.

"And I'm not asking you to be with me. I just trust you enough to ask you to do this. I'm comfortable with you."

"But why are you acting like your virginity is some kind of disability?"

"Because... I don't know."

"Not every relationship ends like Chloe and Kevin's, you know that, right?"

"Oh, yeah?" I crossed my arms over my chest. "And why are you not with your first right now... whoever she is?"

"Because I've never had a first."

"Wh- what?"

We held our stares. I squinted my eyes, scanning his face for any hint he was joking, but the look he wore was serious.

"No. Way." My jaw dropped instantly. There was almost a full minute of silence between us.

"Wait," I said next. "Are you saying you're a virgin?"

He nodded. "Yeah, I am."

"Seriously?!"

"*Yes*, seriously."

"Wow." I shook my head slowly. "I just thought your virginity was a thing of the past—"

"You obviously thought wrong."

"You've had so many girlfriends since freshman year though."

Way too many to keep up with. Whereas I'd dated one and almost two, I was nowhere near the amount of teenage love affairs Hassani indulged in.

"Having a girlfriend doesn't mean you have to have sex with them. People do other things besides have sex in relationships."

"Do they though?"

"Yes, they do." He smirked. "At least I do other things in mine."

"Are you saving it for marriage or something?"

"Not exactly, but then again, maybe?" He ran his hand down his mouth. "I really don't know to be honest with you. Never really thought about it."

"Well, that sucks." I dropped my body back against my mattress. "What am I going to do now?"

CHAPTER 12

$\mathcal{H}$assani

"Wait," my father yelled out to me. "You forgot this, Hassani."

When I turned toward his voice, a huge smile pushed my cheeks back.

"Your mother would have my head if I forgot to put it on you before this race."

It was the gold necklace I wore the day I took my first steps as a child. My mother claimed the day after I started wearing the chain, I went from toddling to running and haven't stopped. She swore it was a good luck charm.

"Dad, that thing don't fit me anymore, you know?"

The sun was out full force that day. Not a cloud in sight. Blue stretched across the sky as voices fluttered the air like butterflies.

Behind me, bright brick red covered the running track, tatted with white lines and the matching numbers.

"Come quick, nuh boy," my father said, gesturing with his head. "You want for them to fire that gun and you're not in position."

"They know better than to start the race without me."

"Ha!" He laughed, reaching over the metal railing of the stands toward me. From his fingers dangled the gold necklace, with the letter H pendant catching the light the most. "Let's not find out if they will or won't. Here."

I lowered my head, bringing my chin to my chest. He reached a little further, draping the chilled chain around my neck, securing the clasp at the nape immediately.

My father patted my back twice, his smile so big I could see his gums.

"You got this," he assured.

"I got this."

My mother wanted so badly to be there that day, but someone had to run the bakery. That woman was so A-type with everything she handled back then. Still is actually. My father had been working full time at the bakery since 9/11. After the attacks, he made a choice not to work for someone else. Building new relationships in a working environment was too hard to fathom after losing so many colleagues.

"Go, go." My father shoed me away with his hands. "And remember what I always say. Start with the—"

"End in mind," I finished, backing away. I tucked the chain inside of my track uniform's shirt then patted my hand against it.

"Good luck, Hassani," I heard to my right in the stands.

"Hassani, bring home the gold," I heard to my left.

Just as I fixed myself to face forward to head to my starting blocks on the track, I glimpsed Ayla. She and her two friends, Chloe and Raina, descended the concrete steps. Her attention was on their conversation, only meeting my gaze once. A smile crested her lips, making me smile too.

"Good luck," she mouthed from a distance.

Things had kind of returned to the way they were after the night at her house. She took me completely off guard when she leaned in for a kiss. Even more taken aback when she asked me to be her first.

I lifted my hand and did a soldier's salute, and her smile grew even wider.

It's like I said, Ayla was a beautiful girl in high school and had the personality to boot. Every other week I was fanning one of my guy friends off her trails before he could even think to approach and ask her out. I always told them that it was because I didn't want my guy friends getting with my girl friends, and that was kind of true. But honestly, I knew exactly the reason I didn't want them asking her out, much less dating her. I just refused to admit it out loud.

"Hassani," my couch shouted to my left. "Put some pep in your step and get into position."

With that, I jogged to my block.

It was the last meet of the year, my last meet in that high school. In three weeks, I would be a high school graduate, readying myself to attend Langston University.

In front of my block with the other runners either to my left or right, I kicked my legs out then hopped in place, repeating the action until I felt my heartbeat pick up pace. I rolled my head around my shoulders, inhaling and exhaling the air in even breaths, warming up to what was to come.

I never got nervous before a meet. Never obsessed or anxiously stressed over coming in first place. My father had always taught me that a man cannot think through labored breathing and if self-doubt shrouds his thoughts.

"Never dig up in doubt what you planted in faith," is what he'd always say to me about everything I was nervous about that I prepared for. He recited that quote so much that it became an innate thought. So innate, whenever my nerves became overactive, his voice would calm them immediately.

"On your marks," the voice announced, the tenor echoing around the field.

The sounds of people cheering like a swarm of cicadas muted the moment myself and the rest of the runners crouched down in front of our blocks.

"Set," the voice said this time.

All I could hear was the sound of my heart pattering.

Then I waited.

Waited for my ears to ring.

Waited for my breathing to hitch at the echo.

Bang!

The shot fired, and I immediately took off. Once upon a time, I flinched at the sound of the firearm going off. I used to flinch so bad, my father took me to a local gun range in Long Island and we spent an hour just listening to the sounds of metal triggers being pressed and bullets blasting out the mouths of guns. Then we spent another hour shooting those guns ourselves.

My father knew I was fast on my feet back then. He also understood I would lose a lot of races if I hesitated even for a second, flinching at the sound of a gun going off.

The wind brushed against my face as I raced toward the finish line. I saw nothing and no one else, refusing to pay anything, even an ounce of my attention. My focus were the curving white lines ahead of me. Not on the sound of people cheering from the stands or the flashes from cameras, both disposable or from the professional cameras owned by cameramen sent by local newspaper editors to capture the event on film.

High school athletics was big in our town, so the turnout was insane. There were people who attended, whose kids didn't even attend the school. The town knew Garvey High for two things - our football team and track and field.

The muscles in my legs tightened as I passed my first competitor. We were competing against 5 schools. Each runner I passed my courage built to so high to past the next one, my ears burned.

I inhaled and exhaled at an even pace, as always. Pumping my arms and landing on each foot evenly. I gritted my teeth and swung my arms back and forth harder the moment I approached the last runner. He was fast, lightning fast. He was shorter but quicker and a lot lighter on his feet. Every time I gained momentum, he'd gain more. So, I pushed harder. Pushed so hard my right ear popped, but I passed him and was finally in the lead. Then I pumped my arms even harder than that, creating a distance I could be comfortable with. I was inches away from the finish line when I finally glanced over my shoulder to see I'd created more than a comfortable distance. I'd created so much distance a car could fit between myself and the fast runner behind me.

The second I crossed the finish line, I turned my head to look for my dad to see him jumping in place while holding up and pressing down on an air horn. That air horn was a staple at all of my races, and my father blew it obnoxiously every time I crossed a finish line. I loved hearing it every time.

Without even thinking, I searched for Ayla next to see her jumping up and down while clapping her hands. Watching her celebrate me almost made my heart burst out of my chest. I'd finally slowed my pace a few feet past the finish line, dropping to my hands and knees to catch my breath. Sounds of people cheering and the cheerleaders shouting their cheer routines were like a wave of noise. It was the most beautiful sound I'd ever heard; one I'd never tire of hearing to this day.

After the meet, after two interviews for two local newspapers, and after the customary team picture with our new trophy, I swaggered out with my dad wearing my new gold medal around my neck.

We were just a few days shy of summer, so the day was longer, keeping night away for a few more hours.

"Is that the superstar?" I heard behind us. "The one who just set a new record for the fastest sprint at Garvey High?"

My father turned before I did, and he laughed when he saw who it was.

"Why yes it is," my father answered. "I'm glad you recognized me."

Ayla giggled. "Oh yeah, Mr. Franklin, you were skillin' it out there."

He chuckled, and so did I.

"But I meant the other superstar."

"Ah, of course." My father grabbed my gym bag off my shoulder. "I'll take this to the car. Meet me there when you two finish talking."

Ayla tapped me on the bicep with her fist. "You took off like a bullet out there."

"Well, you know how I do."

The two of us stood apart for a moment out there, not saying anything. Ayla smiled, then dropped her eyes down to her sneakers, kicking a lone pebble out of her way. "I know we have spoken little since the other night but—"

"I heard my mother and your mother talking the other day. Your mom is about to leave town again this weekend?"

She nodded. "Yeah, to help my aunt with planning her wedding."

I moved in closer. "Maybe I can come over this weekend so we could study?"

Her brows wrinkled. "Hassani, graduation is in three weeks. Tests are done—"

"For college." I looked her right in her eyes. "So we're ready."

She stared at me for a moment, still confused. Suddenly her brows relaxed, and a smile pulled at her lips.

"*Oh,*" she said, just above a whisper. "Okay, yeah, sure."

"Yeah?" I asked to be sure.

My virginity had never been a hinderance in the way it clearly was hers. I knew my dad told me years ago that I should nurture my friendship with Ayla and not ruin it by dating her. I'm sure if I asked him, having sex with her would be a hell no in his eyes, but the idea of her giving herself to someone else who I knew wouldn't appreciate her gift the way I would, rubbed me wrong. My focus had always been running. My father had fostered a discipline in me that was unshakable. I spent so much time doing extra-curricular activities independent of track and field that I didn't have the time to even think about losing my virginity. Sex was always on the brain, though. I was a teenage boy, of course sex crossed my mind daily. And masterbating every now and again was as normal and consistent as breathing. Sex wasn't a constant conversation. Not until Ayla put it on my radar. And ever since she did, I couldn't think of anything else. Now the same energy and assertiveness I put toward winning my track meets, I would apply it to what we were about to do.

"Yeah," she answered. "This weekend then?"

"Yup." I licked my lips, and she looked away shyly. "This weekend."

CHAPTER 13

yla

I'D BEEN ANXIOUS THAT ENTIRE DAY. DIDN'T GET TO SLEEP THE NIGHT before. My mother announcing her departure and her plans to see me the next night sent my heart pounding at a rate that concerned me.

"Are you okay?" she asked as she lugged out one of the two suitcases she planned to travel with to Silver Spring. One suitcase contained my aunt's tailored wedding dress, the other suitcase held her shoes, toiletries, and the clothes my mother planned to wear while in Maryland. I followed behind her with a black garment bag draped over my arm. In the garment bag was a dress my aunt told my mother to bring, just in case they went out for drinks that night.

"I'm fine." I made my way to the back of the car. "Why do you ask?"

"You're shaking."

I reached my hand to press the button on the trunk to pop it opened and froze for only a moment before recovering. "Am I?"

She snickered to herself. "It'll only be for a night. Just like the last time. You could always come with me, you know."

"I'm fine, ma, promise."

But that was the furthest thing from the truth. I questioned my decision to agree to tonight. Hassani took me off guard when he hinted at giving me what I'd asked of him two weekends ago.

It made sense back then. He was someone I trusted. I really didn't want to end up like Chloe or to worse, be actually so in love with whoever I gave myself to, I risked my heart breaking in two.

About an hour after my mother's taillights disappeared in the distance, I called Hassani to inform him she'd left.

He told me, "I'll be there by 8."

He was on time, showing up dressed like he was just going out for a night with friends to an arcade.

"What up A. Boogie?" he greeted the second he stepped over the welcome mat.

"Hey, hi." I squeezed my lids shut, then opened them quickly. "What up?"

He chuckled to himself. Hassani toed off his sneakers while sniffing the air. "I smell pizza."

"Yeah." I pointed toward the kitchen. "It just arrived a few minutes ago. Extra cheese and pepperoni, right?"

He nodded slowly while holding a grin on his lips. "Like always."

We ate in silence mostly. We were so quiet in my kitchen I could hear tiny droplets of water falling from the faucet. My mother promised every weekend she would get someone out to the house to fix it, and every weekend the problem remained the same. She had a lot going on, so her empty promises went unjudged.

I picked at the diced pineapples, adding the chunks to my tongue one at a time between slices, and Hassani did what he always did - dip his head back as he angled the tip of each slice over his mouth.

Every time we'd make eye contact, we'd look away quickly.

After a while of that, we both stopped to look at one another and burst into a laugh.

"How are we going to do this if we can't even look at each other?" he asked.

"We can close our eyes," I suggested, but I knew he had a point.

"Look, Ayla—"

"Please don't back out of this," I interjected. "I might not be sure of a lot of things, but I'm sure about this."

Hassani held his stare with me for two beats before he inhaled deeply, then let his exhale out as a sigh. He sat back in his seat for a moment and stared past me.

I bit inside of my lip. The droplets from the faucet seemed to get louder in our minute-long silence.

"Aight, then." He pushed his chair back and stood to his feet. "You ready?"

"Oh, umm." I scratched the back of my head. "We're going to do this now?"

"I mean if you want to wait longer—"

I pushed my chair back quickly and jumped to my feet. "We can go now."

Laugh lines pulled at his eyes as he wore the look of amusement in reaction. "Then let's go."

The walk to my bedroom was different that night, obviously. I ambled ahead and experienced the weight of every foot I lifted on every step on my staircase. My breaths were just as heavy, and I was becoming light-headed as my heart pounded like it wanted to beat out of my chest and run out the house.

I switched on the light in my room the moment we stepped inside.

When I turned to look at him, Hassani had pulled out a CD and a small box of condoms from his pocket.

I gulped the air.

"Figured, you might not have any."

I parted my lips to say something, but nothing came out.

"I meant the condoms." He chuckled nervously. "Obviously not the CD. You have more CDs than I do."

I forced a short giggle.

"We could use yours if you have them," he added. "Condoms. If you have condoms."

"Oh my God." I dropped my forehead into my hands when the moment became too real for me.

"Ayla," I heard him say in front of me. He was closer now. I could tell this from the scent of him that now perfumed my space. "We don't *have* to do this."

I squeezed my lids shut, knowing he was right. Starting college as a virgin wouldn't have been the worse thing. Who would know? It was stupid to feel this obligation to have sex before then. Well, I realize that now. But back then, going into another day not experiencing something my friends had experienced already, some long before me, just didn't seem like something I wanted to do.

"I'm fine. It's fine," I told him.

Hassani bent his legs at the knees so his face was in line with mine. "You sure?"

I folded my bottom lip into my mouth and bit down on the fullest part.

"I don't want you to feel just because you asked me to come here to do this and I'm here now, that you have to do something you don't want to do. It's not that serious, okay?"

I stared into his eyes, watching as my overhead lights danced along his pupils. The hazel in his eyes was more prominent. His pupils looked gold. The way he looked at me with such care and compassion warmed me. I knew had it not been for me asking him to do this, he would have never tried going there with me. So many nights we spent in my room, innocently studying or me tutoring him or us eating pizza just as friends. Not once did he ever cross the line. Not once did he ever make me uncomfortable in his presence. I was eighteen, but even I understood not all guys my age were like Hassani, and I didn't want to find out what my first time would be like with a guy that wasn't like him.

So, I stepped forward and into his space. This time he didn't back away. I relaxed my shoulders and lifted my arms, wrapping my forearms around the back of his neck.

He said nothing when I balanced myself on the arches of my feet, aiming my lips up at his. Catching the hint, he lowered his mouth as I was rising even further for him. His eyes closed first, and I followed suit. The second our lips touched; a shock ran through me like an electric current. It made the tiny hairs on my arms stand in response. Our kiss started as a peck and then another, and before I knew it, our mouths had opened, and our tongues had left their safe spaces. I exhaled in his mouth the moment our tongues entwined. I lifted my eyelids slightly to see his eyes still closed. The sight of him so into what we were doing made me melt against him.

We stayed like that for another few seconds before he gently broke our kiss.

I stepped back swiping the side of my finger below my lip delaying making eye contact with him. Hassani closed the small distance I created between us, placed a finger beneath my chin to lift my head so my eyes met his.

A simple smile appeared on his lips, one that was sexier than the ones he'd flashed before it. "Don't act shy now."

I smiled in response.

"You can't act shy kissing me like that."

My smile became a laugh and before I could say anything in response, his mouth was back on mine. This kiss was easier than the first, more passionate as well. My lip-locks with other boys before Hassani were always missing something, but I often thought it was just me.

Maybe I wasn't positioning my mouth properly. Perhaps I was trying too hard.

But with Hassani, our kiss flowed naturally like water.

He broke our kiss again, this time to pull at the hem of his graphic tee, pulling the shirt completely up and over his head.

Following his lead, I gripped the bottom of my tee and pulled the shirt over my head too, removing it.

Hassani wasn't modest about staring past my bra and directly at the peaks of my breasts. In fact, he lost patience and was all over me after that.

The bed was our landing spot after we rid ourselves of the rest of our clothing. We laid beneath my covers dressed in only our underwear minutes later.

He reached for the box of condoms he brought over and pulled at the flap, ripping the packaging open and retrieving a condom.

Hassani stared at it for a moment, placing the condom in the palm of his hand and lowering it to the comforter, his view descending with his movements

"Do... do you know how to put it on?" I stuttered.

He snorted a laugh. "I'm a virgin, not an idiot Ayla."

I dropped my head forward and smiled.

"I just..." He exhaled. "Are you sure you want to do this—"

"Can you stop asking me that?"

"I want to make sure—"

"The question is - do *you* want to do this with *me?*"

He exhaled again.

"Because it seems the only person who's having doubts is you."

"Nah, I just—"

I kicked off the covers and stepped off the bed. "Don't feel like you have to do this because I asked Hassani. It's cool if you back out." I folded my arms. "I mean, it would hurt my feelings just a little, but I'd get over it. I already know I'm not your type."

"Can you stop saying that?"

"Why?" I shot back.

"Because you not being my type isn't true." He smirked up at me. "Do you really not understand how beautiful you are to me?"

He moved to my side of the bed, scooting to the edge and toward me. Hassani grabbed me by my hips and pulled me closer, so I was standing between his sprawled legs that hung off the edge of my mattress.

He dropped his head back and stared right up at me and told me, "I wouldn't want my first to be anyone else. I put that on everything."

I darted my eyes from left to right, reading his. He didn't blink, not once.

"I just want to make sure you're good now and that you'll be good after. That *we'll* be good after."

That was all I needed to see to nod my assurance. "It's like I told you, Hassani, I won't make things weird. I promise you that. So yeah, I'm good now and I'll be good after. We both will be."

He said nothing else. All he did was lift his hands to the sides of my panties and hooked his fingers along each band and pulled. Hassani kept his eyes on me until my panties dropped to my ankles. His touch left a trail of goosebumps on my legs. I stepped out of the cotton underwear when he broke eye contact to glimpse me below the waist. He leaned in, pulling me close, only stopping when his lips pressed into my stomach's soft skin.

I thought I'd faint. Something so small sent a chill running down my spine like cool water. I shivered in response. Hassani gently lowered me to the bed, trading places with me to stand so he could remove his boxers.

I remember my mind going blank the moment I laid eyes on his erection. He was longer than I imagined, thicker too. The length of him jutted out the second he freed himself, intimidating me with each bounce it did in response to his movements.

"I'll go slow," he promised.

Everything moved in slow motion after that. The crinkle of the condom again, the rip of the wrapper. The tight grip the condom created as he rolled it down from the head to the root of his erection. And when he positioned himself between my legs, I took a deep breath and held on to my exhale.

His breaths were heavy, his heart raced. I knew these things because he pressed his chest to mine right before he angled himself so the head of his hard-on rubbed against my softness.

I gasped.

He chuckled softly. "You think you can relax for me?"

I nodded, dropping my knees to either side and exhaling when I did. The next few minutes were a series of tries and fails. Between my thighs might as well had been a steel door because it refused to give way, and Hassani was just as lost as I was on how to change that. We grunted and sighed, neither one of us saying anything to each other during the awkward silence. For me, my silence was out of fear of saying the wrong thing. In that moment, I couldn't think of anything I wanted more than *that* and with him.

I was seconds away from just giving up when he crushed his lips against me. The kiss came at a surprise, my eyebrows shooting up over my eyes, but when his tongue entered my mouth in search of mine, I met him halfway, looping our tongues together.

I became even wetter between my thighs as evident by the squeak of the condom. He tried again, and this time the head of him slid in just a bit easier.

Hassani exhaled in my mouth and I wrapped my arms around him immediately. Another inch became two, my walls expanding, a sweet ache rising in me.

I squeezed my eyes shut, widening my legs so he could sink even deeper.

His pumps started off slow and within seconds they became gradually concise.

It was impossible to feel past the pain. I opened my eyes to his and watched as his face contorted into the most beautiful shape.

He groaned in angst. "I'm—"

I held him tighter, wrapping my legs around him to hold him in place when he tried to break free.

"Shit," he whispered before his eyes rolled to the back of his skull and his mouth fell open.

I clasped my palms to either side of his cheeks. Hassani dropped the weight of his head in my hands, then he squeezed his lids closed. Another guttural groan shot from his lips. This one was so deep, the groan resonated inside of me. He shuttered and pumped, then shuttered some more, throwing off his pace, completely unable to control either action. I held him tight, in awe of the view.

When he pulled himself free, the throbbing between my thighs took the place of his warmth. He dropped beside me on the bed, and I followed him with my eyes.

Hassani's chest rose and fell as he struggled to catch his breath. His erection slowly deflated until it laid against his thigh flaccid, his release whitening the inside tip of the condom.

I lifted my gaze to him. "Did you just—"

"Yeah," he confirmed and emphasized his response with a nod. "Did you?"

I shook my head.

He closed his eyes tight.

"But it's cool." I squeezed my thighs together, hoping to calm the ache and another feeling slowly rising inside me. "I heard that most girls don't their first time."

"I'm sorry," he whispered.

I wrinkled my brows. "For what?"

"For *that*."

"Hassani—"

"My dad has always joked with his friends about men who can't satisfy the women they're with."

"Well, you're not *with* me."

"But—"

I sat up, pressing my back to my headboard. "Hassani, it's *fine*." I cringed when I crossed my ankles beneath the covers. "Satisfaction was never the goal, anyway."

"Damn." His brows wrinkled, and he dropped his view to the blanket covering me. "Please tell me I didn't hurt you, too."

"No." I shook my head. Although the pain was definitely present, the pain was an ache I welcomed. "You didn't hurt me."

"Then we can go again." He reached toward my night table. "I got like two more condoms."

"Down boy."

He laughed, bringing his fist to his mouth to cover.

"I'm fine," I assured him. "*We're* fine."

He stared at me for a moment before I broke eye contact to turn my face away to hide my smile.

"You wanna know what's crazy though?" he asked.

When I turned to look his way, I noticed the gigantic smile he wore on his face. Hassani added, "I think I like pineapples now."

"Oh my God, shut up!"

We both fell out laughing.

I may not have enjoyed sex my first time, but I found pleasure in something I wasn't expecting... watching Hassani enjoy me.

CHAPTER 14

$\mathcal{H}$assani

I spotted her the moment I stepped out of the school's main exit. I'd been waiting for my last class to end so I could find her.

I thought it was all in my head, but looking back at things now, I was right to think Ayla had been avoiding me since that night. There wasn't an hour in the day after we had sex that I didn't playback the night's events. I wondered if I was wrong for leaving when I did about an hour after we finished. I questioned if I should have called her when I returned home to make sure we were still good. I wanted to give her space. I needed mine too.

Sex for the first time wasn't what I imagined. It was way better. And it kind of sucked she didn't experience what I experienced.

"Ayla," I shouted as I made my way closer to her.

Although her back faced me, I noticed her hesitation to turn around.

She promised she wouldn't make things weird, and it seemed she was holding true to her promise. I hoped I could too.

I lifted my hand to my mouth and blew into my palm, inhaling my breath to make sure it didn't reek. Never did I ever do that with her or any other girl.

"Stop trippin'," I told myself as I closed the space between us.

The closer I got, the more in view some guy appeared. From afar, it looked like she was just talking to him. But up close, it seemed they were doing just a little more than that.

She turned in my direction to greet me. Ayla wore a smile she struggled to hold on her lips. Her eyes told me everything else I needed to know.

I focused past her at the guy who stood close to her. Too close for my comfort.

"Where you been all day?" I asked as I approached her. "You didn't come to math."

"I had a yearbook committee meeting," she answered. "It was the last one before we go to print, and I still had photos to submit."

Ayla joined the yearbook committee the first day of senior year. She took all the pictures. According to her, she needed something to add to her college applications since she wasn't a student athlete and since she liked photography; it seemed like a simple decision. She was our graduating class's valedictorian, but that clearly wasn't enough. Leave it to Ayla Samuels to be an overachiever.

School was just about over with only a few days left for us seniors. Not much learning happened around that time, so missing class at that point wasn't cause for concern from our teachers. Especially when the absence was school related.

I still felt something was off with her.

I peeked over her head at the guy who stood behind her with his eyes locked on me. He stood tall, a few inches shorter than me though. Dressed like he'd climbed out of a Ralph Lauren catalog, the guy eyed me, sizing me up and probably curious about my relationship to Ayla.

I chucked my chin in his direction and asked, "Whats up?"

"Nothing much," he answered swiftly. The guy maintained eye contact with me. I didn't even know a guy like this was even Ayla's type.

This can't be anyone important to her.

She was my focus again when I moved my eyes off the guy and settled my view on her, hoping she'd get the hint without me having to ask who he was.

"Oh," she spoke. "Cordell, this is my friend Hassani. Hassani, this is Cordell."

I stared at her for a few seconds before asking, "and Cordell is..."

He answered, "Her boyfriend."

My brows shot up instantly. His words hit me in the gut like a ton of bricks. I thought I'd lose my footing. I couldn't believe I heard correctly.

I mean, he had to be mistaken.

Since when did that happen?

I was just with her two days ago and nothing about her having a boyfriend came up.

"And her prom date," he added, because he hadn't dug the knife deep enough into my chest.

"Her boyfriend," I repeated. Saying the words made my tongue heavy.

She shook her head and waved her hand for emphasis.

"It's new," she clarified. "We made things official last night so... it's new.

"Hmph," I huffed. I was really at a loss for words. We were just together. Our relationship had evolved to a level I fantasized about constantly but that I didn't want to jeopardize our friendship over.

Is that what is happening now?

I stared at Ayla for a moment. Doing my very best to communicate with her using my eyes. She did her best to analyze me, and I did my best to hide anything she'd be able to identify.

I forced myself to take a breath and forced a smile on my lips, praying neither she nor Cordell noticed how hard it was to do both.

"Well," I started, "then, it's nice to meet you Cordell."

"Thanks, same," he replied, not missing a beat.

I tried my hardest to control my breathing. There was no way I would break my cool facade for anyone. Not even Ayla.

I could have stood there with them for a few minutes longer. Deep down I wanted to but to more so show the guy his presence meant nothing, but I couldn't. I couldn't bear to hear someone claim her as theirs even though there was no chance I would be able to. Just seeing them stand at the distance they did in front of each other was making my stomach churn and I couldn't understand why.

She'd promised not to make things weird, and I had to make the same promise.

"Anyway." I tugged at the strap of my backpack. "I gotta go." I peeked down at Ayla for only a moment, maintaining the tight smile on my lips that hurt my cheeks because of all the tension. "I'll call you later, Ayla."

I brushed past them, not even making eye contact with her again. It was important I created enough distance between us because I wasn't sure how and what I would do if I remained there with them.

I had no intentions of calling Ayla that night. Unsure what I would say and concerned with how well I would say anything, I never reached out to her.

Instead, I called Jessica Delano, a girl who ran on the girls' track and field team. She'd been dropping hints about wanting me to ask her out to prom, and now was the perfect time to do it.

I knew back then distractions would be necessary to deal with what Ayla and I did. She'd worked her way into a part of my heart I didn't even know had space for someone other than close family. Ayla was no longer just a friend, for real this time. She'd become something else. And that something else would boggle my mind for years to come.

I laid in bed that night with Ayla strong on my brain understanding entirely, things could never be the same between her and I... and a part of me kind of liked that.

yla

PROM WAS... UNDERWHELMING. THE ALLURE OF IT LOST ITS LUSTER because of my date.

Cordell was clingy. The entire night, he needed to be every and anywhere I was. I get it. He didn't go to my school, and this was my prom, but damn, I needed to breathe in air. Air he didn't exhale.

"You want something to drink?" he asked. We stood against a wall at Dania Perez's house. Really, it was a mansion she never shied away from bragging about. It was an hour after prom. For weeks, she'd been promoting her little house party at her parents' big house they didn't even stay in. It was one of the many properties her parents owned, a party house. The place had no furniture and was built from the ground up with the intention of hosting parties there, making it the perfect location to host an after-prom event for at least 60 graduating seniors.

"I can get you a cola or something," Cordell pushed.

I fought not to roll my eyes. On the outside, Cordell asking would've seemed like a sweet gesture. As I think about it now, he would have been the perfect boyfriend... for someone else. For me though, he was a distraction, one who was literally distracting me from my undercover stalking.

From where Cordell and I stood, Hassani was my focus. For the fourth time that night, he pulled Jessica Delano to the dance floor to dry hump to yet another dancehall reggae track that banged out of the overhead and floor speakers.

"Or maybe you want a ginger ale?"

I watched as Hassani wound his waist up against Jessica, her barely able to keep up. I twisted my lips to one side as he pumped his pelvis back and forth to match the melody of the song. She giggled, even though I couldn't hear her laughs over the track. Her teeth were on full display, eyes glittering beneath the barely there lights overhead. Girlfriend was in bliss.

"I'm fine," I finally answered Cordell through my teeth.

"Well, I'm going to go get something. I'm thirsty. Wanna come with?" He trekked a few feet ahead of me, holding out a hand. He looked good that night. Dapper midnight black tuxedo, no tail, to match my black opened-back slinky gown. My mother had designed and sewn it for me. Tailored the dress just right so the hem swept the floor, but not enough to make me trip.

"Sure, I'll come with you," I told Cordell, reluctantly taking his hand as my view drifted over to Hassani again.

Hassani and I had spoken little since the day in the school yard a week prior when he ran into me and Cordell. It was never my intention for Hassani to learn of Cordell that way. I didn't want for him to learn of Cordell at all. I honestly thought I'd timed Cordell and my exit perfectly, until Hassani approached

Cordell and I walked toward the bar at the other end of the room. Dania hosted the party in the grand living room that was as big as our school's auditorium. Cordell held tight to my hand, forcing the threading of his fingers with mine. We were feet away from Hassani when Hassani peeked up from his date to lock eyes with me. His view on me lasted all but half a second before they were back on his date.

Jessica would more than likely talk all about their date for the rest of her natural life. The girl talked too much, period. That was the only reason I knew about her and Hassani hooking up in the backseat of his new BMW. His father bought it for him as an early graduation gift with plans for Hassani to drive back home every weekend once Hassani started school at Langston U. Learning Hassani and I would attend the same university in the city excited me before we hooked up. Now I dreaded it.

"Here you go." Cordell handed me my red cup of cola. Once the drink was securely in my hand, he draped an arm over my shoulder.

Jessica had shared the news about her and Hassani one day while in the bathroom. She'd pranced in with her three friends to check her makeup in the mirror. I don't think I've ever seen her without makeup or out of the bathroom because, duh, that's where the mirror was.

While I stood in the stall, handling my business, more than ready to finish up and exit, she paralyzed me with her admission.

"Hassani was so big," she bragged through her girly giggles. "He could barely fit it all inside of me, but we made it work."

"Did he make you... you know?" One of her friends inquired, her voice trailing off as the bathroom door opened and they all stepped out one at a time to exit. The door closed before I could hear Jessica's answer.

"You all right?" Cordell asked in my ear.

I turned to look his way. "I'm fine, why?"

He leaned in again. "Because your crushing your plastic cup in your hand."

I peeked down to see the cup slightly crumpled in my grip. Guiding the rim to my lips, I chugged the cola until the cup was empty.

"I'm fine," I repeated. "I just need to use the bathroom." Setting the damaged cup down on the bar, I patted him on the chest and added, "I'll be right back."

"I can walk you," he suggested.

"I'll only be a minute."

"It's cool, I can—"

"I'm going to walk myself to the bathroom, Cordell. Alone," I shouted over the music. "Stay here. I will be right back."

I didn't even wait for a reply. Honestly, I needed a break from him. He'd been my emotional support dog for the entire night and didn't even know it. I needed a minute.

Just outside the grand living room in Dania's parents' unfurnished home was a long hall. Down that hall, according to her, were three bathrooms, all available for use so no one had to wait in line. Like I said, the unique design of the house catered to the hosting of parties like the one held that night.

In one of those bathrooms, I peed, and washed my hands. It was a single bathroom, a half bath I would learn. It had a large vanity and sink, and of course a toilet. A floor-to-ceiling mirror that laid flushed against the wall with a frame made of onyx was the centerpiece of the restroom. Dania's father was in the wines and spirits business and owned a tequila brand back then. By the size of their party house it was safe to assume he was successful at what he did.

I dried my hands with one of the single folded napkins, dropped the crumpled napkin in the wastebasket, and stepped out.

Besides the muffled lyrics from the song playing and the hum of the bass, the hall leading to the grand living room was quiet. There had to be at least 60 people in and outside of the mansion, but not a single person in the hallway. I took large steps toward the grand living room, passing the second bathroom door and soon the third.

The instant I passed the third bathroom, I felt a grip on the space between my bicep and forearm. Before I could even think to gasp, scream, anything, someone pulled me into the bathroom.

"Hassani?!" I shouted the moment he got me on the other side of the door and I recognized his face. I balled my hand into a fist and punched him on the arm. "What the hell is wrong with you? What are you doing?"

"*Shh*," he shushed, locking the door.

"*Shh* my ass." I placed my hands on either side of my waist. "What's up?"

He said nothing. Just closed the space between us, taking my face in his hands and leaning in for a kiss. I backed away, and he caught me by the small of my back.

"What are you doing?"

"Making up for the last time." He leaned in again, and I didn't stop him this time. Didn't even think to. Just closed my eyes and waited for the soft warmth of his lips against mine.

Because I'd been missing it?

Hassani wasted no time searching for my tongue with his. He moaned when I met him halfway. Pulled me closer when I wrapped my arms around the back of his neck. Hassani pressed his body close to mine, leaning his forearm against the wall behind me for stability. He dipped his head to one side and slid his tongue even further into my mouth, and I welcomed it. Craved it like it was the only thing able to keep me alive.

He traded my lips for my neck, kissing me from my jawline to the space inches away from my collarbone. I'd later learn that was my spot, a spot that made me lower all of my inhibitions, making it impossible for me to put up a fight even if I wanted to.

"What about Jessica?" I asked between breaths.

"What about Jessica?" he panted.

He smoothed his hand from my neck to over my breast, caressing it for only a moment before he continued with his exploration. Against my stomach, I could feel him growing in the seat of his pants.

"Aren't you two together?" I whispered.

"She's just my date."

"She said you two had sex."

He paused and leaned back to make eyes with me.

"I overheard her speaking with her friends in the bathroom," I told him. "So, I know."

"You don't *know* enough to conclude anything," he affirmed.

We switched from the wall to the vanity, the move orchestrated by Hassani and Hassani alone.

He lifted me by the waist and placed me on the surface. His hands picked at the fastenings on his tux, undoing the buttons on the jacket one at a time until the tailored garment fell to the floor by his designer shoes.

"Isn't she your girlfriend?"

"She's not," he corrected.

"She's not? Then who is she to—"

"Don't worry about that. Don't worry about *her*." He took my hand and briefly pressed it to his hard-on. "Worry about this."

My heart raced, and my tongue laid flat against the roof of my mouth. He gathered the fabric of my dress in his hand, rolling up the hem, only stopping when it reached my thighs.

"Why not?"

"Why not what?" he asked, pecking me once on the lips.

"Why shouldn't I worry about her."

Hassani kissed me from my cheek to the maze of my ear. And right before dropping to his knees in front of me, he said, "Because she's only practice."

I pushed myself as far back on the vanity as I could. "What?"

He dropped his head between my legs and grunted. "I didn't like the way things happened between us at your house that night."

"It was fine..."

"You weren't satisfied."

Yes, I was.

Just seeing him so vulnerable was satisfying enough.

"We didn't do it for me to be satisfied," I protested instead. "Remember?"

"I can't accept that." He kissed a trail up my thigh. "I refuse to accept that." Hassani spread my legs, and I let him with little resistance. "Let me fix it."

Hassani buried his lips between my thighs and sucked and licked me in places I didn't know could bring me so much pleasure. Made my body defy my control by trembling against the grips of his hands. He held me in place as he skated his tongue against the bundle of nerves only I had touched before that night. He groaned against my flesh like I was an actual meal. It was my first-time experiencing pleasure like that, but it couldn't compare to when the effects of his actions made my body vibrate uncontrollably while I came on his tongue.

He stood to his feet and pressed his hand to the mirror behind me. Covered his hard-on with a condom using only one hand. He slid in me gently but with a confidence and familiarity he was lacking the first time he and I had sex. He found a rhythm quicker than our first time, too, pumping his hips like an expert or what I perceived to be an expert at 18-years-old. Hassani moved in me like someone who had not only been practicing but rehearsing for something big.

I had no control over my body. My eyes rolled, my body shuddered and vibrated again. I hugged and released him inside me in ways I couldn't stop, even with increased focus. The pressure build up had me clawing at his back that was still covered in his white button-down shirt. I screamed my pleasure in that bathroom, feeling my voice become hoarse.

What was happening? I wondered when my body felt like it would implode.

He groaned in time with his thrusts, holding me close and in place with one hand. Hassani maintained his balance with the hand he hadn't moved off the mirror behind me. Our eyes met when the sensation hit, causing me to arch my back and drop my head back between my shoulders, and he held me the entire time. Rocking with me, continuing to collide his hard with my soft. I came undone against him, wrapping my arms around him the moment I came down from a body high I didn't even know was possible to achieve outside of a wet dream.

He showered my neck with kisses, kissed his way to my lips, and gave me the most soul-stirring kiss that made me feel like I could experience all the previous sensations just from his mouth alone.

He detached himself from me slowly. Never moved his eyes off me as he discarded the condom in the trash and fixed himself up.

I slid off the counter, my legs feeling worthless the second my feet touched the floor.

He caught me with one arm before I could lose my balance. "You good?"

I nodded, embarrassed. "I think so."

He grinned.

I turned away shyly to face the mirror and noticed my rouge lipstick everywhere but on my lips. Instantly, I thought of Cordell.

"Oh my God," I whispered, pressing my fingertips to the mess around my mouth.

Hassani smirked behind me, something I caught him doing from his reflection in the mirror. I balled my hand into a fist and turned to punch him against his shoulder, but he ducked out of the way.

"It isn't funny," I sneered, a smile appearing a second later. "I look horrible right now."

"You look beautiful," he insisted.

I refused to hold my smile back after hearing him say that.

His smile came as easy as mine.

"Now what?" I asked.

"We go back and party," he answered.

I furrowed my brows.

I could have pushed for more of an explanation. Questioned the real reason we did what we did when we were clearly in that house on dates with different people. But I didn't.

He exited first, leaving no more words to ponder over. I stayed behind for five minutes more to fix myself as best as I could.

I returned to the party ten minutes later to find Hassani standing against the wall with one foot pressed against the surface while the other laid planted to the floor. Jessica stood beside him, rambling about nothing, I'm sure, while his eyes watched my every move.

"You were gone a while, huh?" Cordell asked the second I returned to the bar. "Everything okay?"

Hassani and I stared at each other from across the room, only breaking eye contact when smiles pulled our lips up.

"Yeah," was all I replied with. It was all I could think to say back. The only word I could utter as inside me mourned Hassani's absence.

I still forced myself to ignore the feelings surrounding what happened between us in Dania Perez's bathroom. Because what happened wasn't the favor I asked of him when we first had sex. It wasn't even the continuation of that favor. The way he moved between my legs and conjured my release out of me was as if he had something to prove, like a point he just had to make.

The decision we made to have sex again was also the start of an understanding. An understanding between Hassani and I that would remain unspoken for years and that started the clock on the beginning of an end neither of us saw coming.

PART III
FALSE START

4-YEARS LATER...

CHAPTER 16

yla

"Ayla," Hassani panted beside me. "Where's your head right now?"

The impact of the asphalt against the bottom of my feet as my sneakers pounded against the hard surface sent a ripple of waves throughout my entire body.

"Where else could my head be, Hassani?" I answered through breaths.

"You look spaced out."

"Stop making me talk!"

He laughed as he picked up speed. "Keep up then."

We were running around our university's track. I'd been complaining about putting on weight and wanting to lose a little before graduation. Instead of listening to my complaints, Hassani talked me into going on his weekend run.

I struggled to pace my breathing the whole time. "I can't believe I let you talk me into this."

"Oh, you love it."

I rolled my eyes but didn't dare say something in response, mainly so I could keep the breaths I could take in my body flowing.

Running was like walking to Hassani, and running was like pushing the Empire State Building with my pinky nail to me.

"Lookin' good, Hassani," a girl shouted from the bleachers.

Hassani chucked his chin her way.

"Appreciate it," he said before focusing his attention on the track ahead.

I glanced in the voice's direction to find the meanest glare on the girl's face as she shared a look with me.

"Problem?" I shouted at her. All she did was twist her wrist and hold her hand in front of her face so her palm faced me. You know, the universal gesture for "bitch, whatever."

That was par for the course. Every girl who knew Hassani absolutely hated me. But they always did an outstanding job of showing only their shining faces and sweet smiles with him. Did it so well, when I told him all the girls he has either called girlfriend or played bed Olympics with hated me, he accused me of being overdramatic. This was one reason he and I remained friends and only friends for as long as we did.

"So, you're going to act like she didn't just snarl at me like some kind of Pitbull?"

He looked at me for a moment before focusing forward. "I promise you that was all in your head."

"Yeah, okay."

"Ready to move in to you and Sunni's new place?" I knew he was forcing a change of topic and I refused to make a fuss about it.

"More than ready," I huffed. "Still helping me move in?"

"Still tutoring me?"

"What if I say no?"

He flashed a sly grin. "What if *I* say no?"

I sucked my teeth and focused forward. That made him laugh.

It felt like it was only yesterday we started our first year at Langston University. After four long years, eight semesters, and two summer class sessions to catch up, we were only weeks away from graduating. College was very similar to high school for me only in college, I didn't get assignment reminders or got ridiculed for not showing up to class.

For most of my college life, I lived in the dorms. But after convincing my mother it was time for me to move into my own place in anticipation of my new job at a local school in Manhattan, she supported me.

"I bet your cornball boyfriend can't wait to come and visit."

I wrinkled my face before I turned to glance Hassani's way. "Well, that was random."

"No, it wasn't."

"Yes, *it* was."

"We were talking about your new place, and that was just a thought I had."

"Yes, a random thought."

"Hmph."

A few paces up ahead I added, "And he's not my boyfriend."

"He sure gets the privileges of one."

"Barely." I cringed at the burn in my lungs. "He gets the same privileges as you."

"And *that's* the problem," he mumbled.

I reduced speed. "Huh?"

"Nothing." Hassani clenched his jaw then quickly relaxed the tension. "Don't slow down. Let's finish this last lap and call it the day."

"Ayla," my mother said into the phone.

I'd just rolled over off my back with the phone pressed to my ear. The call came in after eight that night as I laid in my dorm room alone. With plans to move out in a few days, I packed all my stuff in boxes. Myself and my roommate, Sunni, were moving off campus.

"Mom?"

"Baby, I need you to drive with me down to Silver Spring."

I peeked at the time on my desk clock. Turning in early wasn't even like me, but between the run with Hassani earlier in the day paired with all the packing I'd been doing all week long after classes, exhaustion finally won. Even though I wasn't taking any of the furniture, getting things ready for my move to my first apartment took a lot out of me.

"Ayla, are you there?"

"Yeah, I'm here, mom. Why do we have to go to Silver Spring at this hour?"

"It's your aunt."

I sat up immediately. "What happened?"

"I'll tell you everything in the car."

Three and a half hours. It took us three and a half hours to drive out to Silver Spring. My mother caught me up on everything along the way.

"She's completely broken," was how my mother introduced the conversation.

What she revealed next left my jaw hanging open for most of the ride. Aunt Laurie's husband of four years had started a family behind her back. Apparently, he'd been cheating for three of the four years of their marriage, and the product of his infidelity were two children.

"When did he tell her this?"

"He never told her. Laurie found out after the woman called her cell phone looking for him." My mother shook her head as we turned onto Aunt Laurie's block. "When Laurie confronted him, he told her everything, and packed a few of his stuff and left."

Outside her townhouse, her lights were the only ones on, on the block. The neighborhood was a nice one, only townhouses as far as the eyes could see, with a private practice at every corner.

My mother and I climbed the cement stairs and the closer we got to the front door; the louder things got from inside. I rang the bell, and we both waited, and the person who showed up to the door, I didn't even recognize.

"Can you believe this motherfucker?!" Aunt Laurie shouted.

My eyes bulged at her language. I'd never heard her speak like that. Her appearance was none better.

Aunt Laurie flung the door opened, and the doorknob slammed against the wall behind it. "I'm throwing the rest of his shit out. They have to go right *now*!"

She stomped away from the door mumbling a few more expletives leaving my mother and I standing on the welcome mat looking at each other.

My mother took a deep breath and crossed the threshold. "Laurie, come here."

"He had the audacity, the audacity, to tell me he loved me and he's sorry but he's leaving. He's sorry?!"

I ambled onto the property, my eyes growing wider with each step I took. The place was in shambles like a storm hit it. There were men's clothing strewn all over, shoes too. Most of the items were in shreds or had slashes in the fabric. Shards of glass glittered from the floor; broken fine china scattered everywhere. The scene resembled the aftermath of a raid.

"Two kids!" Aunt Laurie hollered. Her mascara ran from her eyes like her makeup was escaping her fury. My new uncle was nowhere in sight and that was a great thing.

Her hair was wild and one side of her yellow silk shirt hung off her shoulder. She was a fragment of herself. Certainly not who I grew up looking up to.

"Laurie," my mother whispered. "Have you been drinking?"

Aunt Laurie ran her fingers through her hair. "I'm *fine*, Sonia."

Mom shook her head. "You don't look fine."

"Well, I will be fine once I get all this junk out of here." Her eyes moved around the room wildly. "Everything in this house he bought. All of this *shit*," she shouted, swiping her hand against a tiny roman pedestal, knocking over a hand blown crystal vase to the floor. The vase landed with a crash, startling me. "And he was playing house with some *bitch* in the same city as me?"

"Laurie, sit down," my mother insisted. Her tone was as if she were addressing a child.

"I don't *want* to sit down."

"You're upset."

"Of course, I'm upset, *Sonia*," she replied, annunciating every syllable in my mother's name. "I gave up everything for that asshole. Every-fucking-thing!"

I couldn't move. My feet felt melded to the hardwood beneath my Converses. In all the years I'd been in the presence of my aunt, never had I ever seen her in rare form like she was the night we showed up to her house.

She and I locked eyes, and she closed hers for only a moment, a tear escaping.

My eyes watered at the sight of her, and my bottom lip trembled.

She opened her eyes to me, and that one tear became many. My aunt fell to her knees, and she slapped her hands to her eyes to cry into her palm.

I went to her quickly, wrapping my arms around her.

Mom stood over us, sniffing back her tears. "I'm going to brew some coffee to sober you up."

I peeked up at my mother and she ran her hands down my coils and curls that were pulled back into a low ponytail. "Stay with her."

I nodded, leaning my head on my aunt's shoulder.

"I'm so sorry, Aunt Laurie."

With that, her cries became audible. Her shoulders shrugged uncontrollably as she bawled in my arms. I couldn't believe this was happening, had a hard time believing my carefree aunt with the bubbly personality was now this worrisome woman on her knees, surrounded by chaos and with her heart as broken as the vase beside us.

"Never do it, Ayla," she whispered. The powerful stench of gin on her breath made me cringe. "Never *ever* love a man more than he loves you, you hear me?"

I looked into her bloodshot eyes.

"Ain't none of them good," she added. "Your daddy was the exception, but he was an anomaly. They don't make them like him anymore."

I wrinkled my brows, noticing when my heart sank.

"Because these jokers these days..." She wiped away her tears and sloppily sniffed back the ones waiting to fall. "Every one of them will promise you the world, then ruin yours without delivering on a single one of their promises. And I knew better. I *knew* better." She slapped the floor with an open hand. "Don't do what I did - trust them. Trust not one of them. Don't you ever do that. Do you hear me—"

"Laurie, stop it!" My mother shouted from across the room. I'd never heard my mother yell at anyone until that night. Her eyes moved to me next. "Ayla—"

"I'm fine." I hopped up from my seat. "I'll start cleaning up."

"Ayla, baby—"

"Mama. I'm. *Fine.*"

But that was a lie. My aunt's words and the conviction in her voice when she spoke them would loiter in my memory for years, causing me to make choices, fearing the worse instead of hoping for the best.

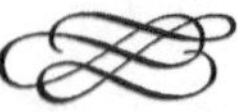

yla

"A. BOOGIE, PUT YOUR BACK INTO IT, WOMAN, COME ON!" HASSANI shouted above me.

"Yeah, no," I replied, peeking in front of me before climbing the last flight of steps. "I don't think so. You told me to speed up during our run the other day and I'm still sore because of it."

I pushed, and he pulled the opposite end of my night table until we'd reached the top of the flight of stairs. The sun blazed that day; the clouds floating overhead like nosey neighbors temporarily shading us from heat. And I was moving into my first apartment off campus. The place was a two bedroom walk-up in SoHo. Real chic like but kind on my wallet since I was splitting the rent.

"Look," he grunted, "I can't put my back out messing with you. Why couldn't you have hired movers?"

"Because movers cost money and I don't got it like that."

The second we stopped in front of my new apartment door,

Hassani dropped his end of my table and it made a loud thud beside the six or so boxes he lugged up the stairs moments prior.

"Hey!" My voice echoed down the hallway. "Don't drop my stuff like that."

"Oh, my bad. I didn't mean to mishandle IKEA's best."

I kissed my teeth.

"Open the door."

I arched a brow and folded my arms.

He pressed his palms together and smiled. "Please, beautiful."

As if I could resist returning the smile.

I'd been waiting to move into the new unit since the start of the month. With only five weeks left in school, I thought it was best to find a place of my own. Technically, it wasn't of *my* own. I moved in with my college roommate and best friend, Sunni. But it was ours. No curfew but now a new obligation to pay rent. Adulting was exciting and nerve wracking to me around this time.

I turned the first lock with the key on my two-key keyring.

"And I hope y'all got the air on in here with y'all cheap ass."

"No, you didn't," I said through my laugh, twisting the second key in its lock.

"Where is Sunni, anyway?" he asked. Hassani pulled on his t-shirt's collar to puff air into his shirt. "And why isn't she helping you pull cheap furniture and one hundred boxes up five flights of stairs."

"First." I turned to face him. "My stuff is not cheap. They are budget friendly."

He twisted his lips to one side in a yeah right fashion.

"Second..." I shoved him against his shoulder. "You helped me move six little boxes, you big baby."

"They felt more like one hundred boxes filled with rocks to me," he mumbled.

"Third, Sunni is working just as hard as we are. She got a little furniture she's moving in here right now."

That part was a stretch. Sunni was definitely moving in but she hired movers. She actually had *it* like that. The quote the movers gave her for the job was way too much for my budget though. But I figured there was no way they'd be done moving her stuff in before Hassani and I, since I planned for us to start early. Plus, Sunni had far more things than I did with her bougie ass.

The moment I pushed open the door, an air-conditioned breeze hit us in the face scented by a dark cherry candle aroma. Neo soul streamed through the air. Sunni lounging with her legs hanging off the arm of the couch came into view next. There were boxes everywhere, all taped and sorted in their proper locations.

"Sunni?" I started. "Don't tell me you're done."

She sat up for a moment only to wave at us before returning to her lounging position.

"I am," she sang. "The movers just left half and hour ago."

"Movers?!" Hassani questioned behind me.

I shut my eyes tight refusing to turn around.

"Why they couldn't move your stuff, Ayla?"

"They cost too much."

"Woman!"

I twisted quick. "Don't even start. I told you I got you on tutoring for your statistics final. This is your payment. So you hush."

He kissed his teeth and brushed past me to make his way over to the air conditioner that blew air on high speed.

Sunni chuckled as she swung her legs off the couch arm to stand to her bare feet. "Anyway, I'm about to hop in the shower and head out to meet up with Josiah."

Sunni and Josiah had been with each other since our third years at Langston University. He was the president of the debate team, and Sunni was studying criminal law. To say the two of them were the perfect match would be an understatement.

"Thank God the air is on," Hassani uttered from his spot in front of the AC. He'd widened his shirt at the hem and damn near wrapped the fabric around the unit.

"Stop hogging up all the air." I dropped myself on the comfy couch.

"You good." Hassani left his position in front of the AC to join me on the couch. "I just did all the work, anyway."

The second he plopped down on the couch beside me, the cushion beneath me made me bounce up.

Hassani and I had found a place in our friendship that was between friend and something else. The something else had become unspoken. So unspoken, us having sex seemed like a distant memory that I'm sure he'd forgotten... maybe. I hadn't but he and I were different. And with the amount of women he's been with since then, I was sure us doing what we did in high school was the furthest thing from his memory.

"So, what you gettin' into tonight?" he asked.

"Just chillin'. I might get in some more studying for my English final that's in a few weeks."

The thought to explore anything more than what we had never occurred to me. I didn't want a boyfriend. I had a guy friend around that time who I entertained and who had a nasty habit of trying to find himself in a permanent space in my life. His interest in making things permanent between us seemed to grow even more the closer we got to graduation. I'd given him the excuse that I wasn't looking for a boyfriend because my studies took priority. Now that school was almost over, the excuse would no longer shield me.

Hassani huffed. "Just chillin', huh?"

After Hassani and I hooked up in Dania Perez's bathroom during our prom's after-party, he called me the next day and we conversed like nothing happened. We both skated around the topic of that night like we were competing for the gold metal in figure skating at the Olympics. He didn't bring it up, and I certainly didn't either. And here we were, four years later.

"How about you?" I asked.

He leaned back in his seat, stretching his arms high above his head and over the neck of the couch. "I'm going to swing by Sienna's room after this. See what she wants to do."

"Hmph," I huffed this time.

Sienna was a name that was coming up more than usual. She performed on our school's dance team, and she and Hassani had been doing the dance of friends with benefits since the end of sophomore year. She was your usual dainty and prissy princess. Hair always done, nails too. She spoke in a high-pitched enchanted princess voice; one you'd recognize from a Disney cartoon. Almond eyes and full lips naturally tinted an innocent pink hue. Skin just as warm as her name. Sienna was perfect for Hassani, at least in my eyes.

"She told me she wanted to watch this new movie that just dropped," he added, "so I'll probably grab it on bootleg."

I rolled my eyes. "Why don't you just take the girl to the movies? I'm sure she'd appreciate the date."

"I don't want to confuse her."

A laugh burst through my lips. "Confuse her?"

"Yeah." He sat up. "Sienna and I have kept it real casual, and I'd like to keep it that way."

I shook my head.

"She's been hinting at wanting more between us for the past few weeks, and I don't want to confuse her with something like a date and make her think we could be more than what we are doing right now."

"And what are you two doing right now?"

"Fucking," he declared without taking a new breath.

I scoffed out a laugh.

"Some good old fashion are-you-free-when-I'm-free fucking. No strings attached of course."

"You are such an ass."

"I'mma get some ass later, that's for sure."

I shoved him away from me.

The chime of my phone on the kitchen counter where I dropped it off when we entered, pinged behind us. I peeked that way, only to turn back around to find Hassani's hazel-greens on me.

"What?"

"See, I don't know why you're acting all brand new," he said through his laugh. "Like you and ol' boy ain't doing the same thing SiSi and I are doing."

"SiSi? Man, please." I kissed my teeth. "Dwayne and I are not even on the level of renting a bootleg. We do not know what we look like eating together. Lastly but more importantly, I have never ever given that man a nickname, which is more than what I can say for you."

My phone pinged again.

"Cold world." He whistled. "And despite all that, he still sticks around. I don't know if I should applaud you or fear you."

"Whatever."

"That's probably him hitting you up right now, pimpin'."

I crossed my arms and shrugged my shoulders. "I am not a pimp."

"You know he's a cornball, right?"

Admittedly, Dwayne was exactly that. He was handsome, very easy on the eyes, but had the charm of wet plaster. Our conversations were stale, so we barely talked. His company was so-so, humor nonexistent. He was safe and predictable and I liked safe and predictable. We met while in-line in our campus's coffee shop. He picked up my order by accident and I had to chase him down to get it back. Dwayne cracked a weak joke he thought was funny, and I laughed to be polite. He asked me for my number, and I didn't want to hurt his feelings by telling him no. I answered his call when he pocket dialed me by accident two months later. I kept answering his calls when he finally called on purpose.

Our talking eventually led to us hooking up a week later in my dorm room. The sex was bland at best, which was good for me. Yes, the one reason I even kept him around, the sex, was far from anything to talk about. But I preferred it that way. I saw what good sex did to some girls on campus. Made them cry when the boys attached to the sex broke their tender hearts or didn't reciprocate the feelings or love those girls gave to the ungrateful few. No thanks. Big pass.

Dwayne was safe and totally predictable, and even though I didn't love him, I loved that about him - his predictability.

"No, he isn't a cornball," I defended. "He's a nice guy with his head on right."

"That's a lot of words to say he's corny."

"And Sienna's fast, but you don't see me pointing that out."

"*And Sienna's fast,*" he tried to mock in my voice but his voice was too deep. "What are you, 80-years old? You and your old-head sistren discuss that over prune juice and coffee cake at bingo."

I balled my lips to keep from laughing.

"Anyway." I stood from my seat. "Thanks for helping me move. I got you on tutoring for the next few weeks. That's enough time to get you ready for your statistics final."

"Thank you." Hassani was on his feet too. In the last four years, his height doubled. He now towered over me, and nothing annoyed me more than that. "Want me to bring your boxes and side table inside?"

"No, I got it," I answered with a smile. "You've done enough to earn your keep."

He leaned forward and kissed me on the cheek, instantly warming me up.

"Uh-uh, back on up." I shoved him away playfully. "I don't know where those lips been."

He licked his lips and chuckled softly; the response doing nothing to calm the heat building in me. Thankfully, he turned and took steps toward my front door.

"I'll call you," he told me right before he closed the door behind himself.

I made my way over to my kitchen counter to check my phone. The moment I got it in my hand, I saw two texts from Dwayne.

Dwayne: Done packing?

Dwayne: When can I come over?

I sighed, pecking at the keys on my phone, agreeing to a night to have him over, not at all anticipating his company.

yla

THE MATTRESS CREAKED WHENEVER THE HEADBOARD DIDN'T BANG. MY
white sheets made a rustling sound beneath me while I did my best to
maneuver my hips so I could feel something, anything.

Dwayne grunted over me, holding his eyes in a tight squeeze. With
every pump, he exhaled all the air inside of him. When he wasn't
doing that, he was lifting his torso off me, balancing himself on his
hands that laid aside my body. Checking every so often to see if my
expression changed.

I tried to appease, offering an understanding smile, tucking my
lips into my mouth, and closing my eyes whenever I felt any
semblance of pleasure. But right when I thought I felt something, he
switched his pace and threw off the rhythm.

This was nothing new. Dwayne was on brand that night like he'd
been every other night we were intimate. The bed would be the
loudest in the room and he would meet his body with mine like a
jackrabbit. On the outside, it would sound like much was happening

between my four walls, but there was nothing worth getting excited about.

It's not like I could depend on his words to get me in the mood. He remained mute from start to finish. As if talking was a crime he wasn't in the least bit interested in committing.

He shuddered against me as he neared his end. All I could do was sigh in relief because instead of coming, I was thankful he was about to get off me.

As always, he lowered himself against me, pressing his lips to my neck. Not exactly kissing me, but panting against my skin. And I let him. Let him catch his breath against me. I even wrapped my arms around him for good measure.

Dwayne inhaled sharply and rolled off me. Dropped onto the pillow beside me while still doing his best to gain control over his exhales.

It was the third night in my new apartment. Sunni was out with Josiah yet again. I didn't have to worry about her interrupting Dwayne and I because she already told me her plans to spend the night at Josiah's.

Dwayne rolled over on his side once he could breathe without struggle, and planted a kiss on my cheek, draping an arm over my bare stomach.

"That was good," he said beside me.

To you.

"Mm-hmm," I lied.

I turned to face him and offered him another one of those polite smiles. I really wanted him out and knew I wouldn't have to wait long. He was as predictable as the five seasons. In a moment, he would roll over once again, then stand off the bed to head into my en-suite.

I drew straws with Sunni for that en-suite.

He did not deserve to use that en-suite.

As predicted, Dwayne rolled over, planted another kiss on my cheek, and hopped off the bed to head to my bathroom.

Once, while I still lived in my university's dorm, I took initiative and pulled Dwayne into a cuddle. It was unlike me to do that, but I needed the comfort. Hassani had just introduced me to Sienna hours earlier, and after our first meeting, I knew Sienna wasn't like the other girls he introduced me to. I just knew she'd be around for a while. The aftertaste from the meeting left a foul taste in my mouth and I needed validation. So, knowing Dwayne's routine, right after he rolled over to plant a kiss on my cheek, I turned to him and wrapped my arm around the back of his neck. I asked him not to go to the bathroom just yet because I wanted another round.

"I have to shower," is what he told me. "When I get back out, maybe?"

"Why do you feel a need to shower immediately after we have sex?"

"Why don't you?" he sniped back.

Since that day I never asked again nor did I have the desire to.

While the shower water drummed against my tub's floor, I remained in bed, my eyes trained on the ceiling. I crossed my ankles beneath the blankets and twiddled with my thumbs, waiting.

Five minutes later, Dwayne joined me in my room again with a towel wrapped around his waist.

"You got some good jets in there."

I nodded. "Yeah, it's pretty good."

"You should consider installing one of those fancy shower heads you can detach."

I focused my attention his way.

"That'll be perfect for me to get all those hard to reach spots whenever I shower here."

"Whenever?" I questioned. "Making plans already, huh?"

"Hoping to."

I chuckled to myself, swinging the blanket off me and grabbing my gray cotton robe from off the floor. "Let's not get ahead of ourselves, Dwayne."

"About that," he said, approaching me. When he was close, he grabbed my hands and held them in his, waiting for me to give him my attention. "I was wondering if you were ready to take this thing to another level."

"This thing," I repeated. "And what *thing* is that?"

He crinkled his brows, but the smile that appeared on his lips moments ago failed to subside. "Come on Ayla, do I really have to spell this out for you?"

"Oh, you're going to have to Soul-Train-scramble-board-it for me, Dwayne, because we've spoken about this."

"Yes, and now that we're graduating in a few weeks, I think we can explore an actual relationship and not this instability."

"Instability."

"Stop repeating the words I say."

"I'm just confused where this is coming from."

He huffed while dropping my hands. "So, what? Are we supposed to go another two years just being... whatever the hell we are? I want to introduce you to my parents. Hell, I might want to move in with you soon."

Oh, hell no.

I held my hands up. "You need to slow all the way down. In fact, come to a complete stop."

"What the hell is that supposed to mean?"

"Dwayne." I tied the belt around my robe and approached. "A relationship is the furthest thing from my mind."

He tilted his head to one side.

"We're graduating soon, that's true, but I can't commit to a relationship."

"Is that right?" He scratched at the side of his fade. "But I bet if Hassani told you the same thing I'm telling you, it wouldn't even be a question."

I inhaled when I should have swallowed, causing my spit to go down the wrong pipe. Or was I just that shocked Dwayne said what he said?

The moment I got control over my breath I said, "You have officially lost your mind."

I moved past him, headed to my bathroom. Inside, I stood over my sink, retrieving my toothbrush to start my nightly routine. I had every intention of ignoring Dwayne and his nonsense.

He had other plans.

"Tell me I'm wrong," he challenged, barging into the bathroom.

"You're wrong, Dwayne."

"You know I see the way you look at him, right?" He crossed his arms and moved in. "Your eyes light up whenever you two are in the same room. You stop everything every time he calls. It's been like that for as long as I've known you."

"You're exaggerating."

"Not even a little, Ayla."

I rolled my eyes.

"It's a wonder why you're not with him. He's always around."

"*He's*, my friend."

"He's your friend." He scoffed. "Why haven't you ever answered my question about him?"

I exhaled loudly and grunted for needed emphasis. This was a discussion I never enjoyed having with Dwayne. A discussion I never enjoyed having with myself.

"Maybe you should go," I told him.

"First, answer the question."

"And what question is that?"

I knew the question. I knew the question well.

"Have you two ever been in the kind of relationship *you* and *I* are in?"

"Like I've always told you..." I lifted my eyes to glare at his reflection in the mirror in front of me. "You and I are *not* in a relationship."

He threw his hands up. "Deflection like always. Typical Ayla Samuels. Are you going to finally answer the question after all of these years or what?"

"There isn't one to answer."

He shook his head.

I hated this part. Hated this topic of conversation. I knew the answer he was looking for, but giving Dwayne the answer he was always fishing for would put me face-to-face with a truth I really didn't want to meet head-on.

"Look, I'm tired of this shit." He crossed his arms once again. "We either make this thing official between us or it's over."

"We have nothing between us to end, Dwayne. You've always been free to go."

He sighed and dropped his chin to his chest momentarily before looking up at me again.

"Why don't you tell Hassani you love him."

I whipped my head so fast in his direction I felt my bone crack. "What did you just say?"

"Tell him you love him because clearly you do." He threw his hands up once more. "Just tell him already, so you can put us all out of our misery."

"I don't know what you're talking about," I pressed through my teeth.

He stared at me for a moment, his chest rising and falling with composed force.

"Who the hell damaged you, Ayla? Honestly, *who*?" He gritted. "And before they did it, did you have a heart? Have you ever learned how to love?"

I squinted my eyes at him. "Just because I don't want to skip into the sunset hand-in-hand with you, D, doesn't make me a villain."

"Well, Ayla, you are in my love story."

"Love?!"

His head dropped forward once again, his shoulders sagging in defeat. Dwayne used the time to gather his breath, and possibly what little patience he had left for me.

To the floor, he told me, "If I walk out that door Ayla, I swear I'm not coming back. I won't call you, and I most definitely will not see you again because frankly I can't keep doing this to myself. I won't. This will seriously be *our* end."

I stared at him for a moment. He was serious, his resolve clear in every word spoken. I tried my hardest to search within the deepest parts of me for any reason to speak up. To stop this. Because yes, he was right, this wasn't right. We'd done this thing between us for long enough. Any sane person would've called it quits months ago, but here he was, begging. Even when he sensed my heart was with someone else, he was pleading with me to make room for him. I realized in that instance I'd wasted enough of his time.

After almost a minute of silence, I dropped my view to the faucet and turned it on, then drew a thick line of toothpaste over by tooth-brush's bristles. As I raised the toothbrush to my mouth and before I started brushing, I mumbled, "Please close my door when you leave."

<h1 style="text-align:center">CHAPTER 19</h1>

Hassani

"YOU HAVE THE PRETTIEST EYES, HASSANI. I SWEAR."

"Oh yeah?"

She giggled beside me, tossing her head back to move her long jet black hair off her shoulders. "Yeah. But you already knew that. You *know* you're fine."

On a Friday night, I sat with one leg on the bed and the other on the floor of my friend Sienna's dorm room. This would be one of the last times she and I hung out like this with graduation approaching.

"I feel like I'm always showering you with compliments."

"And you know I love for you to bathe me in them baby."

She giggled again. "Hassani!"

Sienna was a sweetheart. Real sweet girl. Had the most bubbly personality. She was a real girly girl. I liked her because of that, her feminine energy. She wasn't afraid to be soft around me. I liked that a lot.

My phone buzzed in my pocket and I dipped my hand into my jeans to retrieve the device.

It was a message from Ayla.

I kept her name saved under A. Boogie.

I was reading the message from her, which was only her reminding me of our tutoring session for the following day when Sienna sighed next to me.

I turned to look her way to find her eyes down on my phone. Quickly clicking the button to darken the screen, I placed the device in my pocket just as quick.

"So, you'll be at her new place tomorrow?"

I wrinkled my brows.

"How do I know about Ayla's new place?" she asked, reading my mind. "Her bestie Sunni told a friend of mine who told me about them moving off campus."

"Oh."

"Oh," she mocked, trying to imitate my voice. "That was yesterday, right? Were you going to tell me or were you going to go to her apartment to do God knows what without me even knowing?"

"God knows what?" I asked as calmly as I could. Personally, I didn't think she deserved a response. We weren't in a relationship and I never made her feel like we were anything even close to that. Still, I didn't want to disrespect her. "I know you read the message. You read it well enough to know I'd be at her place tomorrow."

"I'm not comfortable with you two being alone off campus."

I leaned away while scratching the back of my head.

"On campus, I know there's a curfew."

Plus, a few of Sienna's girlfriends had dorms on the same floor as Ayla and Sunni's old dorm room and could have reported back to Sienna if Ayla and Sunni still lived on campus. I knew Sienna would never admit to that though.

"I'm just going over there to study."

"You're always so weird about Ayla." Sienna slammed her back against her white tufted headboard and folded her arms, pouring on an extra dose of dramatic by pouting her lips.

I closed my eyes and exhaled a long breath before opening them again. "Weird how, Sienna?"

She turned to face me quick as if she'd been waiting to answer. "You call her your friend, but I know there's something more between you two, I just know there is. I can *feel* it. You're always hanging out with her, but you've never invited *me* to hang with the two of you. I know I'm not officially your girlfriend, but I'd like to think I'm special to you. Aren't I?"

"Sienna, Ayla is a friend," I told her. "She's been my friend since high school."

Telling her that yes, she was right, would have sent the night in a direction I didn't care for it to go. Because yes, Ayla was more than a friend to me. If I had it my way, we would have been more a long time ago but Ayla never showed me she wanted more than what we were and honestly? I was enjoying life as a young man unattached. Or at least I knew I was supposed to enjoy life unattached. I wanted so bad to believe my father when he said these were the years when I didn't have to be serious. According to him, settling down could wait until later. I wasn't sure how much later but I figured I'd just go with the flow.

"Is she really?" Sienna asked in a soft voice. "You can tell me if she isn't just your friend. I won't get mad."

I knew that was a trap. She *would* get mad. Because the truth most times hurt and would hurt in this one too.

"She's *just* a friend," I maintained.

"So... you two have done nothing physically together? It's always been platonic?"

I pinched the bridge of my nose. "What did I just tell you?"

Sienna moved in closer, kicking one leg over me to straddle me. She leaned forward in her seat on my lap to press her lips to mine. I closed my eyes and let her because this was what I even came over to her room to do. Not talk about my relationship or lack thereof with Ayla. Thinking about my friendship with Ayla made me feel empty. It's always felt that way since the night in her room when we were intimate our first times. I thought I noticed a shift the second time we hooked up after prom but nothing came of that night.

Our first time, after leaving Ayla's house, I swore to myself I would perform better. Because to me, she deserved that and more. And I thought eventually she'd come around because most girls did with me, but she never did. So, since she never talked about us, I never brought us up. I was sure there was no Ayla and I. She started as a friend, and I believed that's all she would ever be and if that was the only way I could have her in my life; I would accept it.

Sienna licked at my lips, encouraging me to part mine. She pressed herself firm against me below, rolling her hips and rubbing herself against the erection growing in my jeans.

"See," I whispered against her lips, sliding my hands up her neck and burying my fingers in her hair. "*This* is the only friction I want between us."

I felt her smile against my lips before pressing her lips against mine once more. She kissed me down to my neck, over my chest, slowly making her way to my lap.

I lolled my head back against her headboard and let her unbutton my jeans, unzip it, and pull out my hard-on.

I opened my eyes enough to make eye contact with her through the slits of my eyes.

She moaned at the sight of my dick, lowering her mouth to flick her tongue over the swollen head. I closed my eyes once again and forced myself into the moment. Picturing the one *woman* Sienna would've had a fit over if she knew I was thinking about *her*. Especially after I barely convinced Sienna she had nothing to worry about when she was absolutely justified in being concerned about Ayla. Because all Ayla ever had to do was say the word and I would drop everything for her, including Sienna.

CHAPTER 20

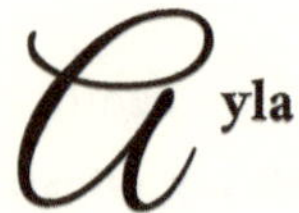yla

"So, what's the answer?"

Hassani took a moment to do the math in his head. We were going on hour two of tutoring, and he'd grasped statistics better than I was expecting.

"You're taking too long." I shuffled the bowl of microwaved popcorn. "Any longer you forfeit your reward."

He bit at his lips, rolling his eyes up to focus on my ceiling.

We were in my new apartment, in my room, on my bed, with small hills of textbooks surrounding us. Besides tutoring him, I was studying for my trigonometry and English finals. I couldn't believe that in a few days, I would be a graduate, the holder of a degree, and one step closer to doing what I loved full time, teaching.

I'd been training at a nearby school. A prep academy in the city with a 40k tuition and that just about every elitist wanted their kids to attend.

"Hassani, what's the answer?"

"Why are you rushing me?" he asked softly. "You don't trust me or something?"

"I do."

"Then know I got this."

I arched my brows and tapped my fingernail against the metal bowl.

After another few seconds of him thinking in silence, I said, "If you want, we can go over the problem again—"

"73," he affirmed. "The answer is 73, right? "

I balled my lips to keep from smiling but failed horribly at holding back my smile. "Correct."

He clapped his hands slowly, building it up to a quick applause for himself. He'd grasp the lesson quicker than expected. I was proud of him.

"It'll shock me if you don't pass your final." I picked up a kernel of popcorn and tossed it his way. He caught it midair with his mouth and chewed with a smile on his lips. "Looks like that job in DC is yours."

For two summers, Hassani had worked a summer internship in DC at one of the top architectural firms in the country. He'd always been clear that track and field was his passion and a way to get through school without hurting his parents' checkbooks, but a career in architecture was the dream that would pay. He did such an outstanding job in his internship, the CEO at the firm he interned at promised a position was waiting for Hassani when he graduated.

"So, what you're saying is…" He grinned. "I'm the shit?"

I laughed while shaking my head.

"And I'm the easiest study you've ever had?"

I folded my lips into my mouth. "I didn't say all that now. It took you one hundred years to get this far."

He chuckled.

To be honest, tutoring Hassani was always a good excuse to be in his company. He never failed to keep things interesting.

I parted my lips to say something more in response when his phone chimed with a text. On cue, mine did too.

We both glanced at one another before reaching for our respective phones. On mine was a text from my mother. She often sent me messages to check on me. I visited home at least twice a month. Driving back to Long Island to make sure all was well. My mother began dating once I graduated high school, and I moved on campus. She'd met a few men, but nothing came of their outings. Their dates never went past the second date, so I never got to meet them. My mother never had to say it, but I could tell she was searching for my dad in those men and was continuously coming up short.

Seems my aunt in her drunken stupor was absolutely right.

"That cornball checking in on you?" Hassani asked, pulling me from my thoughts.

"Cornball?" I tried to mock in his voice.

Hassani scoffed a laugh.

"It was my mother," I admitted. "If you must know cornball and I are no more."

"Oh, you two broke up?"

"We were never in a relationship to *break up*, which was the reason for him and I being no longer involved."

"And why is that?"

I huffed a sigh. "You sure are in my business when I recall your phone going off the same time mine did."

He dropped his head forward to scratch the back of his head, letting more than a few seconds go by without a response.

"Uh-huh," I teased. "That was your girlfriend, huh?"

He pointed at me. "I told you Sienna is not my girlfriend."

"Yet."

"Nah." He shook his head while closing the textbook, tossing the thick book on my floor. "Sienna and I... we have an understanding we're both cool with."

I grabbed my textbooks, stacking them one on top of the other before placing them on my night table. "And why are you taking so long to get her off the bench?"

"I should ask you that?"

I stared at him for a moment and he did the same. After clearing my throat and shifting in my spot on the bed, I asked, "Why do you say that?"

"Why haven't you dated anyone since high school?"

"I've dated."

"I mean, had a boyfriend."

"You haven't had a girlfriend."

"We're not talking about me, Ayla."

I licked my lips before folding them into my mouth.

"It seems like there's always a wall up for these dudes."

I fanned my hand in the air. "Whatever."

"And I'm not defending that guy, believe me I'm not. Dwayne was a cornball and all wrong for you, but he wasn't a bad guy."

"I can't do relationships," I blurted. "I just... can't, okay?"

"Why, though?"

I shook my head, looking away.

"Nah, don't clam up on me, A," he protested. "You can do that with everyone else, but with me? You know better."

I turned to focus on him again.

He scooted closer to me on the bed until he was directly in front of me.

I closed my eyes and exhaled.

"You can talk to me; you know that, right?"

My view dropped to my fingers where I spent the next few seconds picking at the old neon orange polish on my nails.

Hassani didn't rush me. Didn't push me to respond. He never sat back either, remained right in my space, in front of me, waiting.

"You won't laugh?"

"I promise I won't laugh."

"I'm scared," I whispered.

"Of what?"

I closed my eyes for a moment and sighed.

I'd opened them to him, tilting his head and dipping his forehead low enough so our eyes would meet. "Tell me."

"Of loving then losing."

"Losing?"

"Hassani, please."

He leaned in with a slight smirk on his lips. "We got all night and you know I'm more stubborn than you."

I snorted a laugh.

"Tell me what you mean by losing. Losing in what sense?"

"In *all* the sense."

He sat there waiting.

I puffed my cheeks with air and blew it out my mouth. I took another deep breath and, on my exhale, said, "I fear loving someone as much as my mother loved my father and losing them, never being able to recover from the loss. I'm scared of loving someone so much I change who I am so I can keep them. I fear being so invested in a relationship that once I'm blindsided by some bullshit, I lose my entire mind. But more than all that, I'm scared of losing myself in someone else."

Hassani sat there silently, his eyes moving around me. I assumed he was absorbing everything I admitted to fearing.

"That's fair," he uttered low. "How you feel is fair. What you fear is emotionally valid. But is it logical?"

"I never said it made sense."

The chime of his phone interrupted the brief silence between us. He lifted his phone's face off the bed to glance down at it.

"You can go if you have to."

"I don't have to, nor do I want to," he told me without missing a beat.

"It's going to piss her off if you don't at least respond to her text. I know it would piss me off."

"Don't worry about that. Don't worry about *her*. Worry about this; what we're talking about."

His words caused my breathing to hitch. They sounded simple and if the words were said in that order by anybody else it wouldn't matter. But coming from Hassani, his response instantly transported me back to Dania Perez's bathroom on prom night when he said the same exact thing.

"What was that?" he quizzed.

"What was what?" I countered.

"That look."

I shook my head, kicking one leg off the bed to step off... better yet, to escape the conversation. "What look?"

"I don't know how to describe the look, but it was something." He turned to face me. "What did you just think about?"

"Nothing."

"Clamming up again?"

I raised my hand to the bridge of my nose to pinch. "It's stupid."

"Nothing you say is stupid."

"Can we just drop it?"

"Sure, right after you tell me what you thought about. Especially if it has anything to do with what we were discussing."

"It has *nothing* to do with what we were talking about. Trust me."

I reached for my books to remove them from my bed. Hassani placed a hand on top of my hand to keep the books in place.

"Talk," he demanded.

"Prom night," I asserted.

The wrinkles in his brows relaxed.

"Dania Perez's after-party."

Hassani's eyes softened with recognition next.

"In the bathroom. When I asked you about Jessica Delano. You told me not to worry about her either. You called her practice."

He dropped his head to his chest to hide his smile.

"And you know what? I've never really been clear on that."

"I thought I was crystal clear."

"You never talked about that night."

"Neither did you," he retorted, standing to his feet in front of me.

There was silence between us again. Hassani looked down at me while I tilted my head back to look up at him. My heart was racing, my stomach muscles tensing up the longer we stood there, inches a part.

"What was Jessica practice for?"

"You," he replied with no hesitation.

"Me?"

"*Mm-hmm...*"

"With what goal?"

He licked his lips slow and allowed his eyes to fall to my waistline. There was nothing to see. I wore a hoodie with our school's logo across my chest. I paired that with a pair of biker shorts. But the way Hassani focused his attention on my body, you would think I was naked.

"To make your body do what it did that night."

I bit my bottom lip, and he moved in closer. The elimination of space sent my pulse racing, my heart galloping like a thousand horses.

"It's like I told you, I didn't like the way things went the first time."

"It was your first time."

"It doesn't matter. I underperformed." He closed more space between us, and I stepped back. "You deserved better. So, I wanted to give you better."

"Overachiever." I smirked while pressing my back to the wall behind me. "You forget - I wasn't expecting anything from you that night. What I asked of you, you delivered."

He pressed one hand to the wall behind me and buried his other hand in my hair. I couldn't stop the moan that escaped my lips. Hassani leaned in and said, "Only delivering what you asked wasn't good enough."

"Hassani—"

"*Shh,*" he shushed.

I exhaled through my mouth.

"As much as I love hearing my name roll off your tongue..." he moved inches in front of my mouth. "Just, *shh.*" Less than a second later, he crushed his lips against mine.

The move made me gasp but him wrapping his arm around my waist to hold me in place made me exhale my hesitation through my nose. Hassani moved in even closer than before, something I didn't think was possible. His tongue gently slid against my mouth before I offered entry by parting my lips.

He exhaled a moan, bending his legs at the knees to lift me.

Against the wall, he held me up, never losing momentum in his kiss or strength in his arms.

A part of me was screaming, *"We shouldn't do this."* We'd been good those past few years.

No, we never discussed what happened prom night.

Yes, I thought of that night often, but I never allowed myself to think, what if?

What if we addressed those feelings that were conjured up the night we hooked up?

What if prom night was the start of something beautiful?

Hassani moved me off the wall and gently laid me on the bed, his lips remaining on mine. We kissed like we hadn't seen each other in years and honestly; we hadn't. Not this side of one another, at least. We kept this side of us hidden. Not forgotten, only locked away. A mutual understanding that went without discussion.

"You want me?" he asked against me.

His voice was heavy with intention. The guy who made me laugh and made me feel safe sounded like he was a man in waiting. A man in want. And it spoke to a side of me I'd ignored for too long.

I nodded my answer, and he shook his head.

"I need to hear you *say it*, Ayla."

I rolled my head backward so our eyes would meet. He was staring down at me, not once blinking, just waiting for me to respond. So, I whined my waist against him, brushing myself against his growing hard on. I watched as a smile pulled at the corners of his lips. He pressed himself firm against me.

"Don't get me wrong, all this you're doing down there is nice," he whispered, lowering his lips to my neck. "But I can't hear that."

"I want you," I told him.

Those three little words escalated everything. It encouraged the removal of our clothing so they littered the floor beneath my bed. Our breathing was heavy, exhales against each other's skin, causing perspiration. With nothing keeping him from between my thighs, his hand went there. He cupped the shape of my pussy with his hands and ran the tip of his finger against the spot where my clit hid behind the seat of my panties. When that wasn't enough, he slid the fabric to the side, and dipped one finger than another inside of me.

"I got you like this?" he asked.

I nodded again.

"I don't like that." He slid his fingers even deeper until his fingertips grazed something even softer inside of me. "I don't like you holding back on me."

I arched my back the second he made contact.

"*Speak* to me, Ayla." Hassani took my bottom lip between the bite of his top and bottom teeth while pressing his thumb to my clit.

"*Ooh*," I grounded out.

"*Yes*." He guided his finger deeper. "More of that."

He stroked me with only his fingers, moving in and out, repeating the action while creating invisible circles on my clit with the pad of his thumb.

My head started spinning, at least in my mind it did. I fisted my sheets, doing my best to hang on to something while the feeling of floating took over.

"Hassani," I whispered into the air, right before Hassani pressed his lips to mine again. This time he kept them there but removed his fingers. Distracted me so well with his tongue dancing against mine that the crinkle of the condom sounded so far away. Absent of his touch inside of me, I peeled my lids opened to see him staring at me. And when I parted my lips to say something, my thoughts escaped me as he tunneled into me slow.

My jaw dropped the deeper he settled. We kept our eyes on each other until he was so deep, no more of him could fit. But that was nothing compared to when he started pumping his hips back and forth. He moved to a rhythm only he could hear. Never losing pace, maintaining his focus no matter how much I moved beneath him. I tried to match his stroke, roll my hips to his cadence, but his attention to perfection knocked me out of focus, something I was more than okay with. He didn't waste a single thrust searching for my spot. He'd acquainted himself with it the second he sunk deep into me. My walls throbbed against the length of him, contracting and releasing the more he kept pace. The friction caused a sweet heat between us that served as a catalyst to my first shudder. Soon my body was vibrating. Vibrating like it did the night he had me with my legs wrapped around him on a white marble vanity. He changed positions with me in that instance, taking his place beneath me. He grasped my waist with each hand and guided my movements. This position was foreign, I honestly didn't know what to do. I would've sat there frozen in confusion, but Hassani coached me through it without saying a word. Gripping my ass and my waist interchangeably until I found a rhythm that would rock me to my core. I dropped my head back between my shoulders. He sat up, immediately pulling my legs behind him and meeting each roll of my hips with an upstroke of his own. The chorus of our moans were louder in volume and in sync now, and the sound of his will not to hold back sent a wave of goosebumps down my body making me shiver against him. At least I thought it was a shiver. At the tail end of whatever it was, my body shook uncontrollably. I lost my rhythm or the ability to keep my eyes from rolling. But he held on and rocked into me, over and over. Did it so consistently I experienced a pressure in the depths of me I graciously surrendered to. The sounds that came out of me I had never heard. The feeling that swept over me was just as new.

"*This* is what I like," he groaned in my ear before leaving a kiss there. "Get lost with me, beautiful."

Breathing became an afterthought. I honestly, in that moment, couldn't care less about inhaling anything. Because if I drowned in that thing I'd created with Hassani in my room and on my bed that night, my death would have been a beautiful moment and worth living so I could die just like that a trillion times again.

Hassani

She made the cutest sounds as she slept. Not exactly snoring, but almost humming with every exhale she released. I laid beside Ayla with my eyes fully focused on her. I'd risen an hour before and remained next to her as she slept. I could have left the moment I opened my eyes to avoid a conversation after what we did, but when I glanced at her to find her sound asleep beside me, watching her became my new favorite pastime.

Her bedsheet laid against her body so delicately. The fabric contoured to her shape without her even trying. Sun lines beaming through her window blinds, kissed her honey-brown skin, enticing me.

She stirred a little when the golden glow from a sun ray flashed against her eyelids. Her subtle movement caused the top of the sheet covering her breasts to shift, offering a peek at her areola.

I thought about helping myself to a taste. The night before I had the right one in my mouth, both nipples at separate times between my teeth. We allowed ourselves to indulge in several rounds on every square inch of her bed. Several rounds and too many positions to keep track of with us showing how much we'd learned over the years.

Last night was not the plan... at all. Getting into Ayla's mind was always like breaking into a safe, so I could only imagine how much she kept her heart under lock and key.

I watched how she treated the guys she involved herself with along the years. Like they were replaceable. But with me, she always made me a permanent fixture. Immovable. Everyone else could move like pieces on a board, but me, I stayed.

I loved that

I loved always having a place in her life.

I loved... *her*.

The moment the truth crossed my mind, I hopped off the bed like the sheets had caught fire.

My sudden jolt shook the mattress. Ayla stirred again for a bit, then blinked her eyes opened while I pulled on my boxers.

I reached down for my jeans, stepping into the legs one at a time.

She grabbed the sheet and lifted it higher over her breasts as she sat up in bed.

"Good morning," I said to her, leaning forward to grab my shirt off the floor next.

"Mornin'."

She tucked her lips into her mouth and rubbed them together.

We held our stares with each other, neither of us saying anything. Her lips relaxed into a serene smile, and I responded by smiling big.

"Shut up," she whispered.

"I said nothing."

"You didn't have to." She rolled her eyes playfully. "I know what you're thinking."

"Impossible."

There was no way she could know I was debating with myself internally. Debating over where I wanted to be in that instance which was not on my feet with my clothes on. I wanted to be back inside of her.

The chime of my phone on her night table broke our focus on each other. Both of our eyes moved to the device when it chirped.

I approached it, immediately recognizing the name when I saw it.

Sienna: I'm on my way to your room, but I'm going to stop at the coffeehouse. What do you want?

"Shit," I spat low. Not low enough.

"What is it?"

I exhaled sharply. "I gotta go."

A frown weighed Ayla's lips down only lasting for a few seconds. I would've missed it if I blinked. She forced a smile soon after and when I parted my lips to say something about it, about *this*, about last night, my phone chimed again.

Sienna: I'll get you an espresso.

"Go," Ayla asserted.

"I'll be back."

"No." She shook her head. "Just—"

"Ayla, I—"

"Last night was last night," she interjected. "Let's not make it more than what it was."

What it was, was life altering. What she didn't understand was I had never felt so grounded, so at home in a woman, like I felt when I was with her. Because it was more than the sex. Something happened between us that was cosmic. I had no idea how to explain that to her in words.

While I tried to figure out how to tell her, my phone rang in my hand this time.

"I just need to meet Sienna at my room, so she doesn't feel some type of way."

"Hassani, it's okay—"

"She's *not* my girlfriend," I blurted. "I don't owe her any explanation regarding where I am but—"

"She's not your girlfriend, *yet*," she replied low.

"Ayla..."

"Just *go*. I promise I'm okay."

I stood there for a moment, listening to my phone go off in my hand a second time with a call. My eyes bounced from the device to the woman I realized I loved.

But did she love me even half the same?

I wondered in that moment why Ayla wouldn't give in to me. Show me there was something there because what I experienced the night prior with her was something I'd never felt before with anyone else. Not with any of the girls I spent time with before or after her. The fact she wouldn't even fight for me, when it was only she and I in her room alone, bothered me at my core.

Why didn't she see I was worth the fight?

Why didn't I see she was too?

I clenched my teeth at the thought, feeling the pressure in my jaw. I turned to my sneakers I toed off the night before when I arrived for what I thought would only be tutoring.

After slipping my socked feet in and lacing up those sneakers, I turned to say, "So—"

"I'll see you around," she affirmed, snatching her eyes off me, eliminating the opportunity for me to respond.

So, all I did was nod, and exited her room, closing her door behind me.

As hard as I tried and trust me, I tried, it was difficult getting what Ayla and I did the night before out of my head. The way she wrapped around me like God made her only for me was playing tricks on my mind.

I believed all I needed to do was give her space. I thought just as I was thinking of her; she was thinking of me. Things had to be changing between the two of us, they had to be. The night before felt too real for things to remain the same or to go back to the way things were between us.

I was back on campus, one floor below the floor housing my dorm room. After the elevator opened on my floor, I exited the car and marched toward my dorm room. The moment I turned the nearest corner, I saw Sienna standing in front of my room's door. I tried to step back around the corner unnoticed, to hide from view, but she'd already turned to find me out of my room.

"Where'd you go?" Sienna asked. In her hand was a beverage carrier with two paper cups of coffee wedged in the holders. "I told you I would be right over."

I forced a smile onto my lips. "I had to handle something."

She examined my tall frame silently for what felt like the longest time before she locked her eyes on mine. "You didn't sleep here last night."

A statement. Not a question. She was being direct, and that threw me off.

I swallowed hard. "What?"

"You did *not* sleep in your room last night."

"I don't know what you're talking about."

"Hassani." She took a breath to keep calm. "*Don't* play with me."

I shook my head as I closed the space between us, pulling out my room's key.

"You're wearing the same t-shirt and jeans you wore last night when I stopped by here," she spat behind me.

"I threw on whatever this morning to step out for a minute."

"To go where?"

"For a... a walk."

"Really?"

I exhaled and pushed opened my door.

Sienna stepped in behind me and slammed the door behind herself, placing the carrier down on the table by the door. She stomped into the room and grabbed me by the arm to turn me to face her. "Where did you go, Hassani?"

"Why are you trippin' right now?"

"Because you smell like her!" she yelled. "That floral shit Ayla likes to wear? It's all over you right now. You should've invited her back here with you because all I can smell is Ayla." Sienna's bottom lip trembled as she shot daggers with her watery eyes. "You fucked her, didn't you?"

"What are you talking about?"

"You told me you were going to her apartment to study. You thought I forgot?"

"Nah-no," I stuttered.

I forgot I'd told her. The fact she remembered threw me off even more.

That's the thing about lies. You can never tell just one.

"And you returned here this morning, which means you didn't sleep in your room last night."

"I already told you." I turned to face her. "I stepped out to take care of something—"

"You just told me you went for a walk."

"I—"

"Stop lying to me, Hassani," she whispered, choking back a cry. Sienna's fair skin reddened right before my eyes. Her chest rose and fell with emotion, and even though I'd never made her think we were anything more than what we were, it pained me to know I was behind her feeling hurt in that instance.

She threw her hands up in front of her. "I know we're not together. I know I'm not your girl. Fine. *Cool.* But at least have enough respect for me not to lie right to my face."

In a perfect world, I would've been honest. To pour my heart out to her and tell her the truth. To tell anyone besides myself how I was feeling so I could get some of the hurt off my chest. Because I'd discovered that morning, I was in love with someone who probably didn't feel the same way I did. If there was anyone who would've understood the torment in that, it would have been Sienna.

But I didn't.

Instead, I closed the space between us and took her face in my hands. I cleaned her cheeks of her tears with my thumb and she closed her eyes, leaning into my touch.

"Stop your worrying," I told her.

"I want to be with you, Hassani." Sienna lifted her arms and wrapped them around the back of my neck. "I've *always* wanted to be with you since the first day we met."

I darted my eyes across her face while I considered the thought of us. She was beautiful, bright, and a good girl. Sienna never held back with me, making it easy to read her. She wasn't Ayla, but maybe that was a good thing… or so I believed.

In my short consideration, I determined we'd be good together. She was honest about wanting to be committed to me, and that was a start and my final determining factor.

I could learn to love her.

"Okay," I whispered.

She tilted her head to one side. "Okay?"

"Let's do it."

"Just like that?"

I nodded. "Just like that."

"Why the sudden change of heart?"

"Because…" I swallowed the lump forming in my throat. "You're a good girl and you're good to me. School is almost over, and I don't want to lose any of the good we've created. I think we can continue to be good together."

She crossed her arms and balanced most of her weight on one hip. "And you're not settling right now?"

"Settling?"

"Yes," she challenged, lifting a brow. "Settling."

I am.

"I'm not," I assured instead.

I didn't have the balls back then to admit to her or myself that Ayla bruised my ego that day. Ayla, showing no signs of reciprocating how I felt for her, broke me a little inside. I wouldn't dare tell Sienna she was my Plan B. My consolation prize.

Sienna stared at me for a moment. I did my hardest to maintain eye contact, forcing sincerity in my eyes. *How low could I be, right?*

"Aw, Hassani!" she cooed in front of me, lighting up right before my eyes.

The biggest smile I'd ever seen grace her face appeared on Sienna's lips, a smile that reached her eyes effortlessly. A second later, she pulled me down into a kiss.

I admired her bravery. Wished I had the same guts and fearlessness to be as honest with Ayla.

But would it had mattered?

Probably not.

Ayla made things clear there was no use in trying to change anything between us. And to me, honestly? I had no fight left in me to change her mind.

I needed acceptance. I needed to be wanted, and Sienna was more than willing to give me all that and more.

So, I chose her.

CHAPTER 22

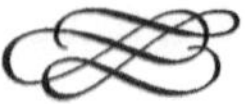

yla

Buzz. Buzz. Buzz.

I stared at my vibrating phone; my eyes fixed on Hassani's name as it flashed across my device's screen. Again. He was calling me for the hundredth time that day. Well, at least it felt like the hundredth time. Because every time my device rang, he was my incoming call.

Buzz. Buzz. Buzz...

I twisted my lips to one side, staring at my phone. Really staring at the name, partially considering answering but having no plans to do so because I feared what we'd talk about. We'd more than likely discuss what happened the night before, and I just... couldn't.

The night before was a moment in time I wanted to remember forever but forget all the same. What we did, what we shared, what he made my body do under his control? The English language had yet to produce such words to describe what he made me feel under his care. It was beyond the sex. Beyond the orgasms. Beyond his physical touch. The feeling was rooted in something else. And that *something else* scared the shit out of me more than anything I could ever conceive mentally.

"And why didn't you answer?" Sunni asked, interrupting my thoughts. His call had distracted me. I stared at his name on my screen for so long I forgot Sunni was there with me.

I lifted my gaze off my phone and focused on her.

The phone started buzzing again.

She pointed with the tip of her spoon at my device. "Aren't you going to answer it?"

I picked up my phone and pushed the button to silence the call.

Her brows wrinkled. "Ayla, what the hell?"

I pinched the handle of my spoon between my fingers and scooped up a spoonful of Lucky Charms.

It was the next day after Hassani and my hookup. Acknowledging that fact made me cringe. We'd done well going through our entire college experience, not even broaching the subject of what happened between us in high school, only to have sex right as we planned to march down the aisle to accept our college degrees.

"Hello?" Sunni tapped the kitchen table twice with the tip of her acrylic nail. "What the hell is going on here? Am I in a warped universe right now?! When did you start ignoring calls from Hassani?" I parted my lips to respond when she added, "I'll tell you when - *never* until today."

"I'm just not in the mood to *talk* with him right now, Sunni."

She tilted her head to her right. "Does this have anything to do with all the condom wrappers I found in the trash earlier today?"

"Shit." I shut my eyes tight, then slapped my hand to my forehead. "I knew I forgot to do something this morning."

"*Mm-hmm.*" She spooned another small mountain of cereal into her mouth. "Trash day was today, and when I checked the trash to see if you'd thrown it out, I noticed you didn't. Also noticed the confetti worth of condom wrappers in the trashcan."

"Sunni—"

"Conveniently the day after your study session with Hassani."

"Please, don't."

"Did y'all at least sleep after? Seemed like the only thing that made y'all rest was running out of rubbers. There were so many wrappers in the trash."

I dragged my tongue over my teeth while looking away.

"I can't *believe* you two finally hooked up!"

"I really don't want to talk about it."

"No worries." She shrugged a shoulder. "The condoms in the trash spoke loud and clear. What was that, three packs?"

I dropped my head back between my shoulders.

Sunni waited for me to level my head and to focus on her again before she allowed a smile to settle on her lips. "I love this for you. I've always liked you two together—"

"Sunni, stop this."

She squealed with delight while leaning back in her seat. "You two would make the cutest couple, make the prettiest babies. I swear."

"Hassani and I are *just* friends."

"Oh, girl, uh-uh." She wagged her finger in the air. "Any other time, that would fly. But after I saw what I saw in that trashcan this morning, *that* is not a card you can play anymore. Just save it for the people who don't know what happened between the two of you last night."

I closed my eyes and shook my head. At the mention of the night before, flashes of last night triggered the type of response from me that forced me to cross my legs tightly under the table.

"Ayla," Sunni said softly.

I opened my eyes slowly to make eye contact with her again.

"You know it's okay to be in love, right?"

I forced a pinched expression onto my face. This was not the conversation I was looking to have with her that day. On any day, actually."

"What the hell are you even talking about?"

She sighed. "I see the way you two look at each other. Especially the way you look at Hassani."

"Sunni, quit."

"You treated Dwayne like crap when that guy practically worshipped the ground you walked on."

"Oh, please. You *hated* Dwayne."

"For you. *Yes*, I did. Detested him more than a winter day," she added while holding up a finger. "But he is not my point. You always have this block up in relationships that I just don't understand."

I slid my chair back and stood up.

"And there you go, again. Running."

I shook my head.

"Running from this conversation the way you're running from Hassani."

"Okay, Dr. Phil."

"Joke if you want." She shook her head as she focused down on her bowl. "But he will not wait forever. No one with the right sense God gave them is going to wait this long for someone to come around. You're scared and I don't know why. Do *you* even know why?!"

I balled my lips, growing angrier by the minute. Sunni never held back, and I loved and hated her for it.

"One of the bravest girls I know becomes a coward whenever the focus shifts to matters of the heart," she continued. "How perplexing."

I looked away.

"I may not be the brightest bulb in the box like you are, but I know you need to get real with yourself and fast."

"All this over some damn condoms in the trash?"

"Don't you *dare* minimize it!" she snapped back. "Besides, this is way bigger than the condoms, Ayla. And you know it."

I stood over the sink, opening the faucet to fill the bowl with water. We were quiet in the kitchen again. I trained my eyes on the flow of the tap. "Let's say I tell Hassani how I feel and he doesn't reciprocate… then what do I do?"

"You move on knowing that you put your heart out there."

"Only to have it broken?"

"It's *okay* to be in love," she repeated. "It's okay to be vulnerable and to tell someone how you feel without knowing they'll say it back. It's okay to be naked, truly *naked* with someone who will appreciate it. You telling Hassani you love him and him not saying it back will take nothing from you. In fact, it will help you grow, Ayla. Because it's okay to be in love. Really it is."

I considered her words for a moment. Let them marinate in my conscience, allowing them time to resonate with my heart.

All the women I knew who had been in love either had that love taken from them or had that love break their heart into pieces they couldn't put back together. My aunt was a semblance of herself after her divorce. My mother still watched videos of my father like a tv junkie would binge their favorite rerun as she cried herself to sleep at night, even till now. My girlfriends every other week were out here complaining about some guy they gave their heart to, only for those same guys to betray and hurt them shortly after. Sunni was the only success story I knew, and although I believed she and her boo would go the distance in their relationship, she was the exception and not the rule.

I wasn't up for the game or the gamble.

"Maybe to you it is," I commented lowly, shaking my head for emphasis. "But for the rest of us mere mortals, it's not okay. It never is."

CHAPTER 23

yla

"Congratulations class of 2008!" Our dean shouted over the PA system.

I looked over at Sunni, and she did the same with me. We grabbed each other's tassels and moved them from the right to the left side of our caps, then punctuated the move with a scream.

"Congratulations best friend," she shouted.

"Congratulations to you too, bestie," I echoed.

A wave of screams and shouts created a sound bath around us, our voices I'm sure traveling for miles as we all celebrated with hoots and hollers.

I was a college graduate - holder of a bachelor's degree in early childhood education.

My cheeks hurt from smiling so much. I felt the light tap on my shoulder before I turned to find my mother standing there with a bouquet of colorful flowers and at least five different graduation balloons.

"Congratulations, baby." She wrapped her already full arms around me and I returned her hug, hugging her just as tight. "Your daddy would've been so proud of you, I swear."

Just the mention of him made me choke down a cry and blink back my tears.

She stepped out of her embrace with me and ran her hand down the side of my cheek, cleaning the tears that escaped my eyes. "Mama is so proud of you too."

I tightened my lips to hold back my already bigger than life smile, but really it was no use. "Thanks mom."

"Aye, there's the other graduate," I heard behind us. His Jamaican accent couldn't go unnoticed or have him mistaken for anyone else.

"Hey Mr. Franklin," I greeted when he approached with his wife, Hassani's mother. He pulled me into a tight hug and Mrs. Franklin did the same before handing me another bouquet of flowers.

"Aww, you didn't have to," I told her.

"You're right gorgeous." She smiled. "I wanted to. Congratulations.

"Thank you." Without thinking, my eyes drifted past them in search of their son. "Where's Hassani?"

"Over there with his friends," Mr. Franklin informed. "He should be over shortly."

"Hey Mrs. Samuels," Sunni greeted behind me. When I turned, I saw Sunni's parents accompanied her.

"Sunni!" my mother shouted, marching past me and toward Sunni with outstretched arms. "Congratulations."

"Thank you!" Sunni beamed in her hug with my mother. "Ma, Pops, this is Mrs. Samuels, a.k.a. mom number two."

We all laughed at that. Sunni had driven home with me several times during our four years at Langston University. She moved from Virginia to New York to attend LU. Going home to VA wasn't always as easy as just driving down the I-495 with me to get a home cooked meal at my house.

While Hassani and my parents huddled together with Sunni's parents, greeting and introducing themselves formally, I searched the yard for a familiar face.

"Looking for me?"

I turned quick toward his voice to find a smile already waiting for me on his lips. His hazel-green eyes glittered under the May sun, highlighting everything that was beautiful about them.

Truthfully, nothing would compare to the way he looked at me the night we were intimate for the first time since high school. His touch heightened all my senses. His eyes appeared more sultry. I would never, *could never* forget how he sounded while deep inside me.

I shook my head to rid the thought and forced a wider smile.

"Congratulations." I extended my arms for a hug and he obliged, pulling me in and close to his heart. I closed my eyes in our hug, inhaling the deep woodsy, sweet notes in his cologne.

"Congratulations," he conferred in my ear before leaving a kiss there.

Hassani and I hadn't seen each other since the night we hooked up. After I ignored enough of his calls, he opted to text me. I replied to those. We continued to exchange texts to check in on one another. The last text was him letting me know he'd passed his statistics final. Every time he'd offer to stop by, I'd tell him I was busy getting ready for graduation, but I was ducking any chance of getting him in my sight or worse being alone with him.

I couldn't make sense of what happened between us that night. At no time while we were intimate did I think to stop. I didn't want to, not even when we had fallen asleep from exhaustion. The feeling of being in his arms, of having him between my thighs, felt so natural.

Like home.

I stepped out of our hug and glanced away when I felt my nipples pebbling behind my graduation gown.

I delayed looking up at him.

"You look beautiful," he told me.

For the occasion, I'd visited a salon the day before for a press that laid my coily curls into a silky, slinky style. My tresses fanned the space where my bra straps hid. He reached forward and pushed one side of my hair back behind my ears. I couldn't believe myself when I closed my eyes at his touch.

"So, what are you and your mom getting into after this?" he asked.

I brushed my hand down my hair. "Lunch at my favorite spot in Brooklyn."

"Juniors," he confirmed.

"You know it." I nodded. I twisted my lips to one side before releasing them long enough to ask, "Wanna come?"

He pointed behind him with his thumb. "Sienna's parents invited me and my parents to lunch."

I jerked my head back. "Sienna?"

"Yeah, we um..." He cleared his throat as he stroked the hairs of his eyebrow with his trimmed nails. "That's why I was calling you, so we could meet up."

I wrinkled my brows.

"I didn't want to tell you through text that she and I made things official between us last week."

The news hit me like a truck. I parted my lips to say something in response, but the words wouldn't materialize.

I knew there was something there between them, something at least growing. The girl saw stars whenever she looked at Hassani. Couldn't keep her hands off him when they were in each other's companies. She'd been patient, sainthood patient. And it appeared to have finally paid off.

"That's great," I forced out. "You two make a cute couple—"

"I'll end it," he blurted.

I blinked hard in response.

Hassani peeked over his shoulder and I followed his line of vision to find Sienna with her parents standing feet away in the courtyard engaged in conversation with each other.

With his eyes back on me, he told me, "I'll end it with her if you tell me to."

"What?" I whispered.

He swallowed hard, shutting his eyes for only a moment before refocusing on me. "If you tell me there's something here between you and me, I'll end it with her *right now*. I swear."

I shook my head.

"Nah, don't do that!"

"Don't do what?!" I asked low.

"Clam. Up." He glanced over his shoulder again then refocused on me once more but this time moving closer. "Don't do that right now."

Voices traveled around us, full of cheer and genuine joy. Graduates passed us with smiles pulling at their lips with their parents wearing the same expressions. The scene around Hassani and I didn't match how we were feeling. How *I* was feeling inside. Conflicted, confused.

"Do you understand what I'm telling you?" he asked, glaring in my eyes. "I'm willing to end my relationship with Sienna to be with *you*."

My eyes darted across his face. His chest rose and fell with such force I felt as if they were my breaths I was inhaling and exhaling.

"Hassani, *why* would you do that?"

"Because I love--"

"Hassani," Sienna shouted for him. I moved my eyes to over his shoulder to see her and her parents closing in.

"Just say the word, A," he whispered to me. "*Please*."

"I can't."

"Come *on*, Ayla," he stage whispered this time. Hassani took my hand and held it tight. "*Just* tell me."

"Congratulations, Ayla," Sienna gloated behind Hassani before hugging him from behind. "We did it!"

He released my hand immediately.

I forced a smile. "Yup, we sure did."

I peeked up at Hassani to see him stare at me for only a moment before cutting his eyes away.

"The entire gang is here," Mr. Franklin announced behind me before joining the group with Mrs. Franklin and my mother in tow. "Your mother told us you two are on your way to Brooklyn to celebrate."

I turned to face him. "We sure are."

"I would have loved for you to join us and Hassani's girlfriend and her parents but there'll be other times I'm sure, before Hassani goes off to DC."

"Don't even fill my ear about DC in this moment," Mrs. Franklin said, extending her arm up toward Hassani and taking his cheek between the pinch of her fingers. "I just want to enjoy my baby while he's here."

"Well, we should get going then," Sienna insisted. She moved her arms off Hassani and grabbed one of his hands, threading her fingers between his.

I watched the whole thing, my stomach turning at the sight but still refusing to do anything about it.

When I look back at it now, I realize how stupid I was. He was willing to change the fate of things by telling me he would choose me. But I couldn't let him do that. Back then, I knew my heart wouldn't be all in it.

At least I *thought* I knew.

For years, that day played in my memory like a bad rerun.

Hassani and I would talk for a few weeks after that, off and on, always through texts. When he finally moved to DC a month later, the texts got even less until we stopped sending texts altogether. When he hadn't reached out to me for my birthday the following year, I knew that was it for us. Friendship wise, relationship wise - both had finally met its end.

And I accepted that. At least I thought I accepted it. Until I received the news of all news five years later.

PART IV
GO

PRESENT DAY - 5-YEARS LATER...

CHAPTER 24

MAY 2013 - NEW YORK, NEW YORK

$\mathcal{A}$yla

"BYE, MS. SAMUELS!" THE TINY VOICE OF ONE OF MY STUDENTS shouted a few feet away.

"Goodbye, Kenny!" I yelled back while waving. I stood on the steps of Park Avenue Prep, facing the expansive school play yard, seeing off my students on a Wednesday afternoon. Five years into teaching pre-k, and I hadn't grown tired of it since.

"Bye, Ms. Samuels," another child shouted, twisting in their father's arms to wave at me.

I waved back, smiling so big my cheeks hurt.

My first day at Park Avenue Prep five years prior had my nerves in shambles. I was shaking as I waited in the classroom I'd been decorating since the end of that summer, nervous about if I could deliver on something I'd wanted to do all of my life. It turns out I had nothing to worry about, I was a natural at teaching and building relationships with children, as I'd been told.

"Ms. Samuels," I heard over my shoulder.

I turned toward the baritone voice and smiled when I recognized his face. "Mr. Carter, hello."

He smiled even bigger, extending his hand for me to shake, which I obliged. Mr. Carter, a parent of one of my students, held on to my hand for longer than I did his. When he finally released his grip, I rubbed my hands together and darted my eyes away.

"It's *miss* Samuels, correct?" he asked, curiosity beaming from his eyes. "I want to make sure I'm being respectful."

"It is." In need of a change in subject I said, "Larnell's dad, right?"

"Right."

"Larnell is such a sweetheart," I added, waving at another one of my tiny students as they shouted my name from a distance. "We had an assignment today where we made tiny houses out of popsicle sticks and Larnell was sweet enough to help one of his classmates who was having trouble with their project."

"Is that right?"

I nodded. "He's very helpful."

"I try to teach him the importance of helping wherever he's needed."

I nodded again, focusing my attention elsewhere. I had handed all my students off to their parents or appointed guardians. Larnell himself ran around the schoolyard with another student of mine.

"If I can be honest," Mr. Carter started, drawing my attention back on him, "my real reason for approaching you today wasn't to discuss Larnell."

"Oh?"

"No." He chuckled nervously. The sun above shone in his deep brown eyes. He lifted his hand to create a visor over his view. "I've been working up the courage to ask you out for coffee since the first day of school."

I blinked back my shock, then parted my lips to say something in response but was at a loss for words.

"I've been looking for a ring, but I haven't seen one since school started in the fall."

"Uh-huh?" I tucked my lips into my mouth.

"And you're an exquisite woman who I would *love* to get to know better."

Mr. Carter was handsome himself. Tall, enchanting russet brown skin with red undertones as highlighted by the sun that bounced off his hue. A career man too, who earned a living as a financial advisor to movie studio execs. I learned this at the school's career day three months prior. If I was someone solely driven by looks and money, I might have at least considered his proposition.

"I'm flattered," I imparted. *And I was.* Still, I told him, "But I've made it a personal rule not to date my students' parents."

I'd just made that rule seconds after he asked me out.

He dropped his head momentarily, then nodded to himself. "Totally understandable." He looked up at me again and grinned. "So what you're saying is I should try next year when Larnell is in kindergarten."

I snorted a laugh, and he expressed humor at my reaction.

"Mr. Carter—"

"I'm only kidding," he interjected with a smile. "I just had to take a chance. Would've kicked myself if I didn't."

"I understand."

Larnell ran up to us, purposely bumping into his father.

"Daddy, can we go now?" Larnell pulled on the hem of his father's brown suede bomber jacket. "I want to get ice cream from the ice cream truck before it goes away. *Please!*"

"Yes, yes." Mr. Carter patted Larnell's head and peered up at me again. "Have a great rest of your day, Ms. Samuels."

"You do the same, Mr. Carter," I told him. "Bye, Larnell. You be good, okay?"

"Okay, Ms. Samuels, bye!" Larnell said, pulling his father toward the Mister Softee truck that blared its signature song at the corner.

I waved their departure, holding my smile until they were out of sight. Mr. Carter being Larnell's father was partially my reason for saying no to his coffee invite.

Yes, it would have been messy to date my student's father, especially if I knew it would end in a less than favorable way, because they all ended in a less than favorable way whenever I involved myself with them. The men these days were less interested in keeping things physical. One date meant the start of something long lasting, at least the men I attracted. And I just wasn't interested in getting into anything serious.

Before returning to my classroom to pack up my stuff to head out for my long Memorial Day weekend, I stopped in the faculty lounge to grab the plastic bowls that held my lunch that day.

"Ready for the long weekend?" Michelle, the school's guidance counselor, asked while brewing a new batch of coffee. "I hear you've taken off tomorrow and Friday as well. I met the substitute teacher who will take over your class while you're gone."

"Isn't she great?" I asked, forcing myself to keep my pleasant smile on my lips. Everyone here was always so nosy, all up in the business that didn't pay them. But instead of saying anything about it, I played the politics, like always. "And how about you? Are you ready for your holiday weekend when it arrives?"

She flipped her natural red hair over her shoulder. "Oh, absolutely. I wish it were here sooner, honestly. Do you have anything planned? Going somewhere exotic again? I still think of those photos you took in Brazil and that you showed all of us when you returned."

I smiled.

"But honestly nothing compares to your recent photos from Egypt."

I closed my eyes briefly, reminiscing about my trip there. It was the last place I traveled, and my weeklong visit was an enlightening experience. I found myself in North Africa. Learned a lot of truths about myself that made me return to the states a changed woman. Egypt was also where I realized traveling alone, at least to me, wasn't as fun as it was the first two years after college.

I pressed my hand to the gold ankh chain I wore around my neck that I bought and brought back from my trip only five months prior during the holiday break.

"I'm going out of town, but nowhere exotic this time," I exhaled. "Just to D.C."

"Sweet! To anything fun?"

"To something I'm actually dreading."

"Oh," she groaned.

I pursed my lips. "*Mm-hmm.*"

"I know exactly how that can be." She poured out the coffee into her mug and lifted the ceramic cup to head out. "Try to have a little fun in the mundane. You should waste no off days doing something you don't at least like."

"Michelle," I said while closing the fridge door. "I wish it was that easy."

She giggled to herself before exiting the lounge and closing the door behind herself. I stacked my containers, then grabbed one of the water bottles off the counter and made my way out as well.

I AMBLED THROUGH THE DOOR OF MY CONDOMINIUM AND DROPPED MY bag on the kitchen's island, kicked off my white Converses, unbuttoned my blouse, then wiggled out of my black pencil skirt, flinging it somewhere behind me. I would get to it when it was time for bed, but as for that instance, I wanted comfort. The days were long at school. I started my mornings at 5 a.m. and was in my classroom an hour and a half later. Running behind children under six was an unrecognized sport. But I loved every minute of teaching, even the stressful ones.

Adjusting the waistband of my panties, I padded to my fridge and went straight for the chilled moscato sitting on the fridge's shelf. I twisted the cap off and raised the spout to my lips. I couldn't trouble myself to pour it out into a glass. These days were all about getting from coffee to wine. Stress didn't consume me much, but the weeks had become difficult to get through after the news.

My phone chiming in my purse on the island pulled my attention from the sparkling wine fizzing bubbles on my tongue. I swallowed the moscato and made my way to my phone. I recognized the caller's name and inhaled a deep breath, hoping that breath was full of courage before I answered.

"Hey mama."

"Hey baby."

"What's up?"

"Oh nothing," she answered. "Just getting ready for D.C."

I rolled my eyes closed.

"Speaking of which, did you receive the details for Hassani's wedding weekend activities?"

That.

That is what I'd been dreading.

Been dreading his wedding since I received the invitation months prior.

Of course, I never expected for Hassani to live a life like a monk after our night together.

He made things official with his bed buddy, Sienna, leading up to our college graduation.

She was the bride. Seems she stuck around long enough, just waiting for his "ready" light to switch on. You know, the "ready" light all men have when they decide to pop the question.

Good for her.

As for me, I'd been avoiding his phone calls that had started up out of nowhere. We hadn't spoken to each other in years, a disconnection that happened a few months after graduation. My mother would later reveal that she gave him my new phone number when he called asking for it. Hassani called me for the first time three months ago, literally 24-hours after I received his wedding invitation, and I missed his phone call, thankfully. Only knew it was him because he left a message on my voicemail. Ever since, every time his name appeared on my phone screen as an incoming call, I let it ring out, while staring at his name, waiting for the call to be sent to voicemail.

"Ayla."

I shook my head, hoping to ground myself back in reality. "Yeah, mom?"

"You didn't answer me."

"No," I replied, taking another swig of the moscato, gulping it this time. "I haven't checked my email."

She sighed a heavy sigh that vibrated my ear, encouraging me to put the call on speaker.

"Ayla, baby, they emailed everyone earlier this week, and the wedding is this weekend."

I blew raspberries with my lips, really wanting to say, *"Please don't remind me."* But I opted to say nothing instead.

She kissed her teeth. "At 27, you still like to wait until the last minute to do things like a man I know."

I smiled, knowing she was referring to my father. After all these years of my father being gone, my mother always spoke of him as if he was still here, just away at a really far place.

"Anyway," she continued, "I bought the train tickets for the trip. You know how I feel about flying."

"I know mama."

My mother hadn't boarded a flight to anywhere after my father passed in 2001. Instead of pushing her to do so, I just accepted it. The selfish side of me didn't want her to go too far from me, anyway.

"Well, have you at least picked out a dress for the wedding or the pre-wedding dinner Friday night?"

My brows went up. "Pre-wedding dinner? There's a pre-wedding dinner?!" I dropped my head back between my shoulders and whined, *"Why?"*

"Ayla," she exhaled. "See, now, if you would've read the email sent earlier this week, your butt would've known all about the things Hassani and his bride have planned."

I cringed at the mention of Sienna. I never had a problem with her, never saw a reason to in the past. Ever since learning of their impending nuptials, the mention of her name had me reaching for a bottle of anything with a high alcohol proof. Since all I had in my apartment was the moscato and it was still at arm's reach, I grabbed that and lifted the spout to my lips and poured the wine into my mouth.

"I need something stronger," I mumbled.

"What did you say?"

I took another swig and gulped. "I said, I'm going to go shopping tomorrow while out with Sunni and right before dinner with Aunt Laurie."

"I'm meeting up with Laurie tonight. I'm going to need to get ready in a few."

"Cool."

"But before I go, can I ask you something?"

I sat on the stool in front of my kitchen's island, setting the almost empty bottle of moscato down on the blue sodalite marble surface. "Sure, mom, what's up?"

"Why are you dragging your feet with preparing for Hassani's wedding?"

The question knocked out whatever air I had left in me to breathe. I wasn't expecting it, not from her, not even in the least.

"You're so on top of things for Sunni's wedding, so I know you know how these things work."

"That's different." I dragged my hand down my face. "I'm her maid of honor."

"But Hassani is your childhood friend."

"Mama, I haven't spoken to Hassani in forever."

"Yes, and about that—"

"Mama—"

"Why aren't you answering his calls? I've lost count of how many times that man has called me asking me if I gave him the correct number because since I've given him your phone number a few months ago, he has yet to speak with you. I'm thinking he thinks I'm senile."

I swallowed hard, my eyes darting from left to right, searching for a lie, any lie. To admit to my mother that the reason I'd been avoiding his calls was because I feared not knowing what I would say to him after all this time seemed stupid. Plus, I knew me saying that would have led to her asking another question, and I just wasn't ready to face any ugly truths that night.

"Ayla?"

"The school year is almost over," I blurted. "Things get really crazy leading up to June, and I've just been missing his calls and forgetting to call back. That's all."

After a long pause that led to an uncomfortable silence, at least for me, all my mother replied with was, "*Hmmm.*"

I bit at my lip.

"Okay, well, let me get ready to meet up with your aunt. I'll see you Friday morning?"

"Yes, ma'am."

"Love you, baby."

"Love you back, mama."

I sat at my kitchen island, staring at the near empty bottle of moscato, resolving to getting dressed again to head to my local liquor store to buy something stronger, *anything* stronger.

My phone I still held in my grip went off with a call. When I lowered my view to the screen, Hassani's name appeared.

As always, I held my breath and watched as the call rang for four rings before my phone transferred Hassani's call to voicemail.

I grunted, dropping my head back between my shoulders again. "How the hell am I going to get through this weekend?"

CHAPTER 25

*H*assani

THE WIND WHIPPED AGAINST MY FACE AS I PICKED UP SPEED ON THE track. If my hair had length, it would blow in the wind. For now, my full mustache and beard combo would have to be the substitute. Like always, I closed my eyes for only a second to ground myself in the moment. Running was my soul food. The action fed me in ways nothing else could. The rhythm of my heart whenever I ran on a track paired with the pacing of my breath was like water for chocolate. I loved it.

The sound of another set of feet gaining traction, faded in and grew louder behind me, encouraging me to pick up speed.

"Shit," he hissed a few feet away.

That only made me laugh to myself.

Only two steps from the imaginary finish line, I peeked over my shoulder, like I always did to see Marcus about a foot behind. I raised my arms in the air as my foot crossed the white line, imagining I collided with the traditional white ribbon at the end of a race. Gradually, I reduced speed.

Marcus had just crossed the finish when I turned to face him from up ahead. I jogged backwards, not even trying to hold back my laugh.

"Still too slow, huh?" I teased.

He fanned his hand in the air at me. Probably didn't have enough air in his lungs to clap-back.

When I found out Marcus had been living in D.C. after attending Howard University in the district, I decided to link back up with him. We'd only see each other when we returned home during school breaks. But we always kept in contact between those times throughout the years. While I kept running in college to maintain my full scholarship, Marcus gave up track in his HU days. He got back into running after I moved out here five years ago. He was now a financier at a major bank in D.C. and I'd just started my own architectural firm that was doing better than projected. My clientele list ballooned so much, I only accepted clients through referrals these days.

Life was... okay.

I stopped at the rest area to grab my bottle of water that sat on the side of the track.

"I don't have on those rich man running sneakers you got on," he noted when he joined me. "You know that's the only reason you keep beating me, right?"

"*Every time* we run though?" I asked right before taking a swig of my water. "They're sneakers Marcus, not wings. That's me flying past you with my legs."

He sucked his teeth, and I laughed in response.

The day was a brisk one. The breeze steady, sun high. We were in the middle of spring, so the trees decorated the landscape in various green hues, offering a lovely complement to the scenery.

Every Sunday, Marcus and I met up at the park. Since I would be out of town this upcoming Sunday, we met up on a Thursday instead. Besides it being a lush atmosphere filled with trimmed grass and beautiful shade-giving trees, this park had a track that was almost as big as the track we used to compete on in high school.

"Sienna got us for lunch?" he asked, between sips of his water.

Every Sunday, like clockwork, after we completed our run, my fiancee, Sienna, would have lunch waiting for us when we returned. Since she took time off from work to prepare for the wedding, Sienna promised she'd have lunch waiting, just like she always did on Sundays.

"Yeah, she got us, like always."

My life in D.C. had become predictable and honestly, predictable was good. I had a stable career, a woman who was good to me and loved me with all her heart. My health was great, and the future was bright, but I would be lying if I said something wasn't missing.

Ayla.

Hadn't spoken to her in too long. Our phone calls with each other eventually stopped after we graduated college because it hurt me too much to speak with her. Knowing that she knew how I felt about her and her not wanting to make things between us more than what we settled on being was too much to bear. So I cut all ties.

That was until recently.

"Ready for the weekend?" Marcus asked as we made our way off the track and toward our cars. We drove in separate vehicles but would meet up at my condo a few miles from the park.

"Ready as I'll ever be." I adjusted the strap of my bag that held my running sneakers, face towel, and water bottle. "Did you get your tux?"

"Oh absolutely," he replied.

I asked Marcus to be my best man. Out of all the guys I knew, he seemed like a good fit. Plus, Sienna adored him and he was the closest friend we had out here. So, it only made sense.

"Cool." I pulled out my car's key fob and unlocked the driver's side door. "See you at the condo."

"Babe," I called the moment I returned home. The smell of marinara sauce salted the air. "We're back."

"Okay. I'm in the kitchen," she announced a few feet away.

Marcus and I stepped out of our sneakers while I dropped my gym bag in the closet near the door.

Sienna walked out of the kitchen. She smiled big at me before shifting her eyes over to Marcus.

"Hey, Marc."

"What's up Sienna?"

She made her way over to me and Marcus made kissing noises as she strutted past him.

"Oh, none for me?" he joked.

"Man, chill." I shook my head and laughed.

Sienna gave a little laugh of her own before balancing herself on the arches of her feet to give me a kiss on the lips.

"I smell pasta," I said to her.

"Yup." She nodded, taking my hand. "I know how much you like your carbs after a run on the track."

Sienna Rodriguez was the woman I planned to spend the rest of my life with. She was my college friend who became more during the four years I studied architecture at Langston University. We made things official shortly before graduation and had been going strong ever since. That was the reason I believed it was time to take our relationship to the next step.

It's like I said, she was good to me. Took care of me, listened, and gave me sound advice whenever I needed it. I trusted her and she trusted me, and to me, that was more than enough.

"You always know what I like." I gave her a pat on the butt.

I made my way to the kitchen to see Marcus standing over the stove with a bowl already in hand.

"Help yourself," I offered, my tone drenched in sarcasm.

"Oh, I definitely will. Su casa es mi casa, right?"

"Wrong," I corrected. "*Very* wrong."

Sienna wrapped her arms around my waist from the back. "I'll fix you a bowl, baby."

I grabbed her hand and lifted it to my lips to kiss the back of her palm. "Thanks, babe."

I watched as she moved from behind me to stroll into the kitchen, bumping Marcus away from the stove with her hip.

Sienna would make a splendid wife; I knew she would. I almost hated myself for constantly allowing my mind to wander to what could have been with Ayla.

Ayla.

She'd been on my mind heavy lately, especially now. The weekend should have only been exciting because I would marry a woman who loved me with every breath in her. Except that wasn't the only thing that excited me. Seeing Ayla again did... that's if she RSVP. She hadn't answered or returned any of the phone calls I'd been making for the past few months, and she hadn't confirmed she was coming to my wedding either. I didn't know what to expect because Ayla wasn't a simple person to read. This was the reason I knew she and I could never be and why Sienna was the better choice.

So, despite feeling like my world was just a little incomplete, I ignored that feeling and made a vow with myself to go where the love was... and that love was with Sienna.

Still, I hoped I could see Ayla one last time.

yla

"Do you really need another china set, Sunni?"

"This one differs from the last one."

I shook my head, pointing the scan gun at the barcode on the box.

On a Thursday evening, I accompanied my friend, Sunni, to a high-end department store to assist with adding items to her gift registry. She'd appointed me maid of honor, and I had taken the role extremely seriously.

"At least get this matching glass set here," I offered, pointing at the box a few feet from the fifth china set she instructed me to scan.

"Nope." She shook her head, her tiny ringlets of curls grazing her cheeks. "Only china. I want to get crystal glasses from William & Sonoma."

I cracked a smile. "Bougie ass."

She howled a laugh that made me join in.

Sunni and I were roommates until she got engaged last year to her college boo, Josiah. I just knew the two of them would get married one day. They were absolutely perfect together. After she moved out, and with my mom's help, I used the money granted to me from my father's life insurance to invest in a condominium in the East Village and have been living there alone ever since.

We moved around the fixtures in the store, scanning barcodes and giggling to each other on just about anything. Sunni was so happy to be getting married, and I was just as thrilled as if I was getting married too.

She peeked down at her gold watch, twisting the face toward her to read the time. "Shouldn't you go look for your dress for the wedding on Saturday?"

I inhaled a long, deep breath before blowing it out through my lips. "It can wait."

"Ayla." She stopped mid-aisle. "There's only half an hour left before the store closes. I know you're not high maintenance, but I'm sure you'll need all the time you can get to find something you like."

I pointed the gun at a wine glass set. "You should get this one. I'm going to add it."

"Ayla!"

"What?"

She laid the tip of her tongue against her top right molar and just stared at me.

I folded my arms and stared back. "Sunni, what?"

"*You* tell *me.*"

"What do you mean?"

"You know I can handle the registry stuff while you shop, right?" She placed a hand on her hip. "We've been in this store for well over two hours. I only got but a few more things to add on there."

"It's cool. My shopping can wait." I turned toward the aisle up ahead. "We still haven't looked at silverware."

"Ay-la."

I turned in her direction again. "Sun-ni."

"What is up?"

I tried to maintain a neutral look but knew it was only a matter of time before she saw right through it. I swallowed hard and closed my eyes, exhaling in defeat.

"You are stalling right now like you don't want to go to D.C."

I placed the scan gun down on the display that held an intricately designed fruit bowl. "Because I *don't* want to go."

"Why not?!"

I pushed my tongue against the inside of my cheek and looked away.

"You haven't seen Hassani in forever. I would think you'd want to catch up... and to finally tell him you love him."

I whipped my head her way again.

"*Mm-hmm.*" She tightened her lips together to keep from smiling. "I know what's up."

"Sunni—"

"I always thought you two would stop playing and make things official, eventually."

"Sunni—"

"Especially after the day I found all those condom wrappers in our trash after your little studying session."

I balled my lips to keep from smiling. There wasn't a time in a day I hadn't reminisced about that night since it happened years ago.

"I always suspected there was something between you two, but you used to always insist you and Hassani were only friends." She rolled her eyes playfully. "I thought you claiming him as only your friend was y'all's way of trying to keep things on the hush, hush. It was cute."

"We actually didn't hook up after that night." I bit at my lip. "Before then, we hadn't had sex at all since our prom night."

"Wait, did you just say *prom* night?" She drew her head back and threw her hands up. "As in *high school*?! You never told me about that!"

"I told nobody, Sunni."

"Okay." She placed her scan gun down this time. "*What* is the deal between the two of you? Like for real, for real. Why didn't y'all just—"

"I don't know." I strummed my fingers on my brow. "At this point, I really don't know. We just never took things to any other level."

"Did you want to?"

"No... but then, yes?" I questioned myself out loud. "Hassani was a girl magnet, and I was super insecure back then. I was so unsure of myself. I thought the worse of everything so I'd feel prepared if the worse ever arrived between us. Just scared as fuck of anything that resembled being vulnerable. I was not about to put myself out there, like not even a little." I shook my head. "Plus, we were friends. A part of me didn't want to ruin that either."

"But now?"

I fanned my hand in the air. "It's too late."

"No, it's not."

"*Yes*, it is." I took a breath to keep the tears from forming. "It's been five years. Though I regret not being honest with him about my feelings for him, I would be lying to myself if I didn't realize that *now, right now*, it is far too late for any of that."

"Ayla, but—"

"Would I had done things differently looking back at them now? For sure. That's why they say hindsight is 20/20. But he's got his life now, and I got mine. He's getting married—"

"It ain't too late until he says, *'I do.'*"

I gasped. "How could you say that? You're getting married next year. What would you do if one of Josiah's exes showed up at your wedding with the type of energy you're suggesting *I* go to D.C. with?"

"I'd beat that bitch with my broach bouquet," she spat through her teeth.

I snorted a laugh.

"But you're not Hassani's ex. You're his friend. And just like you haven't stopped thinking about him, I'm sure he hasn't stopped thinking about you either."

"You think so?" I shook my head. "Nah, I don't think so."

Sunni kissed her teeth and grabbed my scan gun off the shelf along with hers. "We are done here. Let's go find you a dress that will show off all those hips and ass you got. I rarely advise this but, I'm going to help you find a dress that will make you look better than the bride."

"Sunni!" I followed behind her as she took large steps to the bridal registry customer service desk. "I'm not trying to cause any drama at that man's wedding."

"Oh, never drama. We're way too cute for that." Sunni placed the scan guns down on the table and briefly thanked the salesperson who assisted us when we first arrived. Sunni marched in front of me, pulling me by the hand to follow behind her. "We'll just call this you wearing your resume."

TWO HOURS LATER, I SAT ACROSS FROM MY AUNT LAURIE WITH A MENU perched up on the table and below my eyes. My shopping bag that held two folded dresses, one for the dinner tomorrow night and the wedding on Saturday, sat at my heels.

"What looks good, favorite girl?"

Aunt Laurie was in town for just one more night, and since boarding a train was in my plans for tomorrow morning, I had to see her before I left.

"The lasagna looks good."

After spending all the time left in the department store until a store associate had to inform us they were closing, Sunni and I split up so she could meet up with Josiah and I could meet up with Aunt Laurie.

"*Mmm*, yes! Let's share the lasagna," she suggested. "I'll get the shrimp Fra Diavolo and we can share that too."

I wrinkled my brows. "What's Fra Diavolo?"

She licked her lips and smiled. "It's this creamy, spicy tomato-based sauce. You'll love it. I had it at least twice a week when I spent that month away in Italy."

I wasn't a fan of trying anything new, but I trusted my aunt. "Okay, cool."

We sat in a tiny Italian bistro only a mile or two away from Times Square. For May, the temperature was mild and married well with the gentle breeze. We opted to dine outside of the restaurant because of the beautiful weather.

"Wine?" she asked.

"Yes, any white is fine with me." I shrugged. "I never can tell the difference."

She smiled big. "Just like your aunt."

After placing our food orders and receiving our food ten minutes later, conversation somehow ended up on the wedding that weekend.

"Your mother told me you and her are heading to D.C. for your friend Hassani's wedding."

I stopped twirling the pasta around my fork for only a moment at the mention of Hassani's name.

"*Mm-hmm,*" I answered with a nod. "We're taking the train out there tomorrow morning. There's a pre-wedding dinner planned for Friday night."

When I looked up at my aunt, she gave me a polite smile. I knew it was a polite smile because I gave the same smile to people I pitied.

"What's that look about?" I asked on an exhale.

"Nothing." She shrugged. "I just thought you'd go with a date or something."

I shook my head. "No date. Just me and mom."

"Sonia is splendid company, but I'm sure you'd enjoy yourself more if you went with a date." She poked her fork in the lasagna. Right before placing the bed of pasta, meat sauce, and cheese in her mouth she asked, "While we are on the subject - why haven't I met any of your boyfriends?"

"I have had none to meet?"

"Are you asking me?"

I fought back my smile. "No, I'm telling you I have had no boyfriends, Aunt Laurie."

"And why not?"

"Because just like my aunt in her heyday, I like to live wild and free. I tried the traveling thing, but it didn't work out as great as I envisioned it would when I was a kid watching her plane hop."

She scoffed a laugh.

"Nevertheless," I continued, "my beautiful aunt used to say how good it felt not having anyone to report to or check in with, and I kind of agree."

"Oh, Ayla." She patted her lips clean with her white napkin. "Your *aunt* does not think or *feel* that way anymore. She eventually learned life is great solo but is fun and exciting in twos, too."

I scratched the back of my neck while looking away.

"After the divorce, when I flew to Italy and stayed there for a month? I realized my obsession with being unattached had a lot to do with me not wanting to get hurt."

The horns of passing taxis and cars sounded like a blur in the background as an accordion-rich song played from the restaurant.

"And then when I got hurt, and I didn't die from the heartbreak..." She chuckled. "And I went away to be by myself again, I learned the only mistake I made was choosing a man I knew wasn't right for me. My mistake was not falling in love."

I tilted my head to one side, deeply engaged.

My aunt smiled from ear to ear. "My time in Italy gave me a lot of opportunity to think, and I realized there are different types of loves, two specifically. The love that's life giving and the love that lasts a life-time. Some of us are blessed to find both loves in one person. My ex-husband gave me the type of love that was life giving until it wasn't."

After that night in my aunt's Silver Spring townhouse, she packed up all of her stuff and booked a one-way ticket to Italy the very next day. She filed for divorce while she was away, something her ex-husband made difficult, but his infidelity sealed his fate. When Aunt Laurie returned, she was better than when she left, but still not her old self again. To this day, I still found it difficult to unsee all that transpired the night my mother and I drove to Maryland.

"Admittedly, I haven't found the man who can serve as my love of a lifetime," she revealed. "But that will not stop me from looking. Love is life. And when I find it again, I'm going to love with my whole heart and give the man I love all the love he deserves."

"But..." I placed my fork down at the edge of my plate and looked up at her. "You told me never to do that."

Her brows slowly wrinkled with confusion.

"That night, the night before you flew to Italy, you said never to love a man more than he loves me."

The lines in her brows relaxed. "Oh, Ayla." She closed her eyes tightly and shook her head. "I should have never told you that."

My eyes watered with tears. I darted my eyes away to keep them from falling. Her warning to never love a man more than he loves me stuck with me the most that night. It was the support beam behind the wall I always kept up with men. So to hear her say the opposite, practically shattered everything I'd ever known to be true in minutes. I questioned who I was without the wall I spent years building and that I believed was in place for a reason.

Aunt Laurie took my hand, forcing my eyes back on her. "I was a mess that night. A complete and utter tragedy and not because I got hurt, but because in that moment, I felt life lost meaning and that was the mistake. No one should have that kind of power over your existence. I allowed myself to lose myself in a marriage because I wanted to be perfect for him. We were all wrong for each other and the signs were there. Even the night before our wedding when I couldn't get a hold of him, but I went through with the ceremony anyway, even when my gut told me not to. The problem was I took vows with the idea of us before I took vows with *him*. Before I knew anything concrete about him I allowed myself to subscribe to a fantasy even when the signs told me not to. All I knew was he had money and liked to travel like me and back then, honey, that was enough... until it wasn't."

"That's what I'm worried about," I admitted. "I don't want to lose myself."

"You've got this one life, Ayla. Please don't spend a single second worrying about something that has never happened to you. My path is *my* path, not yours, favorite girl. Now, *your* path in life and love? That's up to you to create. Stop robbing yourself of creating it because you're scared of getting hurt. Hurts heal, anyway, remember that.

Case in point - I'm dating this man I met at the laundromat of all places." She laughed to herself and I did too. "He's charming, *very* smart, intimidatingly intelligent. He's in transportation and lives modestly. Favorite girl, we are complete opposites and he loves that. I don't have to change my circle qualities to fit into his square life. He's happy and I'm happy, and that's how it should be.

"Don't be afraid of love. It's not a weakness or a curse. It's a present to be enjoyed in the present." She shifted her eyes away, staring out into the distance with a smile. "And even if that love doesn't work out, the growth you experience, Ayla. The lessons, my love." Aunt Laurie leaned forward in her seat to place her hand on my cheek. "Priceless. Take it from me - if you're not growing you're dying a slow death and are amongst the living dead. That's the truth. They weren't lying when they said it is better to love than to not love at all. Being filled with fear is purposefully putting yourself in a box you can never get out of. I wouldn't want that for you."

"What if I'm petrified of getting hurt, though? What if—"

"What if, what if. What. If? What if the world ends? What if you die right here, right now? Life is full of the unknown, beloved, don't allow your energy to be weighed down by the fear of something you've only created in your head."

I looked away briefly to wipe the tear that fell from my eye.

"I read a quote once that said fear is an acronym for 'false evidence appearing real'." She snickered. "That couldn't be any truer. Out of fear, we create mountains that don't even exist. We literally create our own hells."

"But you got hurt, Aunt Laurie, *badly*. You said so yourself."

"But that has more to do with my choices than with letting go of my fear to love. Do you know I was still fearful in my marriage? I made most of my choices with him out of fear. I wanted to be the woman I thought he'd love, so against my better judgement and out of fear of him leaving - which he did anyway, right? - I *changed*, not for myself but to suit *him*. He liked women who were demure and sophisticated. So, I spoke less, bit my tongue more, traded in my deep v-necks for turtlenecks. Ayla, girl, I popped off my acrylics in exchange for clear polish manicures, which by the way I absolutely hated, *hated*, paying for someone to paint my damn nails with clear nail polish."

She cringed, and I laughed.

"I forced a change that wasn't my idea and that didn't benefit me. And I did it out of fear of losing him. And if there was anything I did wrong, it was doing *that*. Not loving him. Because I could have loved him, realized we weren't right for each other, then loved him at a distance. I didn't have to marry him and lose my peace."

"*Hmmm*," I hummed.

"But that's enough about me and that situation, 'cause *that* chapter in my life is *o-v-e-r* and I am done reading it out loud. Praise God." She giggled, twirling her fork this time in the wide dish holding the shrimp Fra Diavolo that sat beside her slice of lasagna. "Excited for your trip to D.C.?"

Before I could stop myself, I winced at the thought.

She dropped her fork at once. "What was that?"

"What was what?"

"That."

"What?"

"*That!*"

Aunt Laurie pointed and said, "I simply mentioned D.C. and your entire face changed."

"No, it didn't."

"*Yes*. It. Did." My aunt stared at me for a moment through squinted eyes. I held my breath the whole time, then looked away to hide any further hints of discomfort.

"Wait, a minute." She gasped. "It's Hassani... isn't it?"

I twisted my head her way again.

"How on earth did I miss that?" She brought her hand to her mouth for only a second. "*He's* the one whose love scares you. That's the only reason you would be weird about D.C. Your mother told me you've been dragging your feet getting ready for your friend's wedding. And now it all makes sense."

I wanted to object to what she discovered, but swallowing my words seemed easier to do in that instance.

"I always loved the way you two looked at each other whenever I visited and he was around, which was very rare. So, believe me when I say there was and probably is something still there."

"Aunt Laurie—"

"Ayla, stop." She held her hand up, halting my interjection. "Don't even try to deny a thing with me. It's *me* you're talking to. And you already know I won't let it fly."

I tucked my lips in my mouth and sat back in my seat.

"Answer me this one thing - has he ever asked you to change or to be someone you are not?"

"Never," I answered without having to think about it. "Not even once. And to a fault because maybe if he *did* ask me to change, things would be different between us."

She smiled big. "You know, your mother always told me you two were only friends, but Sonia can be so naïve about things like this. Something could be right there in her face, and she still wouldn't see it."

"Aunt Laurie, let's just stop discussing him." I snorted a laugh. "Just like that chapter with Ricardo you said was over, mine with Hassani is too. Remember, he's getting married this weekend."

"But is he?" She cocked a brow, then moved her fork away from the Fra Diavolo before lowering her view to cut into her lasagna again.

I wanted to say something in retort, but the words wouldn't materialize. So, I resumed eating too, with her question echoing in my mind.

Hassani

I STARED DOWN AT MY PLATE, BOUNCING MY EYES FROM MY smartphone's screen to the food and back again. It was taking forever and a day for the web page to load.

I knew nothing about weddings and didn't care for the planning of it. So, I delegated much of the task to Sienna, who was more than happy to set everything up. I just wished she picked a better web host for our wedding website.

"So, this is the grilled Chilean sea-bass that we'll serve as the second course of the night," the chef, a twenty-something blonde we - *well I* - flew in from Los Angeles, California. "It's dressed in a warm savory tomato pesto and laid over a bed of spring mixed lettuce, drizzled with a tangy passionfruit vinaigrette."

I broke off a piece of the flaky fish with the side of my fork, forking the fish into my mouth. Barely chewing it before swallowing, I peeked down at my phone again to see the page loading.

It was the night before my wedding dinner, two nights before my wedding. Like I said, I'd taken a hands-off approach to most of the planning, but I insisted on managing the RSVP list for both the dinner and the wedding. I did so, to assist in something pertaining to the event but to also watch out for one specific RSVP.

As soon as the page loaded, I turned in my seat and clicked into the RSVPs. I smiled big when I noticed Mrs. Sonia Samuels's RSVP. But a frown weighed my smile down immediately when I noticed I hadn't received her daughter, Ayla's, RSVP yet.

What is taking her so long to RSVP? I wondered to myself.

"So?" Sienna shouldered me gently against my back, prompting me to turn the face of my phone toward the floor.

I turned to face her. "So, what?"

She sighed loudly. "Hassani!"

"What babe?"

Sienna kissed her teeth and rolled her dark brown eyes for emphasis. "The food. What do you think about the food?"

"Oh." I took another look at the fancy fish laying over the colorful lettuce. "It's aight, I guess."

She sighed again.

"SiSi, you know I don't know too much about this bougie stuff, right? If it's good to you, know I feel the same way."

She gave me a blank stare.

"Not a suitable answer?"

Sienna shook her head. "Not at all."

I flashed a warm smile, and she blushed.

"Don't do that." She held a finger up. "I *hate* when you do that."

I placed my phone on the table, purposely face down. "When I do what?"

"That *thing* where you try to make me forget exactly why I'm annoyed with you. Don't smile all sexy at me is my point."

I licked my lips slowly, knowing the effect doing that would have on her too. She shoved me against the shoulder in response, making me laugh.

"Seriously, Hassani," she whined. "You promised you wouldn't let work distract you for the next few days. You told me you wouldn't engage in work stuff of any kind until after the honeymoon, but here you are," she accused, pointing at my phone.

"You're right." I pushed the button to darken the screen on my device and forced another smile. "I just needed to check on a contract. I'm finished now."

I wouldn't dare tell her I was looking for Ayla's RSVP. Wouldn't tell her I'd been looking for Ayla's RSVP since the wedding invitation, and eventually the email about the dinner went out. That I'd been checking the list online at least five times a day to the point the action of checking had become one of my daily routines.

"Good." Sienna focused her attention on the chef. "This is great, Hilary. What's next?"

Sienna was five-alarm-blaze-pissed-off the day she found out I'd sent a wedding invitation to Ayla. Sienna was well aware that Ayla and I had not spoken in years. She never cared to find out why Ayla and I grew distant after graduation. If you ask me, I think Sienna was just happy Ayla was out of the picture. So, when she saw Ayla on the list of invitees, all of her suspicions about Ayla returned full force.

"Why didn't you tell me you were inviting her?

"Why did you feel a need to invite Ayla?"

"Is there a reason you need Ayla to be at our wedding?"

Those were just a few questions she posed, and I could answer each one without raising no further suspicions.

I never confirmed what Ayla and I were to each other because, technically, I didn't know what we were myself. A part of me just needed to see Ayla one last time, for what, I still wasn't clear about.

Or maybe I was clear, but not brave enough to admit it to myself.

I had an exceptional woman. Sienna was an *exceptional* woman. She was a successful accountant, with an excellent head on her shoulders. She catered to me in ways that men heard about in songs. Sienna never held back, was always opened to being vulnerable. It was never, ever a mystery how she felt about me, and that transparency was relieving.

Ayla was the complete opposite with her feelings.

Closed off.

Guarded.

Walls all the way up and immovable. Just difficult.

So why couldn't I stop thinking about her after all this time?

"Earth to Hassani." Sienna waved her hand in front of my face.

I blinked myself back into the moment, then pinched the bridge of my nose.

"Is all this overwhelming?" Sienna asked, leaning in closer to read me. "It's too much, huh? Yeah, it's too much." She turned to Hilary. "Hil, do you think you can give us a moment? I think hubby needs a moment to digest these menu items. Right, baby?"

Not really.

"Yes," I replied. "Just a moment."

The smile Sienna flashed, one of relief from my response, made my heart ache.

She's always been upfront and honest with me on things that would be difficult to be honest about along the years. That was the reason I asked her to marry me. I admired her bravery to love without restrictions even when the man she loved had his heart somewhere else... which I'm sure she knew deep down. Asking her to marry me seemed like the right thing to do. She'd been a great woman to me, despite my penchant for being distant at times. So, on the last night of our vacation in Miami, I got down on one knee and asked her to marry me. Had my doubts but went through with it anyway because she deserved at least that.

That sounds horrible when I think about it, but I knew I was making the right decision. I was getting older, and I honestly wanted a family. Sienna did too. And I was fine with those plans until I spoke with Ayla's mother a few months ago and learned Ayla hadn't gotten married yet. Hadn't started a family either. After that, I needed a reason to be in the same room as her and inviting her to my wedding seemed like a good excuse.

Please, don't judge me.

"What do you think of the food so far?" Sienna asked, drawing me out of my thoughts.

"They're great. You chose great."

"Are you sure?" She pouted. "You seem to have a lot on your mind."

I do, just not the things you would be happy to hear about.

"The Chicago building project I contracted last December is being put on hold until after the wedding, so I just want to make sure everything is in place for the break," I assured. This was partially true. I had to place the project on hold, but I'd stopped thinking about it a few days ago. "You know, the firm is still very new. We're used to things moving at a certain pace and not being stalled."

I'd started my firm three years ago after receiving the blessing from the CEO of the firm I worked at straight out of college. With his help and his connections, I created and managed a private architectural firm that was thriving immensely.

"Aww, it's okay baby." Sienna leaned in and pressed her lips to mine. She sat back in her seat and winked at me. "I promise I'll be worth your break from work."

Before I could say anything in response, she waved Hilary over, who'd been waiting with her crew to bring the next dish.

With Hilary's return to our table, we picked up right where we left off with the menu.

"This is a broiled steak on a bed of grilled spring vegetables with a hollandaise dipping sauce on the side," Hilary started.

I drowned her out and retreated into my thoughts again. Honestly, I wanted to be anywhere but there at the moment. The chef wouldn't consider my silence rude since, as Sienna had pointed out, this was all overwhelming... but really it wasn't. I just wasn't interested or as excited about this stuff as she was. I also knew Sienna could handle the rest of the dinner's details with no extra input from me.

From the outside looking in, everything looked perfect in my life.

I had the perfect career, the perfect woman, a flawless wedding plan that could rival a celebrity's nuptials, and the prospect of building a beautiful life starting two days from now. My life was about to be complete.

Then why did I feel like there was still something missing?

CHAPTER 28

yla

My hands wouldn't stop shaking.

"This place is beautiful," my mother whispered beside me.

She and I stood feet away from the entrance of Carle's Place - a gorgeous wedding venue with a gigantic cascading waterfall that divided the parking lot's entrance and exit on the property. The building itself resembled an expansive mansion.

The enormity of the property and the reason I was there made my hands shake as soon as my mother and I stepped out of our rental car.

I was good before we arrived. Told myself all I needed to do to get through the night was focus on how happy I was for Hassani. I forced myself to forget all that Sunni and Aunt Laurie told me.

What did they know?

Hassani and my situation wasn't as black and white as they thought it was. I couldn't just *move* our friendship to something else. We hadn't spoken in half a decade, so did we even still have a friendship?

My mother and I took steps toward the entrance.

"Look at those gorgeous Grecian statues," she uttered in awe. "Hassani and his bride have such aesthetic taste."

The mention of his name made my heart feel like it had grown hands and was trying to punch its way out of my chest.

"Oh, Ayla, I really can't believe you forgot your camera at home, beloved," she chastised lowly. "You would have captured such beautiful pictures tonight with your eye for beauty. I just know it."

The last thing I wanted to do was remember the events of that night, much less capture it on film.

I'd left my camera at home on purpose but she didn't need to know that. Revealing to her that I wanted to forget this weekend ever happened the moment we boarded the train back to New York, would have raised too many flags and questions.

We pushed through the turnstile doors one at a time. My hands slid down the shiny glass, and I gasped at the wet handprint I left on the surface. I ran my palms together realizing how damp they were, knowing that if my palms were sweaty, the rest of me was as well. I swiped my fingertips gently over my forehead to check, quickly realizing how damp it was too.

I was practically expelling sweat like the waterfall out there.

Around us were a bunch of unfamiliar faces, all dressed in their best.

With Sunni's help, I'd purchased an all-black designer dress that matched the appearance of velvet but had the texture of silk and formed a tulip-like shape around my hips and above my thighs. The outfit was long-sleeved, which I was grateful for because the extra fabric would mask the sweating I hadn't planned to do. This was the only dress Sunni, and I agreed on. All of her picks had my ass practically hanging out and my breasts damn near spilling out from the top.

I hesitated with allowing my eyes to scan the room, worried my view would collide into the man of the hour.

The thought alone sent me into a silent panic.

I leaned close to my mother's ear. "I'm going to run to the bathroom."

"Right now?!" she asked, turning to face me. "We just got here."

"I need to check my makeup."

"It looks fine. You look beautiful, baby." She switched forward to face the large room of people. "We should find Hassani first. Let's at least let him know we're here."

My head became light.

"You go ahead." I backed away from her, taking steps to what looked to be the bathroom down the hall. "I'll be right back out."

"Ayla, just wait a moment—"

"I'll be really quick, mama."

I didn't stay long enough to hear her protest any further.

"Excuse me," I said to the first person who looked like they worked at the venue. "Where is your nearest bathroom?"

"Up ahead." She pointed. "Just keep straight. You can't miss it."

I forced a smile. "Thank you."

I told myself before arriving at Carle's Place that I would only be there for an hour, two tops. Show my face just to say I was there and then go to my hotel and wallow in whatever feeling I'd leave the wedding venue with after watching Sienna and Hassani together. I planned to drink one drink at the dinner, which would be enough not to get intoxicated so I could drive back to the hotel. But once I got back to my hotel, I planned to drop mom off at her room, head to mine to change clothes and head out to buy a bottle of the hardest liquor I could find at the nearest liquor store.

Once I was inside of the venue's bathroom, I stood over the vanity in front of the mirror. Even the bathroom was gorgeous, with white marble vessel sinks and faucets accentuated by crystal knobs.

I stared at my reflection and took a few deep breaths, doing my best to get it together.

"How am I nervous already?" I asked myself out loud.

How *was* I so nervous already? I hadn't even seen him.

At this rate, I might lose consciousness the moment we actually lock eyes across the room.

There were folded napkins on the bathroom's vanity, an arm's reach away. I grabbed one at a time and patted my forehead, then used another to slide inside the neck of my dress to dab against my sweaty armpits.

"This is ridiculous," I mumbled to myself as I discarded the napkins in a nearby trashcan. I moved my eyes to my reflection in the mirror. "*You're* being ridiculous."

Music started up outside the bathroom and made its way into my space like a muffled hum. The dinner was about to start. My pulse raced even more at that realization.

I was applying powder to my forehead when my phone chimed in my velvet clutch. I retrieved my phone, noticing the message from Sunni.

Sunni: Please don't let this weekend go by without telling Hassani.

I dropped my head back between my shoulders and grunted.

"Sure, Sunni," I mumbled to myself. "Because I'm not freaking out enough in the bathroom."

I grabbed my black velvet clutch and tapped into my messaging app with my thumb, typing my reply to Sunni as I pulled opened the bathroom door with my free hand to meet up with my mother.

I stepped through the bathroom door quickly, immediately colliding face first into a hard chest.

It stopped me cold.

I stepped back, gazed up, and his hazel-greens greeted my eyes before he said a single word.

I gasped and held on to my breath.

"A. Boogie," Hassani whispered.

I parted my lips to say something, but my brain wouldn't compute. Words had escaped me completely. I couldn't believe who I was seeing, even though I'd been expecting to see him that night.

He exhaled audibly, a smile slowly appearing on his lips, making it harder to stay on my feet.

Hassani's eyes left mine and coasted south of my neck.

With his attention on my hips, he said, "You look absolutely incredible, A."

I had a hard enough time remembering to inhale and exhale, much less respond with something, anything.

A compliment of my own, maybe? Because he sure deserved a litany of them.

He looked better than when I last saw him. Everything on him had matured. Hassani's hair was a fade with soft black curly hair sprouting from the top. He had a mustache and beard now. The perfectly trimmed hairs framed his soft plush lips like a masterpiece. His shoulders were broader, arms hillier in his tailored suit jacket. By the time I made eyes with him again, I stumbled back, completely taken by how sultry they'd become.

My. God...

"Whoa!" He stepped closer in my space to catch me before I fell against the bathroom door behind me. "You aight?"

I tried again to speak, but my brain kept coming up blank.

Hassani tilted his head to one side, his eyes squinting the longer he observed me in my stunned state.

I inhaled a stuttered breath, recognizing his stare. He was analyzing me, something I absolutely hated when he used to do it way back when. But in that instance, it calmed me a little, recognizing him as the same Hassani. And that was enough to make me smile.

He smiled with me, then nodded slowly, tightening his grip on my arm while pulling me to him gently. His eyes softened, and he gave me a look. One of understanding. A look that made it clear words didn't need to be exchanged between us.

"Get over here," he whispered, guiding me into a hug.

I closed my eyes as he wrapped his arms around me. I inhaled him once my body settled against his. The exhale I released was so relieving, it was as if I'd been waiting to do it for months, *years*. The feeling that came over me next was so overwhelming, I had to hold back a cry.

He stepped out of the hug to meet my eyes again.

"I saw your mother out there," he explained, the bass in his voice rumbling in my chest. "She told me where you were, and I couldn't wait to see you."

"Hi," I finally squeaked out.

First, he smiled, and then he chuckled. "Hey."

I heard the click and clack of heels approaching

"There you are," The voice chirped a few feet behind him. "I've been looking all over for you."

Hassani and I directed our attention that way. She glowed, more than she glowed while we were still in college, which was saying a lot because she was stunning back then too. Sienna's skin was a match for her name. Smooth and warm like café au lait... heavy on the au lait. Her cat-like eyes shot my way then to Hassani. Her eyes moved like a sharpened pendulum as they moved between Hassani and I once more.

I turned my head to look at Hassani again to see he was still looking at me, with a softer look than hers.

"Ayla," Sienna said, just above a whisper. Her eyes focused on Hassani again. "I should've known this is where you'd be."

Hassani chuckled, scratching the back of his head.

I had to hold back my smile at his telltale gesture of nervousness.

"Congratulations." I looked at him first then turned my gaze on her. "And thank you for inviting me."

Sienna rushed closer, looping her arm with Hassani's. "Well, we hadn't received your RSVP for the dinner *or* the wedding, so I wasn't even sure you were coming."

"Oh." I pressed my hand to my chest. "I didn't realize I had to RSVP."

Well, that was a boldface lie. I knew I had to RSVP. Sunni had been in my ear complaining about her family members who were complaining about needing to RSVP for *her* wedding, so I knew the drill. What was true was I didn't know if I was coming to Hassani's wedding dinner either until that morning when I boarded the train.

"You didn't *have* to RSVP," Hassani weighed in.

"*Of course*, she had to RSVP, babe," Sienna insisted in an admonishing tone while glancing up at him. "How else would we have known the final head count to confirm with the venue?"

She turned to look my way. "You *should've* sent in your RSVP. If you didn't have to, we wouldn't have asked that you do so on the invite. I'd been looking for your response for weeks. I thought you weren't coming."

I wasn't.

Hassani switched his head in her direction with a surprised expression on his face.

"Anyway, Hassani." She rolled her eyes away from me then focused them up at him, "We have to go. The dinner is about to start."

He turned his head my way again.

I nodded, offering him a closed-lips smile. "Go, please."

Those hazel-greens were on me again, penetrating the facade I thought I'd done a good job of making sure was solid for tonight.

"I'm right behind you guys," I added.

Sienna forced a smile my way before twirling on the arch of her designer heels, pulling Hassani along with her by the hook of their arms.

He reached for me and held my hand for only a moment. "Thanks for coming, Ayla."

He kept his eyes on me until he was a few feet away. I blinked back my tears as he slid his hand down to Sienna's, threading his fingers with hers.

HASSANI AND SIENNA HOSTED THE DINNER IN THE GRAND ROOM. ROUND tables with crisp white linen draped over them formed a large half circle. A giant crystal chandelier hung over a slightly elevated platform at the center of the room and served as the dance floor. Hassani and Sienna sat at the curve of the semi-circle with Sienna's parents to her right and Hassani's parents to his left.

Mr. Franklin was beside himself, happy to see me there. Damn near squeezed the life out of me when he hugged me and talked my ear off to my delight. Mrs. Franklin nearly bursted into tears when we embraced. I hadn't seen the Franklins in half a decade, but you would think we spoke the day before with how effortlessly we conversed before dinner started.

My mother and I sat at a table only a few tables away from the bride and groom. Throughout the dinner, the groom and my eyes would meet from across the room. I'd always pull my eyes off Hassani's whenever I noticed our eyes finding each other like magnets. To be honest, I wasn't sure if he ever looked away.

Dinner was an impressive five courses. By the fourth, I'd had enough. I'd purposely drank my one drink as slowly as possible. I still had to drive, but the minimal liquor in my system made the night hard to deal with.

Sienna and Hassani's name together was on everything. On the table settings, floating on the ballroom's floor, flashing from a projector above. They even spelled their initials out in red roses against a white rose flower wall.

It was torture seeing it all. Every time my eyes landed on a wedding detail with their name on it, I took a sip of wine, really wanting to gulp it.

It surprised me how much I held it together. Long enough for the dinner to transition into dancing.

Before I knew it, we were up and out of our seats. Some on the dance floors, others conversing at their tables, like my mother and Mrs. Franklin. The rest of us were at the bar like Mr. Franklin and his friends or standing around the ballroom holding up the wall like me.

"Ayla?" I heard to my right.

When I turned toward the voice, I immediately recognized the face.

"Marcus?"

"Wow," he exclaimed when he was close. "Look at *you*."

Before I could respond, Marcus moved in close and wrapped his arms around me, prompting me to hug him back.

"You look amazing."

"So do you," I returned.

Marcus like Hassani had grown into an even more handsome man over the years. Instead of a beard and mustache, though, Marcus only sported a goatee. He still maintained his slim physique, the one that got him across finish lines when he ran track and field.

"So where's your husband?" he questioned.

"I don't have one."

"Want one?"

I laughed. "Still a straight shooter, huh?"

"Always and forever." He smiled. "Especially when I see a woman over here looking as good as you."

I rolled my eyes playfully. "Oh stop it."

"I'm serious, Ayla." He bit his bottom lip while smiling.

"Let me guess." I tapped my chin. "Did you finally get serious and pursue a career as a male gigolo like your favorite movie?"

He hollered a laugh, and I joined in.

"Nah, finance. But I still need a hobby."

I giggled.

"Tell me this, though." Marcus moved in closer, leaning his arm against the wall beside us. He licked his lips and asked, "How on earth did you get even more beautiful since high school?"

I tilted my head to one side and balled my lips to fight my smile.

"How?" he whispered.

"I see it's a Garvey reunion over here," I heard behind Marcus. Hassani approached, draping an arm across Marcus's shoulder. Marcus playfully shoved Hassani away, and they pretended to square up, taking their positions in fighting stances. These two had always been like this, with their little friendly rivalry. Independently, they were very competitive. But up against each other, it almost seemed toxic. I never really understood Hassani and Marcus's friendship, but they were close. Clearly close enough to maintain a friendship that lasted this long.

My calm breaths became harder to take again, with Hassani only inches away once more.

His eyes were on me when he asked, "What are you two over here talking about?"

"Wouldn't *you* want to know," Marcus teased.

"I would," Hassani countered.

"Well, if you *must* know." Marcus focused on me and said, "I'm working my way up to asking Ayla to be my date for the wedding tomorrow."

I jerked my head back, shocked by the admission. "You are?"

"Yeah," Hassani echoed. "You *are?*"

Marcus laughed, and I giggled nervously.

The only person who didn't show amusement was Hassani. Instead, he clenched his jaw twice before scoffing a laugh that was so obviously forced.

"You're a wild boy, Marcus," was all Hassani replied with. A smile had yet to grace his lips, and that's saying a lot about Hassani, who had a smile always waiting on reserve to flash.

Marcus maintained a sly grin on his lips. "You know how I can be."

"Like one big happy family over here, I see," Sienna said, sliding her hands in beneath Hassani's arms and hugging him from behind. "Can I steal my husband away so he can meet a few of my coworkers?"

My eyes locked with Hassani's for only a second before I shifted my attention ahead.

"Of course," Marcus insisted. "Besides, it wouldn't be stealing if he's yours and you're his, right?"

Sienna smiled at Marcus, maintaining eye contact with him while giggling like a schoolgirl behind Hassani. I cocked a brow at that. That seemed like a weird thing to say, but I wasn't in any position to label anything weird that night. I had my own internal war to deal with.

"Come on, baby." Sienna took Hassani's hand and pulled him away from our tiny huddle.

Marcus and I were alone again.

"I'm surprised you two have remained in contact after this long," I said to Marcus.

"Yeah." Marcus nodded. "I knew he moved out to D.C. after y'all graduated from LU and I was already out here. After I graduated from HU, I stayed. So as soon as he moved, we linked up again."

"Ah, I see." I twisted my lips to one side. Being told in fewer words that Hassani's friendship with Marcus was more valuable than his friendship with me, hit me hard in my chest.

"Yeah. Hassani and I actually go running together every Sunday at the park. Went running yesterday to make up for him being away at his honeymoon this weekend."

"Oh, cool." Hearing about Hassani and Sienna's impending honeymoon was like taking a dagger to my throat. I maintained a relatively unaffected disposition though... at least to *me* I did.

"So about that date—"

I released an airy laugh. "Thanks, but no thanks Marcus."

"Really?!" His smile gradually fell off his lips. "Why not?"

"My mom's my date," I lied. "Sorry."

"Aw, man." He slapped his hand to his chest. "You're breaking my heart."

I laughed.

"You know I've been wanting to ask you out for a while, right? I even wanted to ask you to prom, so you saying yes would've made up for it."

I furrowed my brows. "You wanted to ask me to prom?"

He nodded. "Yup. But your boy over there told me not to."

I couldn't hide my shock if I wanted to. "Really?"

"Oh, yeah." He laughed. "Raced me to keep me from asking too. I should've asked you, anyway. It wouldn't have been the worse thing I'd ever done."

I pointed my attention to Hassani, who sat on a chair with Sienna on his lap. He laughed with her coworkers, running his hand up and down her back affectionately. After a short while, he wrapped his arm around Sienna's waist and pulled her closer to him. His arm fit so perfectly around her waist, as if the most high created Hassani's arm to rest there.

A lump formed in my throat at the sight of the two of them together. I'd swallowed it back, but it was hard to ignore that I'd had enough. Especially if I would have to witness them do worse tomorrow at their wedding.

"I'm going to go check on my mother."

Marcus pushed out his bottom lip in an exaggerated show of his disappointment. "Well, aight. I'll see you tomorrow?"

I bounced my head up and down. "Tomorrow."

"Can't say I won't ask again then."

I smiled. "Later, Marcus."

I'd only taken two steps away from Marcus when my phone chimed in my clutch. I slowed my pace and pulled out my device, only to see it was Sunni calling this time. She'd been blowing up my phone with a bunch of texts since her first one from earlier. I guess she grew tired and impatient after not receiving a response to her earlier text. I never got a chance to reply to her after running into Hassani head first.

"Did you do it yet?" Was the first thing she asked when I answered.

I sighed. The DJ turned up the reggae track that spun on his turntable. I decided quickly to exit the grand ballroom to hear Sunni better. "You make it seem like it's so easy."

"Ayla—"

"Sunni." I glanced around me before moving to a nook behind one of the closest walls. "I *can't* do it."

Sunni grunted. "You can't or you *won't*?"

"He seems so settled in his new life and so perfect with her. I just... I can't. I won't. This is the night before his wedding, for God's sake."

"Tell. Him!"

"And what if he does nothing with what I tell him? Huh? Then what?"

"Then that will be that," she answered. "But at least you'll have no questions in your head about 'what if'. You can move on with a clear conscience."

I bit at my bottom lip, thinking. The idea of being rejected might as well be equivalent to death, because my heart honestly couldn't tell the difference. Death and rejection sent the same charge through me.

"Ayla..."

"Okay," I whispered. "I'll, um..." I scratched at my head and released a loud exhale, hoping that when I released my breath, the tension would leave with it. "I'll go back in and if he's by himself, I'll try to tell him."

"Don't try," Sunni insisted. "Do it."

My steps felt heavier returning to the grand ballroom. I immediately shot a glance to the section of the room I last saw Hassani. While Sienna and her coworkers still laughed and talked in their individual seats, Hassani had left her side. It didn't take long for my eyes to land on the back of his head. He stood facing the bar and I could point out any part of him in a lineup, regardless of how many years had passed or how far I stood away from him.

I inhaled a deep breath and let it out slowly through my lips as I closed the space between us. It's like God kept everyone away because for the first time that night, we would finally be alone.

"So, you and Marcus go running every Sunday, huh?" I said to his back when I was close.

He pivoted on his feet instantly, and when he recognized the source of my voice, a serene smile spread across his lips.

"I'm a little shocked by that." I crossed my arms, feigning offense. "Thought I was your running partner."

Hassani stared at me for a moment, holding his smile on his lips. I had to turn away only for a moment to calm the beating of my heart.

"So... she speaks," was his first reply. He waited for me to make eye contact with him again before adding, "And it's a little difficult scheduling running dates with my original running partner when she's been dodging my phone calls for months now."

"I haven't been dodging your calls."

"Ayla," he spoke again. "If my phone calls to you were the red ball used in dodge ball, you'd be the last one standing in a game I never wanted to play with you."

"I..." I opened my mouth to say something in retort but couldn't think of anything to say, so I said once more, "I haven't been dodging your phone calls."

"Oh, so..." He leaned one arm behind himself and against the edge of the bar counter. "She not only speaks, but she also lies now too?"

My laugh tumbled out of my lips before I could stop it. "About me not speaking - I wasn't expecting you to be standing outside the bathroom door back there. Cut me some slack."

"And the other thing? The lie you're trying to sell me about dodging my phone calls?"

"Hassani—"

"*Mmm,*" he interjected with ease. "It feels *so good* to hear you say my name again, though. And that's an irrefutable truth."

I blinked in response. Once I found the courage, I told him, "It feels good saying it too."

Hassani licked his lips slowly, then tilted his head toward the bar and asked, "What are you drinking these days?"

I lowered my shoulders and loosened the tension in my muscles, finally finding comfort in his company again. "moscato."

He jerked his head back. "So... basically juice."

The giggle that escaped me sounded like Sienna's. I guess Hassani had that kind of effect these days. "It is *not* juice."

"Yes it is."

I shoved him against his shoulder. "With the right amount, you can get a buzz."

"A buzz?" Over the music playing in the hall, the bass in his voice still rumbled in my chest. "Let me get you a proper drink, A. Boogie. Please. I beg of you."

I rolled my eyes playfully.

"Sean," he called to the tall gentleman dressed in all black behind the bar counter. "You got Riesling back there? Preferably a bottle from Germany or Cali?

"Let me check," Sean answered. He picked up a bottle of white wine from off a shelf below him. Checked the label and said, "This is Riesling, but it's from New York."

"Uh-uh, that'll turn off her tastebuds since she's used to wine with spin-off caps and all."

I shoved him again, and he laughed.

"How about Prosecco?" Hassani inquired through his laugh.

"Yup, got that," Sean confirmed. "Just poured some out for someone else."

"Cool, bring a glass and the bottle, please." Hassani turned to me and said, "It's not as sweet as moscato, and it's a little on the dry side, but it's sweeter than other wines, so you should be aight."

"And when did you become such the wine connoisseur?"

"I designed a tiny spot for a client of mine." Hassani accepted the bottle from the bartender and poured the wine into a champagne glass for me. "He owned a few vineyards in and out of the country and was interested in opening a winery in upstate New York. He posted a bid to a private forum in search of an architect to create a blueprint for the property, a bid I responded to first." Hassani lifted the glass and handed it to me. "I had to convince him I was the guy for the job, so I spent an entire night studying wines and their notes so I could name drop a few to impress him."

I sipped the wine, rolling the bubbly crisp wine over the bed of my tongue. The taste was light, fresh, tasted a little like peaches, and tickled the roof of my mouth just how I liked it.

"*Mmm*," I moaned to myself.

"*Mm-hmm*," he replied, lifting his short glass of brown liquor to his lips to sip.

"And what are you drinking?" I asked before taking another sip of my new favorite wine.

"A pineapple whiskey sour," he drawled out. His eyes settled on mine, and he didn't blink. He was giving me a strong taste of his energy, just like the drink he held in his grip.

"So..." I cleared my throat, hoping to recover from being spellbound by the intensity in his eyes. "... you're basically sipping on flavored gasoline."

That signature smile I could always depend on being on his lips reappeared, bigger and bolder, showing all his teeth before he scoffed a laugh. "Yeah, basically."

I raised the rim of my flute to my lips to hide my amusement. After taking another sip, I told him, "I remember when you used to hate pineapples."

He looked me right in my eyes and replied, "And I remember when you changed that."

I broke eye contact for only a moment to keep from blushing under his gaze.

"So, a teacher?" he quizzed, gaining my attention back. "At one of the top preparatory schools in the country."

"Yup." I nodded. "Same school I interned at while at LU."

"Congrats. I remembered how hard you worked to secure a position at that school."

"Thank you."

We were quiet again, allowing the sounds of the surrounding music to fill our silence.

"So," he started again.

"So," I echoed.

To someone looking in, Hassani and I were being redundant, unnecessarily peppering our conversation with, "So." But honestly? The buffer that filler word provided relieved the awkwardness that should have been present between us after not speaking for five years.

"The little boys in your class must be failing."

I tilted my head and wrinkled my brows at his comment.

"There's no way anyone is getting work done with Ms. Samuels standing at the front of the classroom."

"I beg your pardon?" Forget blushing. My temperature had climbed several degrees.

"Oh, *please*," he said lowly, taking another sip of his drink. "Don't front. You *know* you're fine."

I smiled while dropping my jaw, all before looking away shyly.

"*Always* been fine," he added.

Our eyes met again, and I had to take a deep breath through my lips.

"Damn," he whispered this time, placing his glass down on the counter. "You look so amazing. *Stunning.*"

"You do too," I said, not missing a beat. "*Really* amazing."

He licked his lips while maintaining eye contact.

The air in the room became suddenly warmer. I took a deep breath and released a stuttered exhale. "Hassani, um, I..."

"Hassani," Sienna sang from a few feet away.

And just like that, the temperature in the room had returned to normal.

"It seems whenever I go looking for you, I find you tucked away from everyone else with a certain someone occupying your time." Her tone was dry, but she wore a convincing smile on her face. It confused me and made me feel uneasy... I'm sure which was her goal.

He laughed while scratching the back of his head. That made me smile again. Nervous Hassani made me nostalgic.

"Anyway, I need you again. I *always* need you." Sienna looped her arm with his and leaned in, balancing herself on the arches of her feet to land her lips on his cheek. I looked away to keep from showing exactly how I felt about it - annoyed.

And why would I be? This was *her* fiancé. They planned to march down the aisle and into the new chapter of their lives in a few hours.

Why was I still trippin' like this?!

"We need to speak with Reverend Connelly before he and the First Lady retire for the night."

Hassani turned to look at me and I did him. "Can you give me a few more minutes? Ayla and I were—"

"No," she answered with more bass in her tone. Sienna had one of those high-pitched girly voices that fluttered in the air when she spoke. It was the quintessential sweetheart tone that made men melt and made her miss congenitally to strangers. Her eyes locked on mine and refused to move. She burned me with her gaze, made me feel like a child who just got caught with their hand buried deep in someone else's cookie jar. Her penetrating glare made me swallow hard, but not hard enough to get rid of the guilt. I was at her wedding dinner the night before her wedding, flirting with her soon-to-be-husband, and she knew it.

"We have to speak to them now," she urged, this time with her usual light effervescent tenor. "Just to finalize a few things. You know they are a little older and being up at this hour is way past their bedtime."

Sienna pointed her eyes on me again, and I couldn't hold my

stare with her. I immediately dropped my eyes to the floor before turning to face the bar.

Hassani started. "Ayla, um—"

"It's cool," I insisted as I turned to face them again. "It's a big day tomorrow and I know you two still have a lot to do."

With Hassani's attention on me and off Sienna, her eyes returned to mine, and she stared me down with a squinted expression.

I forced a smile. "It can wait."

No, it can't!

His brows wrinkled. "Are you sure?"

No!

"Go," I said, looking up at him this time. "Please. We'll talk... tomorrow."

The words sounded like the right thing to say, but the idea of even going to the wedding at that point was looking less likely.

Hassani stared at me for a moment, eyes darting across mine, paying special attention to each iris as if he were trying to mentally compute the exact hex code for the brown in them.

He was reading me.

I needed him to stop.

There was no way I could hold it all together with him looking at me like that. Not in front of *her.*

"Come on babe." Sienna slid her hand down to his. For the second time that night, I watched as her hand relaxed in his, fitting comfortably into the contour his grip provided. Reactively, my stomach turned.

I'd reached my limit.

"We'll see you tomorrow, Ayla," Sienna reiterated. She was the first to turn away and Hassani followed. He turned to glance back at me once before facing in the direction she pulled him.

With the glass back in my hand, I raised the rim to my lips and gulped down the rest of the Italian white wine. I needed something stronger for sure, but for now, I just needed to get the hell out of there.

As I took steps from the bar, it occurred to me I didn't get to tell Hassani how I felt and at that point; it didn't matter.

I fought to keep my eyes dry as I made my way over to my mother, who was engaged in conversation with Mr. and Mrs. Franklin.

"Ayla!" Mr. Franklin shouted as I closed in on their table. I'd spoken to him and Mrs. Franklin throughout the night, but you would think he was seeing me for the first time. "You owe me a dance, young lady."

"Tomorrow," I promised with a smile. "I think I'm going to head back to my hotel room."

"Head back to your hotel?" Mrs. Franklin questioned. "You can't tell me us old folks got more energy than you do. It's only 9 p.m."

I laughed a genuine laugh, and it felt good.

"You all right, baby?" My mother asked.

"I'm fine. I just have a slight headache. I think I might have had too much wine at the bar, maybe." I'd only had half a glass during dinner and the glass of Prosecco Hassani poured out for me, but saying I had a headache seemed like the most believable lie I could give.

Because admitting that it was killing me softly, seeing Hassani do what an almost married man should do with his soon-to-be wife, seemed melodramatic. Admitting that I'd choked back enough cries for the night, and I needed to retreat to my hotel room to lick my wounds didn't sound good in my head and would probably sound worse out loud. Telling them I needed to save the little energy I had left to get through tomorrow, just didn't seem right either.

So, yeah, I lied for the second time that night.

"Well, okay," my mother said, reaching for her purse. "I can go with you—"

"Sonia, we can bring you back to your hotel, no problem," Mrs. Franklin insisted. "Do you mind Ayla?"

I shook my head. "Not at all." I turned to my mother. "In fact, I think you should stay, mama. I'm just going to go right to sleep when I get to the hotel, anyway."

Friends surrounded my mother, so it took little convincing for her to remain seated. The Franklin's had become like family to my mother. How Hassani and I could stay apart for so long would baffle the average person, given the close relationship of our parents.

I left the hall as quick as I could, refusing to say goodbye to Hassani before leaving, knowing I'd have to face Sienna again too. She just kept popping up whenever Hassani and I were in each other's company, and I was completely over it at that point.

The drive back to my hotel was a quick one. The wedding venue was less than a mile from where I planned to stay for the night. Hassani and Sienna had set things up that way so that their guests didn't have to travel very far from their events. I finally checked out their wedding events email while I was on the train from New York to D.C. They planned and curated everything well. The two of them would make a great couple because they'd *been* a great couple.

The moment I slid my keycard into my hotel room door, I threw my clutch on the floor and kicked off my heels. Images of that night played in my head like a bad movie reel, causing my chest to tighten and the tears to pool in my eyes.

My phone buzzing in my clutch stole what little attention I had left to give. It was Sunni again, and I refused to answer. Having to admit that I didn't do what I told her I would do just made me feel even more defeated.

I tried, really, I did, but the emotions that built in me and bubbled within, spilled out through my eyes. I'd lost strength in my legs and fell to my knees, covering my mouth and doing my best to muffle my wails with my hands.

I cried for the fear I let lead me here. The time I wasted fearing something I couldn't even make sense of anymore. Most of all, I cried because of the fear that had now become my reality.

I was too late, and there was nothing I could do about it.

CHAPTER 29

*H*assani

I HOPED HOW I FELT DIDN'T SHOW ON MY FACE AS I SAW EVERYONE OFF. It was after 11 p.m. The DJ, Sienna and I hired for the night, was in the middle of packing up. He'd be back tomorrow afternoon for the reception scheduled to be held in the same spot as the wedding dinner.

I'd searched all over for Ayla after meeting with the reverend who would officiate me and Sienna's wedding ceremony tomorrow after-noon. But when I finished speaking with him and his wife and went looking for Ayla, my mother told me she had taken off to her hotel. It took everything in me not to leave to go after her. I had to stop myself realizing how it would look to Sienna if I did.

I hadn't had time to really speak with Ayla tonight. Probably wouldn't have talked to her at all if I didn't run into her mother in the venue's lobby earlier in the night. Mrs. Samuels told me Ayla ran to the bathroom really quick and would be right out, but I refused to wait. Honestly, I didn't want to share the moment we saw each other after all this time with other people watching. I had to damn near compose myself when Ayla approached me at the bar. I didn't think she'd speak with me tonight. The short time we spent speaking with each other at the bar reminded me of old times. It felt good... *too good*.

So good, I wished I could hit the pause button on that moment with her and never press play again.

As I approached the bar to grab another drink before heading out to catch a cab home, I waved at a friend from college who ran track with me. He was there with his wife of a year.

Seeing Ayla for the first time after all those years was a surreal moment. She'd gotten more beautiful if that was at all possible. Same sharp eyes and bright perfect smile, but the curves in her physique had enhanced so naturally in a major way.

"Hassani, son," my father called from his seat beside my mother and across from Mrs. Samuels.

I approached their table. "Hey dad, what's up?"

"Me, your mother, and Sonia are about to head to our hotels, but I need to have a word with you."

I nodded. "Okay, cool." My attention moved to Mrs. Samuels. "Do you know if Ayla made it back to her hotel room safely, Mrs. Samuels?"

She smiled. "I'm sure she did. She probably went straight to sleep like she said she would."

"*Hmm.* You guys are staying at the Belvedere?"

"The Montrose, actually." She corrected. "On the fifth floor. As luck would have it, her room number has the numbers in your wedding date - 525.

"Oh." My brows shot up. "Interesting."

"Synchronicity... I guess," my mother said next.

My father simply huffed, "Hmph."

I mouthed the hotel's name to save it to memory. "The Montrose is only a short distance from here, so I'm sure she got there safely."

"Speaking of hotels," my mother spoke next. "Sweetheart, did Sienna head out to hers already?"

"Yeah," I answered. "She's staying at the Marriott across the street with her bridal party."

"Cute," my mother answered, taking a sip of her drink. From the time she first met Sienna, she hasn't been a fan. My mother once mentioned how Sienna was competing with her for my love. Mom found it funny, and so did I because Sienna could never win. There was no competition. But as much as she wasn't a fan, my mother hadn't voiced her disapproval of Sienna or my relationship with her. I spoke with my mother first before asking Sienna to marry me, and she asked me if I felt it was the right decision and if I loved her. I loved Sienna, and I told my mother as such, and all my mother told me was if I'm happy, then I have her blessing.

My father leaned over in his seat to place a kiss on my mother's cheek. "I'll be right back, ladies." Dad was on his feet when he gestured in front of himself to direct me in the direction I should walk. "Son?"

"Dad," I answered as we headed toward the other side of the room. "I have little time. After getting another drink at the bar, I'm going to catch a cab home to get some rest for tomorrow."

"Yes, about that," he started, stopping me a few feet away from the table where my mother and Mrs. Samuels now sat alone. "Are you ready?"

I bobbled my head slowly. "Yeah. A little nervous, but that's normal, right?"

"Depends."

I wrinkled my brows. "On?"

"On what you're nervous about."

"I don't understand."

He sighed, dropping his head forward briefly. My father looked up at me and asked, "Call me crazy, but I don't think I saw you smile as big as you did with Ayla with anyone else tonight. Not even the bride."

I rolled my tongue in my mouth. "I haven't seen Ayla in a while, so I was just happy to catch up with her."

"Is that all?"

"Dad?" I questioned. "I'm going to say what you always say to me..."

He chuckled.

I smirked. "Spit it out, old man."

"Okay, then." He took a deep breath and, on his exhale, explained, "Marriage is a very serious commitment."

"I'm aware."

"Are you?"

"Of course."

"Then why are you marrying Sienna if she doesn't make you smile as big as your friend Ayla does?"

Because Ayla doesn't want me.

"Because Ayla..." I swallowed hard. "Because Ayla and my relationship is different. That's it."

"If there's any time you need to be honest with yourself, Hassani, it's right now."

"I *am* being honest."

"The way you and Ayla—"

"Hold up... didn't you tell me *'Anyone but Ayla, son'*? Or am I trippin'?"

"I said it."

"Okay then."

"But I was wrong. And you know I was wrong."

"All I know is—"

"Hassani, you *know* I was wrong, right?"

I clenched my jaw. "You're never wrong."

"Unfortunately, on this, I was." My father exhaled loudly. "Extremely wrong. I should have never told you that."

What?

"Where is this even coming from?" My chest rose and fell like a bull's. I couldn't be hearing this now. Not the night before my wedding.

"The way you two looked at one another tonight—"

"Me and Ayla haven't seen each other in years. We missed each other. Our friendship was great. That's it, and I promise, how we looked at each other tonight was because of that. We were only catching up."

"No. Lies." He shook his head. "You looked at Ayla the way I look at your mother. Like a man in love."

I looked around us. My eyes falling on Sienna and my name etched on everything. Our wedding colors that we chose together sprinkled here and there, mixed in the details. I ran my hand down my face and grunted.

"Why does it feel like you don't want me to marry Sienna?"

"If marrying Sienna will make you happy." He waved his hand in the air. "Then I want you to marry her because I want *you* to be happy."

"Dad, *why* are you doing this right now?"

"Why are you?"

I bit inside of my bottom lip.

"If you're marrying her because you think that is what we all expect of you, stop right now."

"Dad, I'm getting *married* tomorrow. Should you really be telling me this?"

"Yes." He nodded. "Yes, I should."

"Ayla was my first, okay?" I confessed. "In high school, about three weeks before graduation. She and I... I lost my virginity to her... *with* her. She was my first."

My father's eyes grew so wide I thought they'd pop out. He fixed his lips to say, "what," but no words came out.

"That was why I looked at her, *how* I looked at her, but..." I shook my head. "We have made nothing out of that moment, and I'm not about to start now."

"Oh, my God." My father's jaw dropped when what I told him finally set in. "Hassani, are you in love with Ayla?"

"Dad, I'm getting married tomorrow." I affirmed. "I love Sienna and she makes me happy." I nodded with finality. "Done."

He held his hands up in front of him in a sign of defeat, then sand-wiched them together over his lips as if he were about to say a prayer. My father took a deep breath, then looked me directly in the eyes. "Okay. Then, done."

~

IT WAS AFTER MIDNIGHT WHEN I ENTERED THROUGH THE DOOR OF Sienna and my condo. We'd purchased it a year prior, a few months before I proposed to her. Decided we'd only be here for two years, maybe three, because we had plans to purchase a house in Virginia or Maryland.

I sighed as I toed off my dress shoes and peeled off my suit jacket, hooking the jacket on the coat hook near the door.

The condo was dark, and I kept it that way. Being in the dark always helped me think.

I rolled my neck around my shoulders as I made my way down the long entrance hall that led right into the kitchen. The condo was small for my standards. When I first moved to D.C., my parents footed the bill for an apartment close to the architecture firm I worked at after college. I loved that apartment. Became a responsible man there. Learned a lot about what I liked and didn't enjoy living on my own. Sienna had moved to D.C. after accepting a position at an accounting firm after college, too. We didn't live together then, which was my choice because she was more than willing to move in with me. I just figured we both needed our space and at the insistence of my dad, Sienna and I lived apart until a few months before our engagement.

Thinking of my father, I thought back to an hour prior when he questioned my decision to get married.

My parents were always cordial with Sienna. When I told them, we were dating a few days before my college graduation; it surprised them, but they supported my decision to be with her. After they met her, they liked her and never had a negative thing to say about her. Which was why I was having a hard time wrapping my head around my father's change of heart.

"Son, I want you to know I like Sienna, she's a great woman," my father explained right before we parted for the night. *"I just want you to be sure she's a great woman for you."*

I clasped my hand to the back of my neck, making my way around the tiny island in the kitchen. I reached for the handle on our French door refrigerator, pulling it open. The kitchen lit up because of the fridge's light. My eyes scanned the shelves in search of a beer. The moment I spotted the green bottle, I grabbed it and angled the cap beneath the bottle opener I kept on the fridge door that hung off a magnet.

With the fridge opened, I peeled the top off the beer bottle, bringing the spout to my lips to take a swig. Used the light inside the fridge to see my way to the trash bin - at the end of the kitchen – to dispose of the cap. Where the bin sat served as an exit that led to the entrance of Sienna and my living room.

Speaking of Sienna, I nearly lost my footing and choked on the beer I swallowed hard when I saw her sitting on the couch, quietly.

"What the fuck!" I shouted, slapping my hand to my chest. "Woman, what the hell?"

"Hey," she greeted in a voice that was a tone above a whisper.

"Hey?!" I flicked the light switch closest to me. The room lit up. "Sienna, what are you doing here and why on earth were you sitting here in the dark?"

She still wore the white sparkling dress she wore at the dinner. She'd released her shoulder-length hair out of the slick, low bun she donned earlier. Sienna's white heels were off and to the side of the couch, her hands folded on her lap.

"Hassani," she started. "We need to talk."

I grunted. "Babe, you know how much I hate it when you say *we need to talk.*" I chuckled nervously, returning to the kitchen to shut the fridge's door.

Back in the living room, I leaned forward and planted a kiss on her forehead before taking a seat beside her. "What are you doing here? I thought you were staying at the Marriott with your girls."

"I was." She turned to face me.

"And I thought you said you didn't want for us to see each other before the wedding." I peeked down at the face on my watch. "It's 12:45 a.m. It's officially our wedding day."

"I know, but I wouldn't be able to sleep tonight if I didn't get some things off my chest. And I was thinking you wanted to do the same."

I took another swig of my beer while shaking my head. "Nah. I'm good."

She scoffed a laugh while shaking her head. "So, you really think I didn't see that tonight?"

"See what?"

"The way you were looking at Ayla."

I choked on the cough the beer produced when the liquid went down the wrong pipe. That's because I gasped instead of swallowed.

"Yeah," Sienna whispered. "I saw you. When I found the two of you in front of the ladies bathroom I watched for a good few minutes before I approached and honestly, Hassani? That was the happiest I've seen you in a *long* time."

"I haven't seen Ayla in years."

"No." She shook her head. "That wasn't what that was."

I leaned forward to place the beer bottle on the glass coffee table in front of us.

"Sienna." I turned to face her. "Ayla and I are friends, aight. That's it."

"Hassani," she said lowly, "don't lie to me. Just stop it already."

I clenched my jaw and inhaled a stuttered breath, letting it out just as shakily.

"Don't look me in my face and tell me that when I know what I saw."

Her refusal to back down stilled me, but my heart wasn't. It was pounding in my chest.

"If we're going to spend forever together, be honest with me and tell me everything. *Please.*"

I swallowed once more and closed my eyes, exhaling in defeat.

"Aight." I cleared my throat and scooted to the edge of the couch. "Ayla was my first."

She arched a brow. "Your *first* what?"

Damn, she's going to make me say it.

I licked my lips then revealed, "My first sexual partner... and my first love."

Revealing out loud Ayla was my first love removed a weight off my chest I didn't even know was there.

I noticed the moment Sienna stopped breathing, and I wanted to stop it right there, but she was right. If we were going to do this in a few hours, it was time I kept it real.

"She and I hooked up in high school, twice. And after that we were just cool, only friends. She never spoke about what happened those times we had sex and neither did I until two weeks before LU's graduation."

Sienna's brows went up.

"We slept together the night I went to her and Sunni's apartment to study, and honestly, what we did that night, I have *never* felt with anyone else… not even you, but please don't take that the wrong way. Ayla and I… we made love that night. It wasn't just sex. I realize that now."

Sienna inhaled a shaky breath before letting it go through her mouth. She dragged her fingertips over her lips and then placed her hand against her chest before closing her eyes to gather her breath, I presumed.

"We had an intimate friendship is how I would describe it," I continued. "When we were friends, we were friends and when we were intimate, we were intimate. Not one side of our connection impeded the other, and that was that. But that was then, this is now, and I want to be with you—"

"I slept with Marcus," she blurted before folding her lips into her mouth and closing her eyes tightly.

I sat there for a moment, silently denying I'd heard her say what she said. I'm not sure how long I sat there for, but it was long enough for her to continue.

"It was the week you went away on your business trip to New York," she continued, running her fingers through her hair nervously. "You and I had just moved in together. I was pissed you were leaving. I… I thought while you were there, you would see Ayla. And I was in a mood." She shook her head. "Marcus stopped by to drop off the running gear he borrowed from you the weekend prior to your trip. He noticed I was sad, and we got to talking and we just... it just... happened. And I feel *horrible* about what we did. But he was there for me when I needed someone in my corner the most and I appreciate him for that—"

"I didn't go to New York on business, Sienna," I interjected. "I went to get your engagement ring, and Marcus knew where I was going and for what purpose." I leaned in closer. "Marcus *helped me* choose the date to fly out."

She gasped softly.

I scratched the top of my head before running my hand down my face and scoffing a laugh in my hand. "I told you I was going for business because I didn't want you to know, that for a month, I'd been planning how I would propose to you and the last step was getting the ring. I didn't even see Ayla that weekend. Didn't even think to." I held up a finger. "Nah, you know what? Since we're keeping it real and all? That was a lie. I wanted to see her. I really, *really* wanted to see her. But I talked myself out of it because I didn't want to disrespect you. The first time I've seen Ayla after all these years was at the dinner tonight."

She cupped her left hand to her mouth. "Oh my God."

My eyes went straight to her left ring finger. The solitaire diamond was hard to miss. That was the main reason I bought it so every man would know she was taken from a mile away. The flawless diamond taunted me now, winking at the light as the ring sat prettily beneath the ceiling's glittering fixture, a fixture Marcus helped me install when Sienna and I first moved into the condo. I couldn't hold back my chuckle. It was laugh or scream.

"Ain't this a bitch." I laughed this time. "You fucked my friend while I was in New York City buying a ring for your ass. Wow."

"It was a mistake."

"You ain't lying about that."

Sienna scooted closer to me and I shot up from my seat. She held her hands up in front of her, her lips trembling, eyes pooling with tears. "What I did was bad?"

"Bad?" I leaned forward and close to her face. "Nah, sweetheart, it was fucked up!"

I turned on my socked feet, rounding the coffee table as I began pacing back and forth. "I had this fool playing in my face tonight, playing in my face for the past year. I made that conniving two-face motherfucker my best man and you let me?!"

I screamed a laugh this time. Didn't even know it was a thing until I did it.

"Hassani, I'm sorry!"

"Oh, you're sorry?" I clapped my hands once. "Sienna, you say sorry when you step on someone's shoe by accident or when you forget an important birthday. Saying sorry when you fuck your fiancé's best man just won't cut it."

"Okay, okay." She pressed her hands together. In a shaky voice she told me, "If you're willing to look past what I did with Marcus, I'm willing to look past your love for Ayla."

I stopped pacing to face her.

"We love each other, remember?" she smiled, quickly wiping away the tears falling from her eyes. "And I know I will never be Ayla, and I'm willing to live with that. I'm willing to accept I might never have your heart entirely. I can do that. Let's just put all of this behind us and get married in a few hours. I want to still marry you, baby, just like we planned."

The urge to break everything around me pulsed through my veins like a jackhammer pounding through concrete. I looked at Sienna, recalling how she felt against me, understanding that Marcus had felt the same thing. The faces she made with me while I buried myself between her legs. She more than likely made those faces with him too.

I shut my eyes tight when the images became too much to bear.

"Hassani, *please*," she whispered.

I would've given Sienna the world and then some... but honestly? For all the wrong reasons. Out of guilt for constantly wondering what Ayla was doing who she was with because I hadn't stopped thinking about Ayla since the day of our LU graduation. I replayed that moment daily, rearranging Ayla's responses that day, which would have ended in us leaving LU hand in hand. Sienna was valid in thinking I would meet up with Ayla in New York because I thought about it several times. Thought about calling Ayla's mother to get Ayla's number and inviting Ayla out to dinner. And if she would have obliged, I would have put all my cards on the table, poured my heart out until I was out of breath. But I would have been at peace knowing I finally told her how I felt about her. She was my first love, and I was still very much in love with her.

"Hassani," Sienna pleaded from her seat on the couch. Her tears clumped her lashes together and stained her cheeks with black lines. "Please say something."

I stared at her for a moment and then nodded. "Okay."

"Okay?" She perked up. "So... we're good?"

"No, okay to you wanting me to say something. Here's that something - The wedding is off."

CHAPTER 30

$\mathcal{A}$yla

I NEVER MADE IT OUT TO THAT LIQUOR STORE AS PLANNED.

After bawling my eyes out, I laid in bed and stared up at the ceiling. I'd at least changed out of my dress and now wore a pair of varsity shorts and a plain black tee that was two sizes too big.

My mind was racing with the various excuses I could give for missing the wedding in a few hours. None of them valid, leaving me stuck with the decision to attend.

The hour was 3:33 a.m. I didn't have to be up early in the morning, but I would have to be up early enough to mentally prepare for the ceremony and the reception. I'd resolved to getting through the ceremony and leaving an hour after the reception started. I pictured myself sitting at the table, repeatedly glancing down at my watch so I would know exactly when I'd reached my hour limit.

"Maybe I should set an alarm to remind me when to leave," I mumbled.

Soft raps on my hotel room door broke my focus on the ceiling. I turned my head to look that way, still not moving an inch.

A part of me thought I was hearing things. There was no way my mother would come over to check on me. Our rooms were right down the hall from each other, and she'd already called my room's number hours ago to check in and to let me know she made it safely back to the hotel.

The knock came again, this time slightly harder.

I rolled out of the bed and made my way to the door. Pressing my hands flat against the surface, I leaned close to the door to peek through the peephole.

My brows shot up and my eyes widened at the sight of Hassani on the other end.

"Oh, my goodness," I whispered. "Hassani?" I questioned this time out loud.

He replied with nothing. All he did was stare back from the other side. It didn't take long for me to realize what was happening.

"Hassani, go home."

"Open the door."

"Don't *do* this."

"Ayla. Open. The. Door," he commanded, this time more sternly.

Out of all the scenarios I imagined occurring that weekend, *this* was not one of them. It was hours before his wedding, and he was *here* outside my room door? I knew the decision would bring some drama I wasn't at all prepared to deal with.

"Hassani, I'm not letting you in, so you should just—"

"If you don't let me in, I swear to God I'll break this door down, Ayla."

That made me crack a smile.

"Oh yeah? This is a metal core door, Incredible Hulk. You'll break something, but I promise it won't be this door."

He grinned. "Then so be it."

I stared at him through the peephole, noticing the red lines around his light eyes.

"Did something happen?"

"Open the door."

I bit my lip in thought, hesitating for another moment before I turned the knob and the door automatically unlocked. When I pulled it opened, Hassani stood on the other side. The suit he wore hours ago gone and replaced with a white tee and black joggers, white and black adidas shelltoes on his feet.

"Why'd you leave without saying goodbye?" he asked.

"Why are you here?"

He approached, pressing his hand above me and against the door, pushing it open wider for him to enter. I turned to look at him, following his stride inside my room as the door closed on its own behind me. "Hassani, *why* are you here?"

"Why have you never fought for me?"

"What?"

"Why," he questioned, moving in closer, "have you *never* fought for *me*?"

"Fought for you?"

"To be with me. Why have you never tried? There's no way you've felt nothing for me after all this time."

"Hassani."

He shook his head and turned his back to me. "I dated so many girls, slept with *too* many women, searching for *you* in them. I realized that tonight amongst other things."

I bit at my bottom lip.

"I almost got married because I really tried to convince myself that Sienna was my forever." He turned to face me. "When you are."

I blinked hard at that. "*Almost*? What do you mean by almost? What are you... where is this coming... what's happening right now?"

"I love you, Ayla."

His words made me step all the way back. I held my hands up in front of me.

"I love you *so* much woman, and I know you love me too."

My jaw couldn't hang any lower. "You're getting *married* in eleven hours!"

"Forget about the wedding."

"What the fu—" I slapped my hands to my mouth. "What do you mean forget about the wedding, Hassani?"

"I have been *waiting* for you," he stressed with so much fire in his eyes I thought he would self-combust. "I have been waiting for you to keep it real with me. I've been waiting for you to say it. To say, Hassani, I love you and I've loved you from the start."

"Stop it." I dropped my head into my hands. There was no way I wasn't dreaming.

"Stop fearing me," he whispered back.

I lifted my gaze to him.

"Stop being scared that I'll hurt you because I won't. Quit thinking I won't love you the way you deserve to be loved because *I will*. Man, Ayla." He pointed at me. "You deserve the world, and there's no one who knows that more than I do. I love you with everything in me. I am in love with you."

Hassani closed the space between us, and I couldn't move to create more. When he was close, he slid his hands past my jawline, balancing my face in his two palms. He ran his thumbs against the apples of my cheeks and I closed my eyes, reveling in his touch.

"Why didn't you fight for me?" he asked. "Why won't you tell me you love me?"

"I don't know how," I admitted, shaking my head free of his hold. I backed away next, and he followed, only stopping when he took me back in his arms. Somehow, I started crying. Didn't realize it until I felt his thumb brush a tear away. "I almost did tonight. Almost told you how I feel, how I've always felt, but I couldn't. I mean I *can*, but I'm too scared to risk getting hurt by you if I do. Ask me to break your heart or let you go; I can do that. Offering you my heart at the risk of it being rejected? Or me giving it and losing you with no way of getting my heart back?" I shook my head. "I don't know how."

"I would've never rejected your love or you. I know what to do with both."

Hassani ran his hands down my arms, stopping at my hands where he interlocked his fingers with mine.

"Ayla, do you love me?"

I nodded.

"Can you *please* tell me that before I lose my mind convincing myself otherwise?"

I blinked a few times before I parted my lips and told him, "I love you, Hassani. I have *always* loved you and from the start."

He closed his eyes and exhaled deeply. Dropped his head back between his shoulders and smiled. Hassani leveled his head to lock eyes with me again. "Hearing you say you love me is my new favorite jam. Play it again."

I laughed, shoving him away playfully, and he pulled me with him, wrapping his arms around my waist. I circled my arms around his waist and looked up at him. "I love you so much."

His lips were on mine before I could take another breath. He moved me back against the nearest wall. Hassani released my mouth long enough to lower his lips down to my neck to kiss there too.

"Wait, wait… what about the wedding?" I whispered, eyes closed, honestly not wanting him to stop but also not wanting to be that girl either.

"There's no wedding," he whispered back against my skin.

"But—"

"*Shh.*"

"Hassani—"

"Listen," he said close to my face. The warmth of his breath sent my temperature up a notch. "Don't worry about anything outside of us right now. Do you hear me? Because *nothing* exists out there with you here with me."

I raised my hands and laid them against his cheeks.

"I don't know what's going to happen tomorrow, but I know I want to be with you. Do you want to be with me?"

I nodded.

He cracked a smile. "We have to work on your communication because this nodding thing you like to do, I'm not with it."

I balanced myself on the arches of my feet and leaned in, only stopping when I felt his lips against mine again.

The whole moment felt like a dream. One of those daydreams I'd have whenever I thought of us. I always shook those loose though, fearing that if I thought of him too long, I would think him up.

And would that have been so bad?

"Where are you right now?" he asked in my ear.

"Here."

His hands slid down my waist, grabbing me by the curve of my ass and lifting me off my feet.

He carried me to the bed where we undressed and spent more time lips to lips. Hassani's hands were everywhere on me, with more focus and knowledge on what would make me feel good. This was not the same teenager who believed he needed to prove to me he knew what he was doing or who needed a second chance to show me.

We pleased each other with our mouths like doing so was a second language. The taste of him between my cheeks was one I was grateful wouldn't be my last. I slid him in and out of my mouth, watching his head bob back and forth as he fought not to give in but also not to miss a minute of me pleasing him. When he had enough, we traded places, his lips on my lower lips, not once lifting his tongue off my pink bud. He flicked the tip like I covered that part of me in his favorite flavor, moaning on me like it brought him more pleasure to feast on me than it did for me who was being served.

And when he crawled his way on top of me, sliding in with nothing between us, we exhaled, only taking a new breath when he couldn't bury anymore of himself in me. His strokes were well timed, the pressure he moved with the same, his body and my body fitting perfectly together like custom puzzle pieces. I wrapped my arms and legs around him to keep up, moving with him like a boat over water. Whenever I closed my eyes he'd whisper, "look at me," which made my walls pulse every time.

He turned with me, allowing me to take a seat on top, and I rolled my hips to a song only I heard. Hassani's hand gripped me by the waist, and I placed one hand against the headboard over his head for balance. He kept his bottom lip in the bite of his teeth and when it wasn't there it was stretched just like his top lip into a cunning smile that made me ride harder.

"It's a shock no man has claimed you yet moving like that," he whispered into the dark.

Before I could say anything in retort, he sat up and leaned forward, changing our position from the headboard to the foot of the bed with him now on top.

His speed increased, and my resistance weakened. Perspiration covered our bodies and my hair that now stuck to the back of my neck.

The first wave of my release caused me to arch my back and to lower my pelvis innately. He responded by angling his waist so that he'd tap that spot, finding it even when my body jerked uncontrollably. It was as if he had a magnet attached to the head of his hard-on.

He grunted with each thrust he had left to deliver and my eyes rolled without me wanting to stop them. I fisted the sheets in my hands and groaned. The slickness between us elevating the moment. I felt like I was floating again, a feeling I've only felt with him. Hassani told me he was searching for me in those women, but I was searching for him and *this* in other men, constantly coming up short.

My orgasm crashed into me and I gave in, dropping my head back between my shoulders with my jaw hanging low. Hassani's hand cupped the back of my head for support, never losing momentum or interrupting his rhythm.

He bucked, and I shook, moaning like animals in heat, and it was the sweetest sound.

That was only the beginning because as soon as we came down off afterglow, he turned me on to my stomach and got on top, placing his knees astride each side of my hips.

"The days were long, and the years were too while I was away from you," he admitted, slowly tunneling into me again.

I gasped.

"And we're about to make up for all that, A. Boogie." Hassani pressed his lips to my neck and started a new series of strokes. Against me he ordered, "Now, arch your back for me, and let me show you exactly why I have no intentions of being just your friend anymore."

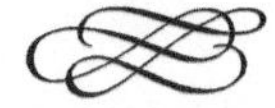

*H*assani

I FOCUSED ON THE NEEDLE AT THE TOP OF THE TALL STRUCTURE, measuring the height of the building visually, deep down, wishing *I* designed it.

The day was cool, not unusual for November, but the day was slightly somber for the love of my life.

Ayla stood in front of the perimeter of the North Pool, staring at the expansive list of etched letters. We'd circled that pool for almost half an hour searching for a familiar name. The pool sat in the footprint of the North tower, the tower Ayla's father and my father worked from when it was the original One World Trade Center.

I watched her stare at the name for a moment before closing her distance between herself and it. She laid her hand flat against the bronze parapet, then ran the tip of her fingers from left to right and back again. She was touching her father's name that appeared amongst over two thousand other names.

We were at the National September 11 Memorial & Museum and

feet away from The Freedom Tower - a building built to pay homage to those who perished during the attacks on September 11, 2001. Weeks before, I watched her struggle with deciding to visit for weeks. She asked her mother to accompany her, but Mrs. Samuels refused, so I insisted I go. I'd done my best to make the day as special and easy for her.

I did not know how she was feeling, but I would do my best to help her carry the pain.

She looked over at me and smiled. I'd given her space, under-standing that if she needed me close, she would tell me. The instance we found the wall with her father's name, she asked me to give her a minute and I was more than happy to.

Ayla made her way over and I welcomed her with opened arms.

"Let's go home," she insisted against my chest.

Home was not exactly my home now. It was hers and would be hers for only a short time longer. She just didn't know it yet.

After that night at Ayla's hotel room, the next morning, I called everyone who was important to inform them the wedding was off. I'd lost count of the amount of tearful voice mails Sienna left me that night. I met with her the next day because despite what she did, there was something in me that felt like I still owed her closure.

"How could you do this to me? She shouted in the condo we shared. "If you wanted to be with Ayla, you should've just been with her from the start!"

I couldn't blame Sienna for feeling how she felt. But yes, I loved Ayla and yes, I could've been with her. That however had little to do with Sienna being disloyal.

Speaking of disloyalty, Marcus wasn't as melodramatic or apolo-getic as Sienna when I confronted him on what would've been my wedding day. I couldn't blame him entirely and really, he had saved me from making what would have been the biggest mistake of my life. Still, I punched him in his face, twice, on sight, for violating my trust, because I don't play that. Since I didn't disfigure his face or dislocate his jaw, I considered us even. I excommunicated him afterwards though, because I don't keep snakes around me, and I subscribe to the saying that when someone shows you who they are the first time, believe them.

Ayla and I arrived at her condo in the East Village when I pulled her close to me the moment we closed her front door. Moments earlier, during the ride from Lower Manhattan via a yellow cab, she was quiet.

She looked up at me. "What?"

"You know if you're not okay, you can always tell me, right?"

Ayla sighed, dropping her head a little. I held her jaw in the webbing between my index and thumb fingers and used her chin to level our eyes.

"It was beautiful and surreal seeing my father's name on the perimeter of the pool."

"Yeah." I ran my palm over her coils, flipping her hair behind her shoulder.

"There were so many names," she whispered, closing her eyes. "I always wondered what he thought that day. If I was one of his last thoughts."

"I'm sure you were."

She blew out a long exhale and leaned into me. "I hope my mom will go there with me one day. She refuses to and I understand why I just... really want her to see it, you know? Seeing his name around that waterfall. It's a feeling I won't do justice to if I described it to her."

"When she's ready, she'll go, just like you. I'm positive of that."

She inhaled a long breath then sighed.

"It took you one year to visit the memorial site. It might take her a little longer, understandably. The memorial and museum aren't going anywhere and will be there when she's ready to visit with you." I wrapped my arms tighter around her and pulled her closer. "Go hop in the shower and I'll order us some dinner."

She nodded against me, then kissed me on the chest through my shirt.

Ayla walked away, and I waited at the doorway.

The first year we were together was a beautiful one, filled with getting to know the us now. While making love had become our favorite pastime, there were moments when it felt like I was using the tip of a pencil to pry open a steel vault whenever it came to discussing our feelings for each other. But things got better, and Ayla became more open and vulnerable with me, trusting me with her heart when she understood I knew what to do with it.

For the time being, I was still in D.C. I took off this day to accompany her to the unveiling of the Freedom Tower. She refused to go in, and that was fine. Ayla toured the memorial site, and to me, that was a major step.

The second I heard the shower turn on, I peeled off my jacket and tossed it on her couch. I patted my pocket and nodded when I knew it was secure there.

I'd been planning how I would do this from the day I decided to do it. I drove to Long Island to speak to my parents about my plans, and the news elated them both. My mother tearfully shouted "finally," while beaming from ear to ear, and my father insisted he help me shop for a ring. Mrs. Samuels was just as supportive and excited when I asked for her blessing, so that was my final encouragement.

I toed off my boots and made my way to Ayla's bedroom in route to her en-suite to check on her. Turned the knob to her bathroom and opened the door, a puff of steam billowing out. The second I got a view of her in the shower, I smiled. Her form through the foggy shower glass enticed me. All I saw was smooth brown skin hidden behind glass, covered with droplets of water. She hummed a tune to herself and that was a relief knowing that although the day was heavy, her spirits were light.

"Why are you watching me," she asked inside of the stall.

"How could I not?"

She giggled. "Did you order the food yet?"

"About to."

"Well, do that because I'm *about to* get out and I'm hungry."

"Aight." I agreed, not moving an inch, allowing myself to get lost in the view.

She giggled. "Hassani!"

"All right, all right. I love you."

"I love you more," she sang.

I left the bathroom, closing the door behind me. Took a few steps to her dresser and laid a folded piece of paper down on the surface and placed a photo beside it. I smiled big at the photo, my heart filling with so much joy I thought it would burst. I'd been working on the project for a year and a half, and it was almost complete. I just knew she'd love it. Ordering dinner would have to wait because I had a question, I needed to ask her, and I didn't want to waste another moment waiting to hear her answer.

∼

AYLA

I STOOD BENEATH THE SPRAYING WATER THAT SHOT FROM MY SHOWER head for one final rinse. It shocked me how okay I was that day. Seeing my father's name on the perimeter of the North Pool brought tears to my eyes. His death had always weighed on my heart, which was why I thought visiting the memorial site for the first time during the opening of the Freedom Tower would break my heart all over again, but it did the opposite. Knowing my father's name was forever etched in a monumental spot was relieving. He'd be remembered.

I turned the shower knob to turn the water off.

Life with Hassani was a life I should have never allowed to take so long to live. The fear of him not knowing what to do with my heart was such a hindrance for me. We could have started this beautiful journey years ago. I hoped God would give us enough time to catch up.

I pulled open the shower door, drying my feet one at a time before I stepped out. Pulling open the bathroom door a second later, I exited the bathroom and entered my bedroom.

"I hope the food is on the way," I said out loud, making my way to my underwear drawer.

On my dresser's surface, there laid a paper, a blueprint to be exact.

After closer examination, I recognized the drawing, but more so what the blue lines formed. Next to it was a printed color photo of a house. It was unfinished, but the layout of the design looked almost identical to the architectural blueprint.

"It's Upstate, about thirty minutes from here, so the commute will be a breeze," he said behind me.

I pressed my hand to my chest, then to my mouth.

"I found an office space to work out of that's about a seven-minute stroll from Park Avenue Prep, so my commute to work won't take me long either."

I was so taken because he'd breathed life into the drawing, the same drawing he showed me as a teenager. I continued examining the color photo. "Is this the—"

"Yup." He answered, moving in closer behind me. "The house I drew at architecture camp when I was fourteen. The same blueprint you picked up off the floor our first day at Garvey."

"You had it built." I finally peeled my eyes off the photo to turn toward his voice. "But you told me that house was for your—"

I turned to find Hassani down on one knee, holding open a tiny blue box. Tucked in the box's slit protruded a diamond ring that sparkled in my eyes.

"Wife," he finished. "It's for her; it's for *us*. I even added the skylights in every room like she told me to."

"Oh my God, Hassani!"

"I went home that night and added the skylights to the design," he revealed. "I thought your idea was genius and deep down I wanted to please you. Looking back at things, I added the skylights because I knew I wanted the house to be for you... for us."

I pressed my hand to my chest.

"I love you, Ayla," he started. "And I'm not trying to waste any more time. It's like I told you, I knew you were the one the moment I stepped into your kitchen when we were 14-years-old."

I bit my bottom lip.

"I have dated enough, I have loved a lot, I have even almost married another woman only to discover that you are the one who owns my heart and I trust it most with you."

"Aw, Hassani."

"So," he started, before clearing his throat exaggeratedly. "I want you to be a little fearless with me in this moment, okay?"

"Okay."

He pulled me closer by the hem of my towel from his bended knee. "I'm going to ask you a really important question right now. It's the last time I plan to ask anyone. You ready?"

I giggled. "I'm ready."

"You sure?"

I nodded, removing any trace of amusement so he'd know I was serious. "I'm ready."

He licked his lips and looked me right in the eyes. "Ayla Samuels, love of my life, the only woman I have ever loved wholeheartedly and without conditions. The only woman on this planet I have *ever* been a one-minute man with—"

"Oh, shut up!"

He laughed then added, "The only woman who was my first and who I have every intention of making my very last..."

I smiled, my emotions building in me, wetting my eyes.

"Baby, will you marry me?"

I nodded quickly, my hair falling in my face. I took a seat on his bended knee and coiled my arms around him before the tears pooling in my eyes could fall. He didn't hesitate to wrap his arm around my waist and to pull me even closer.

"Yes, Hassani," I whispered in his ear. "I absolutely will."

THE END.

Dear Reader:

Thank you for reading *My First, My Last*! If we are friends on social media, you know I planned for this story to be a novella, but the characters Ayla & Hassani had other plans. They were my most frustrating characters I've ever worked with because communication wasn't their strongest suit. And to make matters worse, they had people indirectly (or directly) telling them how to be in relationships. It begs the question - who do we have to thank or fault for our perception of romantic love? For Ayla, romantic love was something to fear because it was tied to the idea of losing herself and her freedom. For Hassani, romantic love was something his father taught him to view as a distraction and something that could wait. Hindsight and making choices out of fear instead of hope was a theme throughout this story. We all know that everything is clearer in hindsight but often we don't have the opportunity to change the course in which our decisions steer us. I wanted to see what would happen if an opportunity was afforded to right a wrong and how it would play out. That was something I could do through Ayla and Hassani.

These two were really a unique pair for me. Whereas with my

other characters in my friends-to-lovers stories (*Just Friends, Girl Code, Last Comes Love*), the scenarios always had one person knowing they loved the other while the other was clueless. However, with Ayla and Hassani, the two of them felt something immediately when they first met, but circumstances made having a picture-perfect love difficult, starting with the death of Ayla's father. The loss happened at what would have been the start of Ayla's dating life. She had the perfect example of a happily ever after right there in her parents, but seeing what being in love is like when one half of that happily ever after has transitioned did no good in Ayla picturing herself surviving a similar scenario. Pair that with seeing her aunt (who Ayla idolized) live out a what's-the-worse-that-could-happen love affair and you have the perfect recipe to feed Ayla's fears.

Then there's Hassani.

Hassani's dad meant well… I think lol. Somewhere in his thought process what he told Hassani was for Hassani's on good. Hassani's father was old school. We all know the type - encouraging the boys to explore all their options while telling the girls to wait for that perfect one. Mr. Franklin wanted Hassani to build himself before creating a romantic bond with someone, which is what most traditional parents want, but maybe dad should have let nature take its course on this one because everything as life has shown doesn't always follow the perfect order.

Ayla and Hassani were kids falling in love and doing grown things they probably shouldn't have done without cluing each other in on their genuine feelings for one another. All they had to do was talk, but if they talked, would we have gotten a story?

I don't think this is it for these two though.

This story was friends-to-lovers and stayed true to form. We witnessed them move their relationship from a friendship to one that became physical.

I think there's more to tell and I've been playing with an outline that would continue their story. What do you think? Would you be so kind to let me know in a review?

Either way, thank you so much for reading and for reading this far! If this is your first book by me and you enjoyed it, you're what I like to call a Brookelynite, so welcome! If you've been rocking with me from a book or many books ago, thank you so very much for your support. I write for me, but I also write for your love of reading so thank you for flipping these pages.

See you at the end of the next book!

Love,
Brookelyn.

P.S. If you're into book visuals, visit my website at https://brookelynmosley.com/my-first-my-last/*to view select scene elements from My First, My Last including Hassani's wedding invitation and the blueprint for the house he drew in architecture camp when he was 14 years old. There's also a little surprise I think you might be interested in when you scroll to the bottom of the page.*

ACKNOWLEDGMENTS

A loving thank you to my amazing husband who is without a doubt one of my biggest supporters. Your support is worth its weight in gold. A gracious thank you to the track stars of today and yesteryears, I appreciate the inspiration. A special thank you to my reading family. To all my supporters across all social medias, I thank you. You all have embraced my brand of writing and I'm beyond appreciative of it. Shout out to the readers who have reached out to me privately to share your thoughts regarding my books. I thank you for keeping me motivated and excited to create new projects for you. When I write, I keep you in mind. Thank you for your support. It's my soul food.

ABOUT BROOKELYN MOSLEY

Brookelyn wrote her first short story when she was a sophomore in high school. Back then she discovered how using her experience as a teen living in Brooklyn to create romantic shorts was just as exciting to her as retail shopping and going on dates. After starting her first semester of college two years later, Brookelyn's creative writing became more of a hobby and something to escape the stress of midterms and finals.

Now in her 30s as a freelance writer, penning short stories and novellas is her everything. While her experience with writing has evolved for the better, her undying love for creating fiction remains unchanged. Brookelyn's focus is on creating contemporary women's fiction with characters based in urban settings. Her stories chronicle the emotional journeys and erotic experiences of women today through her characters and the scenarios they're thrown into.

The motivation behind her brand of writing has a lot to do with what she discovered storytelling provided for her - an escape. Her goal with her work is to create characters and urban worlds that offer a great escape for fiction readers looking for a break from the daily grind of adulting and who prefer to relax with good books and short stories. When she's not freelance copywriting, doing yoga, or showing her husband, son, and daughter lots of love, she can be found sitting at her computer desk, with her legs folded, and a cup of coffee (or a glass of wine) at arm's reach as she types or edits her latest short or novella.

Connect With Me Online!
Twitter: @brookelynmosley
Facebook: http://facebook.com/brookelynmosley
Facebook Reading Group: Brookelynites Book Lounge
Instagram: @Brookelynmosley
My Website: BrookelynMosley.com (FREE short stories!)

Made In Brooklyn.